Wrecked

Love Edy Book Three

I0629333

Wrecked

Published by Razor's Edge

1st Printing
Razor's Edge: trade paperback, Feb 28, 2017 Printed in the
United States of America
All rights reserved worldwide Copyright © 2014 Shewanda
Pugh

ISBN-10: 0-692-84171-7
ISBN-13: 978-0-692-84171-6

Cover art by Regina Wamba

To illness. For showing me how kickass I really am.

To Uncle John, for reminding me.

Love is friendship that has caught fire. It is quiet understanding, mutual confidence, sharing and forgiving. It is loyalty through good and bad times. It settles for less than perfection and makes allowances for human weaknesses.

-Ann Landers

One

On Hassan's last day in the city, after all his bags had been packed, and he'd said goodbye to all his friends, his mother laid out a spread fit for a festival. There were samosas out the ass. Butter chicken, kofta curry, palak paneer, dal makhana, fish and lamb curries. All of it laid before Hassan on a table fit to collapse, as his mother sat across from him, watching him attack it. He'd tucked into a bit of fish and shoved a few samosas down before realizing he couldn't stay away from the butter chicken any longer. While he made a business of eating, she made a business of watching, until she rose and brought him a mango lassi. It made him think of his girlfriend and how she adored that drink.

"I am glad you are going away to college," his mother had said in her accented, lilting English. It took on an oddly wistful tone. Hassan fed her a wary look.

"Yeah?" he said after a moment of awkward silence. He turned to scrubbing a bit of chicken through the delicate sauce his mother always pulled off before speaking again. "Any reason in particular?" He had a feeling that what lay behind those studying green eyes of hers was something more than gratitude at seeing her kid get an education.

"New experiences," she said and picked at a dish cloth she'd carried from the sink, going so far as to pull free a few strands, "are teaching tools for us all. And I am determined to remain optimistic."

His chicken went down like a brick. The unsaid 'despite' of her words hung in the air as smog would: she was determined to remain optimistic *despite* him giving her every reason not to. That was what she didn't say, was what stood between them. So, his lips parted, but then his jaw snapped together. He would get out of Boston 'despite' the bullshit. He had a new agenda 'despite' her efforts, and it didn't include old dramas.

Hassan looked down at his food, unsurprised at how undesirable it all looked now. It resembled blood money: her cheap bribe in payment for what was beyond price. Hassan shoved his plate away and sat back.

Growing up, he'd been told that he looked so much like his mother. He could see it in the eyes, of course, wide pools of green flecked with glittering brass. There was the tone, too, a soft golden that contrasted with his father's deeper coloring. But Hassan was kidding himself if he thought the similarities between him and his mother ended there. Echoes of his mother made up his face, while the build of his uncles comprised the body.

Was that where their similarities ended, he and his mother's? On days like this, when she persisted with the old shit, the dead shit, then yes, that was what he told himself. At the same time, he recognized that same persistence in the gym and on the practice field. He lived by her dogged determination.

Maybe, if the two of them talked—talked and not screamed—Hassan could get her to see how very much Edy held his heart. She'd want his happiness, after all, right?

"*Mām,*" Hassan said tentatively. "*You know that Edy has always been my best friend, right?*"

His mom looked at him as if he'd gone cross-eyed. "*Lawrence is your best friend.*"

See, this was the crap he was talking about. "You think I'm too dumb to know who I'm closest to?" English now. He was pissed and reverting back to his preference.

"*No, I think you're too dumb to think with the right head. And she—she is giving you encouragement to think with the other.*"

She got to her feet and started snatching plates, half spilling them and not caring.

"There!" Hassan spat. "Finally, some truth. You think I'm stupid. And you think Edy's..." He didn't remember standing, but as he looked down at himself, unwilling to call Edy what she implied, he was obviously on his feet.

"I say what I mean!" His mother half-heaved a platter of samosas onto the counter, and in doing so, sent at least half a dozen reeling.

He glared at her. His mom glared back. And at the worst possible moment Hassan realized, that yes, he looked exactly like her. More so than even he realized.

Hassan sighed. "I'm leaving, Mom. Why can't you simply support my decisions? Why do you have to have your way all the time? And the way you treat Edy…" Edy didn't cry about it anymore, but Hassan recognized the wistful look his girl took on anytime she saw his mother. She wanted what they had again.

"You want a *mām* who will endorse impulses and fawn over all you have become. I do not forget the old country nor who we are, as you do. I do not forget our obligations to family or our people. You will remember them as well. You'll have no choice with me as your mother."

Hassan sighed. This was going nowhere. "I've got packing to do," he said and bounded up to his room, slammed the door, and locked it.

She wouldn't get him down. She wouldn't steal his final moments at home or the edgy excitement he had as college finally approached.

And with college came Edy.

Hassan drew back his curtains for a glimpse of her through those ridiculous window bars. She had a suitcase on her bed and clothes piled all around. Neat. Orderly. Both things he wouldn't bother with. He'd shoved clothes in suitcases and duffle bags, fully aware that he required more bags because he wouldn't fold them. Inspired, Hassan grabbed his phone and shot Edy a text.

WHAT A SLACKER. STILL PACKING?

She paused in her work, read his message, and grinned large enough to show teeth in the next house over.

BALLING UP DIRTY CLOTHES IS HARDLY PACKING, she responded.

He burst out laughing.

HEY. THEY'RE CLEAN.

How did he end up on the offensive in this conversation?

THE WHOLE BAG DOESN'T GO IN THE WASHING MACHINE, YOU KNOW.

He rolled his eyes at that one.

THAT WAS 10 YEARS AGO.

Her message came quick: FEELS LIKE YESTERDAY.

He smiled up at her and knew she meant it in more ways than one. A few steps later and she'd closed the space between them as best she could, having traveled over to her windowpane. At the start of their summer, when they'd been locked up in their respective prisons, they'd spend a lot of time sitting on the windowsills text messaging. Sometimes, though, they wouldn't even bother with that, content in the small space they'd created. He got an idea one day. In his desk were a few dry-erase markers left over from a school project. He grabbed a couple and began doodling, not even sure what he'd create, only knowing he wanted it large enough for her to see. Knowing that Edy had the other half of the markers, he wasn't surprised when she disappeared and returned with them. When she did, it was to see a half heart with a ragged inner edge. Inside, a stick figure sat on a window ledge. A flicker of emotion stole over her features at that, before she went to work drawing a half heart to match his, with its own stick figure inside.

They left their doodlings up for the entire summer. The first time Hassan's father saw what his son had drawn, he swallowed uncomfortably and left without speaking. His mother, on the other hand, glared at it, then peered beyond it, as if knowing Edy's window would have the other half. When she returned the next day and washed it off, he drew another one before Edy could even wake and notice it was missing. That went on for about a week, before he heard shouting from his parents' room one night. It caught his attention because they didn't argue much, and when they did, his mother didn't raise her voice at his dad. But this argument was pretty intense. Afterward, his mom didn't spare a glance for the sketch on his window.

Hassan hung out in his room with the television on ESPN. He texted with Edy here and there about a commentator's random comment, but he didn't tell her about the argument with his mom. Ronnie Bean dropped a message about being envious that Hassan was going to Louisiana and that he hoped one day to return home. The north was just too cold for him. Interspersed between the two were Lawrence's practical texts about dormitory check-in time, meal plans, team correspondence, and what to expect when they got there.

Downstairs, he heard his father come in. The yelling kicked off immediately: loud Punjabi that made him go for his Beats headphones and eye his pull-up rail. Maybe he could get a hundred in before bedtime. Maybe he could tire himself out and forget that the Pradhans and Phelps were a complete wreck.

Maybe.

One hundred and thirty-two. One hundred and thirty-two straight pull-ups before his father banged on the door. There was no mistaking a knock like that. Hassan jumped off the rail and let him in, expecting a fight like the one he'd heard.

Once again, his father's gaze traveled over to the window and the half heart and, just beyond it, Edy folding clothes and sliding them in her bag.

A long while passed with his father watching her. When he looked away, it was to study Hassan with an expression that wasn't quite clear. Uncertainty? But why?

"*Bētā*, there are things I would change for you if I could. I hope you know that," his dad said.

Hassan hadn't until then. Or maybe, he hadn't

believed it.

"We will travel to Baton Rouge together," his father said.

Hassan raised a brow. "Who will?"

"The Phelps and the Pradhans. We will travel as we should. Your mother has opted not to attend."

Hassan rolled his eyes, before reminding himself not to bother. This was progress after all. Even despite the news about his mom, he had a hard time hiding his excitement. This was making headway, right? This was something.

"Nathan is important to me," his father said. "As is Edy. We must... mend fences with them." He stood there for a long time after, the air heavy between them, but it wasn't awkward. Hassan understood. "Fold those clothes properly," he said on his way out. "Don't just throw them in."

Two

Wyatt woke with a chill on his back and shoulders. He creaked an eye open, then another and the sight of night's creep into the sky disoriented him as he peered through one massive window pane. The curtains had been swept away and tied. A grubby and fattened pigeon pecked at the bird feeder he'd erected just yesterday. Or had it been the day before?

"Please," she said. "The day's so beautiful. Would you like to go out?"

As if he could deny that voice. As if he wasn't halfway up already for *that* voice. But then disappointment slammed him full on in the chest, jerking him back so that he gawped at a 'he' instead of a 'she.'

"Mr. Green. Please. Your grandfather requires you at dinner."

There was that goddamned manservant who followed him around, à la *Downton Abbey*-style. He found shit to do like wiping down new Jordans after one wear or assembling a collection of cufflinks to Wyatt's liking. Not that he'd known what cufflinks were before.

Wyatt rose, made sure to glare at him, and stepped out onto his private terrace to light a cigarette under the encroaching moonlight. Where had the day gone? He could only faintly care about things, he found.

His grandfather had nearly developed apoplexy the day he'd returned from California with a half-a-pack a day smoking habit. The old man had sputtered, jowls wiggly in a moment of indignity, before informing Wyatt that if he wished to commit slow suicide on cheap cigarettes then it was his right to do so, but *away* from the European tapestries.

"Supper waits, Mr. Green," Geoffrey prompted, as if he couldn't leave him alone. And yes, that was his actual name. It was as if his parents meant to prepare him for a life of exceptional service and dignity from birth.

Yes, Wyatt had actually slept the day away. He preferred it whenever possible. Better that than waking to a gilded cage and empty days.

Silence ensued, the full kind that meant someone else shared your breathing space and that both of you were waiting for something to happen.

"Geoffrey—"

"Sir, your grandfather insists today." He said it like an apology.

More silence. It was fine by Wyatt.

"Sir? A delicate point has arisen that I need to address with you before dinner."

There was always a delicate point that needed

addressing. On day one it had been the dress code: white button up shirts and long sleeves, jackets preferred at the table. Every day. Every meal. On the first night that Wyatt sat across from his grandfather at a candlelit dinner, he decided there wouldn't be a second.

But Granddad had his woolly ways. So, when Wyatt settled for a meal of cigarettes and watching birds drop loads from his new verandah, he got a personal visit from his grandfather.

He hoped to never get one again.

He was the tallest old man Wyatt had ever seen. A stupid thought, he knew, as if people collapsed in on themselves with age—but it was always the thought he had. So, when his grandfather had stepped into Wyatt's bedroom, he stubbed out his cigarette and stood, mouth fumbling with half-formed excuses. Hell, he hadn't expected to make any at all—he hadn't expected the old man to care much about his absence. After all, he'd just spent months in a treatment facility. Wyatt hadn't been at dinner then, either.

"Wyatt, you haven't been trained much in the way of social graces living with that oaf, Roland Green. What my daughter learned under my roof, she quickly unlearned under his tutelage. However," he held up a long, slender finger before Wyatt's nose, "you are no young lady I can merely cart off to finishing school. We must work with the material we have." At this, Wyatt's grandfather twisted his mouth disagreeably.

"You are blood and therefore deserve a chance. But make no mistake of it." He wagged the finger that continued to hang in Wyatt's face. "Should you find my rules beneath you, I will stop checks and tie you up in court. I will disinherit you as I have my daughter. And it will be far easier for me to disinherit a street kid than my youngest child."

Wyatt knew better than to cross his grandfather. But he wasn't afraid of him. He was just an old man, after all. An old man who had given him several million dollars. Theirs had been a business transaction, an agreement, not a reunion. Wyatt could live with that.

"I'll take supper, yeah, but no more of your delicate points," Wyatt said, returning to the present and his personal assistant. That evening he preferred to be blindsided with whatever his grandfather had in mind. After all, the best that could happen was that Edy Phelps wasn't downstairs. And the worst that could happen was that Edy Phelps wasn't downstairs.

Wyatt took a shower and managed to get a good long whack off to an image that only sort of turned out to be Edy by the end. And who could blame him? God, that girl turned into a real figure eight in the end. If only he'd had all the facts at the start of the race, like, back when his greying underwear dropped onto his ripped-up Converses. What kind of choices would he have made then, if he had known that he'd fall in love, get shot, and get a second-place participation trophy for playing The Love Edy Game? He suspected he'd have made the same dumb moves.

As Geoffrey smoothed the white fabric of Wyatt's shirt down onto his torso, Wyatt made a legitimate attempt to bury the voice of his therapist and failed.

"Edy's not a prize to be won, Wyatt. Not by you or any other man."

Dr. Tomkins had clearly never met Hassan Pradhan.

"Sir, I'd like to mention that delicate topic your grandfather has insisted we discuss," Geoffrey said.

"Why?" Wyatt turned to the vanity and scowled. He'd only ever seen one on TV before. They struck him as gaudy and ostentatious, the sort of thing that came with Barbie dolls and a bench, all in miniature.

"I thought it prudent, sir, that we—"

"Why are we discussing this?" Wyatt cut in. "Can't we just say we did? Let's say that I consider myself chastised for… whatever and that I won't do it again." He suppressed the urge to roll his eyes.

"But it isn't a matter of chastisement, it's—"

Wyatt yanked at the knot of his tie. Who wore a tie to a meal? And not just *a* meal, but every meal? They had stupid on autopilot around there.

"Your grandfather likes things a certain way," Geoffrey began apologetically.

Wyatt stared at the man. Then took off.

He shot out before he borrowed one of his father's many crass phrases—and there really were so many.

As he thundered down the cascading, double helix staircase, Wyatt remembered the time he told his third-grade teacher to 'eat hair pie' and got sent to the principal's office. He'd overheard his dad use that expression about his 'annoying bitch' of a teacher after she'd called yet again about Wyatt exhibiting concerning behavior. How was *he* supposed to know that she was actually a lesbian or that 'eat hair pie' meant, er, *that*? But he'd turn around and tell Geoffrey to eat hair pie in a second if he kept on about how his grandfather preferred things.

Despite the rush, Geoffrey managed to maneuver past Wyatt with a slip that would have made Hassan proud.

"Mr. Wyatt Green," he announced once they'd reached the intimate quarters of his grandfather's second dining room. This was where most meals took place, unless, of course, he was entertaining.

Geoffrey stepped aside with a sweep of his arm and a polished table of deep, elegant wood came into view. Wyatt's grandfather sat in his customary seat on one end, Sandra, the Boston cousin who had been Ms. Popularity, sat in the next, while Lottie filled the third place.

Three

"It's hot," Edy complained.

"Of course it's hot. We're damned near licking the equator." Hassan wiped the pooled sweat from his brow and hefted her bag along with his own, which he had insisted on carrying, so that her petite frame wouldn't topple over what with the other two bags she had to carry. He had no idea where all their possessions would go. He worried that both of them had brought entirely too much as they trailed through the airport parking lot in a precarious parade processional leading to some hidden rental car. By the time they found it, Hassan's dad, Ali, had uttered a string of obscenities and drenched his dress shirt in sweat. Hassan, not much better than his dad, asked whose bright idea it was to rent a mid-sized vehicle. This led to a bout of hissed accusations—first his father at him, then Edy at Hassan for ridiculing his dad's efforts, then her dad, Nathan, at her as he warned her to stay out of it, then Edy at Nathan as she countered that he'd never cared before which Pradhan arguments she involved herself in. All this was before they'd even climbed into the ruby red Ford Focus.

Hassan was beginning to think that he should have peeled off with Rebecca and Cam, who had disappeared as fast as they could once the plane landed.

Somehow, Nathan ended up behind the wheel of the Focus, which was unfortunate as he drove like a tortoise in molasses going uphill.

As they rode, Nathan chattered on excitedly about the anticipation of seeing the state capital, a few classic examples of plantation architecture, and soaking up history, of course.

"Any takers for just such an adventure?" he said.

It took a moment for the question to register with Hassan. Not for the first time, the gravity of his earlier deception with Edy took root and buried deep. Any time they traveled, Nathan and Ali had a slew of plans —they were best friends and practically indivisible. They had so many of the same interests, with history being high in a gruesomely long list. Nathan having to ask for company on an excursion that had Hassan's dad all over it painted the grim reality of how one relationship could affect others. A butterfly effect, he supposed. So, how would Hassan play this? How would he fix what he had broken? He knew that, as adults, they were responsible for hashing out their own problems. Hell, that responsibility extended up to and included the insane amount of money his family owed the Bathlars. Still, he was Hassan and Hassan felt an immense sense of duty towards his parents, his girl, and his friends. There was no escaping it. So, he mulled over solutions.

As the wheels rolled on the interstate and Ali's jaw clenched so tight his son could see it from the back seat, Hassan gave his father's seat a quick jab. Then another when that didn't work. What was keeping his mouth shut?

"I have plans to see the Rural Life Museum on the campus of LSU," he finally said. "Perhaps, if you are interested in…"

"Of course," Nathan said eagerly. Maybe too eagerly.

Ali gave a curt nod. "Yes, then. We can make arrangements."

It wasn't until Hassan exhaled and cast a glance over at Edy that he took notice of just how much their dads' relationship affected him. A small part of him, immature though it had been, died with the realization that anything could come between those two men. Strife could take anyone and everyone from him. No one was promised. Nothing was sacred. Maybe unconditional love was a fairy tale. Maybe he'd been a fool to never think otherwise.

❈ ❈ ❈

Wyatt saw and yet didn't see the tall, pale waif of a girl with the thin, smallish smile. But his heart, lungs, and nervous system insisted she was there, just the same.

"Ms. Lottie Davis," Geoffrey announced apologetically.

Wyatt darted a look his way. He barely had time to process the monumental way in which his personal assistant had understated the presence of their guest. Truly, was the man that clueless? That *thick?*

"Wyatt," Lottie said and rose from her seat.

That voice. That dulcet, whispering, hesitant voice. It stabbed at his heart still. As did that quietly expectant way she always looked at him, as if he was worth so much more than —

Wyatt's gaze snapped to the wall. He didn't need this shit. He didn't need this girl in his life at this moment or any other. She wasn't even *there.* After all, there was no one who would willingly put that girl in his presence. Lottie was miles away. Lottie was —

"Sit," his grandfather said. "Now." One wrinkled, liver-spotted hand clenched the table as his gaze dragged to Wyatt's place setting. Across from Lottie.

Jesus Christ.

He walked with stiff knees, crossing the small space with the shuffle of the wounded. As he did so, Wyatt thought back to his grandfather's odd visit to the hospital after he'd been shot. How he'd presented him with the opportunity to unsully himself as if he'd actually cared for him. Days of living with the old man had taught Wyatt better.

Sandra met Wyatt's gaze and held it with steel

magnetism and a serrated edge, dragging him with will-power until he lowered himself in his seat. Her eyes held a world's worth of warning: gray granite reminding him that he could show no weakness at this moment.

They said nothing, that bizarre family of three, unless the clearing of mucus from his grandfather's throat could be counted as a something. Wyatt tore his gaze from Sandra's with desperation and concentrated on the table instead. Every bit of him shook so that he didn't trust himself with a knife or fork. A minute or a million might have passed and in them Wyatt swallowed a thousand times.

"Duck pâté," Dandridge, the head butler, announced and placed a compact square in front of Wyatt. It looked like cat food drizzled in Thousand Island dressing. His stomach did a lurch at the thought. Or maybe it was from Lottie being so close for the first time in four years. Sweat pricked his forehead; bitter chalk coated his tongue.

If only he could figure out what Lottie wanted. What she was doing here.

Sandra cleared her throat. In times of infinite stress, she could be counted on to break the silence. Even if it was better for her to shut up.

"So," Sandra said, "this is some reunion, huh? I don't know who's sweating more, Lottie, you or Wyatt. Maybe Granddad should've sprung for two treatment slots in Maui."

Wyatt groaned and pressed a dampened hand to his face, to his temple. Lottie knocked over her wine and the collective table jumped. Never mind that the old man looked grim enough to disinherit all his grandchildren that day.

Both Dandridge and Geoffrey sprang to action, mopping up the spill with dinner napkins. Meanwhile, their grandfather glared at the spot as if it pulsed and rotted, a living source of foul stenches. Wyatt searched for the ability to breathe.

"Everything alright, Lottie?" Sandra said.

"Stop," Wyatt said, because he knew she didn't mean it. "Just don't."

He looked up to find the two girls staring at each other, Lottie with her sweet, anime eyes and innocence, Sandra with her wolf's grin.

Soon, they were back to the pâté, three newly minted adults and the old man.

"This is delicious," their grandfather announced. "There is a fineness to it worth noting."

Wyatt glanced at three plates, each ornately prepared. Each untouched.

"It is," Wyatt agreed, for the sake of something to say.

Sandra rolled her eyes.

They moved to the larger dining room for the second course and remained there through a succession of largely untouched plates of food that would have lasted Wyatt and his father a week, maybe more. They had prime rib for the main fare, and poked at in silence, with Wyatt mortally aware of the shallow in and out of Lottie's breathing. Of the way she dragged her knife through the meat. Of the fullness of her cheeks as she ate little chunks, always like a chipmunk hoarding its walnuts.

They were so much younger before. He'd only been in the eighth grade. What had he thought he was doing? What could he have meant to do? Wyatt hoped that he would never feel that out of control again.

"He plays games," Sandra said to him, saddling up as they moved into the drawing room. Airy and old world-feeling, the high-arching ceiling and warm, natural tones made that section of the mansion seem both intimate and forbidding.

When their grandfather retired, Wyatt lit a cigarette. Sandra, who had her arms folded tight enough to snap, furrowed her brows. "I don't know if you noticed, but Granddad loves games. Every so often, he strikes a match to see what will ignite."

Wyatt didn't need to be told she meant him and Lottie.

Standing far and away from both Sandra and Wyatt, Lottie feigned interest in a glass case with Olmec figurines. Their grandfather wasn't adventurous like the Phelps: he dealt directly in the art trade so he never actually went anywhere to collect.

She looked through the art instead of at it. She was fidgety, nervous, wired, alive.

"Why is she here?" Sandra asked.

Wyatt blinked at the hostility in her voice. It occurred to him for the first time that she—Sandra—was standing on the wrong side of the room, with the wrong cousin.

"Why do you care?" he said.

"Because she's up to something," Sandra said.

He gave her a long look. "And you aren't." Not a question.

Sandra flashed him a wounded look. Sandra. Wounded?

Lottie wandered over. "I can't stand it," she admitted. "Someone talk to me."

Wyatt finally took a drag on his cigarette. Once, this girl would have never had to ask him that. No, he'd thought that he could upend the very tendrils of society and love his cousin though it repulsed most. Now, only a few years later, he thought it much safer to smoke his cigarette. How telling.

"Why would you come here?" Sandra demanded.

"Sandra—" Wyatt began, but she swatted an arm at him much like when they were kids and he didn't immediately do what she had said. Sandra hated dissent.

Lottie stared at them with orbs bright as a child's. "I thought…" She looked at Wyatt for help.

Sandra sucked her teeth in disgust. "Wyatt, I'm warning you. If you let—"

"Go," Wyatt said to Sandra. He had no idea why

she was being so hard on Lottie. After all, he had attacked her, or so everyone thought. "Leave us alone," he said.

For the first time, Sandra's eyes widened in alarm. "Wyatt—"

"Will you fucking go? Unless you think I'm going to attack her, then by all means stay."

He had never been good at standing up to Sandra's fury, so when her ice blue gaze shot him a look of absolute ferocity, he looked away.

"Please, San," he said, quieter still.

Sandra shook her head. "I'm sorry, Wyatt. But we'll all just stand here in silence before I leave the two of you alone."

And that's exactly what they did.

Four

They checked in at the Hilton Baton Rouge, three rooms between Edy, Hassan, and their dads, then had dinner downstairs after a little prodding and secret coordinating on both their ends. For some reason, Edy could scarcely contain her excitement at the notion of the four of them having dinner together—a staple reminiscent of her entire life that had evaporated overnight.

So, after bellhops and showers, she practically ran ahead of their group, so eager was she to sit down with her dad, her boyfriend, and his dad. It took Hassan snatching her hand as they stepped off the elevator to slow her down.

"Take it easy. This isn't an engagement party. We're not off the hook yet," he said.

Edy knew that she looked at him strangely, but couldn't help it. Engagement party? What an odd thing to say.

"Race you there," she told him instead, though she had on flip-flops. And because he was Hassan he shot forward like a car, unable to help it, never caring to help it. Edy clop-clopped behind him like an idiot, so slow that he pivoted past the check-in desk, weaved past guests and retrieved her like a package, his arm a familiar loop around her midsection. Edy couldn't help the cackle of laughter as they careened in search of food.

"Hassan! Really!" Ali hissed from somewhere behind them. And how could she have forgotten about him? He'd been sheepish about their ease with touching each other long before this relationship. What would he think now that his worst fears had been realized, now that Hassan and Edy were together?

Hassan, like the absolute idiot he could be sometimes, turned around while still holding Edy. For some bizarre reason, it made her laugh harder, reminding her of the time they'd rode a Twirl 'N' Hurl ride at Universal Studios and Ali had begun yelling, which made Hassan laugh, which made Edy laugh, before Ali promptly threw up.

"Hey, you're that new freshman for LSU, aren't you? Hassan Pradhan?" Though the gentleman before them was dolled up in a standard suit and tie, there was no mistaking the buried bayou where he dragged out his speech or dropped the 'n' off Pradhan. There was also no mistaking the light of excitement and certainty in his eyes.

Hassan practically dropped Edy. Good thing she was a dancer with impeccable balance and could catch herself. But she could forgive him. This was, after all, the first time he'd been referred to as a college freshman, and not just any college freshman but one belonging to the SEC. She would give him a minute to get his bearings.

Edy looked up in surprise to find not just Ali behind Hassan, but her father, silent but distinctly interested. He never looked up from the conversation as Hassan and his newfound fan briefly discussed his coming to Baton Rouge, how impressed the man had been with the YouTube videos he'd found of Hassan, and how desperately LSU needed a solid, consistent running back.

"I'll never know how you do it, but I saw you coming down the hall and couldn't believe my luck," the man said.

Hassan shrugged, bashful like. "I'm a student of the game. I owe just about everything to this man right here. He taught me. I hope he keeps teaching me." Instead of simply placing a hand on Nathan's back, Hassan actually pushed Edy's dad forward a step or two.

Edy's father sputtered, then blushed. She'd never seen anything like it in her life.

"Well, sir, Louisiana thanks you," the man said and thrust his hand at her dad with a grin.

"I'm going to find us a table," Ali suggested.

"Oh," the man said, disappointed. "I don't want to hold you." But he looked hopeful, even as he said it.

"No, you two stay. Edy?" Ali said, surprising her.

She followed him down the hall as they went in the direction of the hotel's lounge. No doubt the restaurant would be attached to that. Patiently, she waited for him to say whatever was on his mind.

"I watched you two coming down the hall," Ali said, "running and silly, just like you've done. And when he picked you up, I was horrified for propriety's sake. But then, I realized something."

Edy's breath caught. She wouldn't hope. She wouldn't dare to hope.

"Look at my son. He is smart, handsome, admired. There is no Indian boy better known than him in America. Not one. But what is this worth if he hates himself and the choices he makes? I would not have him self-hate for me."

Edy whipped on him wide-eyed. She had yet to figure out how to breathe. "What are you saying to me, Ali?" She said it in a tiny voice.

"That I love my son. That I love you, too."

Her vision had begun to swim. How badly had she needed those words? What would she have done for them?

"I love you, too," Edy whispered and launched herself at him for a hug.

❋ ❋ ❋

Deep in the pockets of Wyatt's shadowy, senseless dream, he felt another—a bone and sinewy figure of real life imposing just beyond the curtain of sleep. He pushed back at them, seeking rest, seeking peace, and swirled in a misbegotten flurry of shapes and colors. Edy was here, running fingers of warmth through his hair, puffing little breaths on his neck. She darted a hand across his chest and the hand was all he could see, brown fingers tipped in pink, curling and rubbing with every touch. Wyatt inhaled, allowing his lungs to swell near capacity, before grabbing Edy with an arm and pulling her flush. He couldn't stop the painful groan of longing from deep in his chest.

His hands—so greedy now—rushed paths over and across her body even as he felt himself surge. She laughed and swatted at his hands, playfully though. He grew bolder, thinking he might get away with kissing her, before crushing his mouth against hers and gripping her roughly. When she gasped, Wyatt's lashes flew open. Open to face Lottie.

He never knew he could scream without opening his mouth. But he did, all while flinging her from him. Wyatt scrambled from his own bed, tangled in the covers, and hit the floor like a sack.

Was she crazy? Insane? He didn't want to be in the same zip code as Lottie, let alone a bed.

She stared down at him thoughtfully. "Mind if I have a cigarette?"

Wyatt couldn't speak or move or remember if he had any goddamned cigarettes. But the sound of her lighting up kick-started his mind.

"Granddad doesn't like—"

"Fine. Whatever. So, he won't like it, okay?" She took a drag, then another, before offering it to him. Wyatt took it and began to smoke intently.

When his shaking had slowed and his heart finally decided against palpitations, he looked down at the carpet and drew up his knees to his chest. "What are you doing in here?" he said.

Lottie looked at him. "I didn't think you'd mind."

He didn't know how long he stared at her. "I don't know why, Lot. We've got bad blood between us."

She frowned, baffled. "Why? What did I do?"

"What did you do? What *haven't* you done to me?" The good thing about therapy was that he'd spent a lot of time puzzling out the snags in his life; how in such a short time he'd managed to go majorly wrong. It didn't take long for him to realize that Lottie was a significant part of that.

Wyatt stood and stubbed the cigarette out viciously. Though he hadn't anticipated the fury steamrolling in, once it hit him, there was no stopping it.

Lottie watched him, eyes filling dangerously with unspilled tears. "I only came in here because I couldn't sleep."

For some reason, that comment put him over the top. "Got used to sleeping next to Dennis, did you?"

She shook her head. "We, uh, broke up."

They broke up.

Wyatt folded his arms. "Did you break up with him

or did he break up with you?"

She had the decency to blush, at least.

"So, let me get this straight. I take the fall for what your asshole boyfriend does to you and then *he* dumps *you*?" God had a cruel sense of humor.

"Keep your voice down," Lottie hissed.

"Right, because you can't have anyone knowing it was that crazy asshole and not this crazy asshole who beat the shit out of you."

Lottie stared at her. He stared back.

"Why not go sleep with Sandra?" he said finally.

Lottie laughed mirthlessly. "Sandra doesn't seem to be very fond of me now."

"And why is that?"

Lottie jerked a shoulder. "Maybe she can't stand anyone coming between her and the thirty-million-dollar boy."

Wyatt looked at her. That was a weird thing to say. "Sandra doesn't need money. Remember her parents?"

"Yeah. 'Remember' is the perfect word. When will we see them again?" Lottie said.

Wyatt didn't know and wouldn't criticize. He hadn't seen his mom in years and probably wouldn't see his dad again. He did have a more appropriate question though. "Where's Geoffrey?"

"Outside the door waiting to tell us if someone's coming," Lottie flashed a bashful smile. Wyatt didn't return it.

"You need to go."

"I wanted to ask you something first," she said.

"So ask, then leave."

"Where's the girl that got you shot? Is it true she ran off with another guy?"

That clenched Wyatt's jaw. Suddenly, he wished he hadn't stubbed out that damned cigarette.

"Want me to light another?" Lottie offered.

"Yeah," Wyatt said and took a seat on the bed, a safe distance from her.

He had been skeptical when she first asked about Edy, but she seemed legitimately interested, pausing to ask follow up questions about things Wyatt had or hadn't done, about whether he had any pictures of her, and most importantly, lighting up when Wyatt pulled out his phone to share a selfie they'd taken together sophomore year.

"She's beautiful," Lottie said.

"I know," he groaned.

"And you've given her up?"

This time he looked at her. "Have you even been listening? She's in love with another guy. He got the girl, I got shot. Even then, I never had a chance."

Lottie rolled her eyes. "Yeah, but you will."

She sounded so certain, Wyatt slid a look her way. "How?"

"They'll be in college, where they'll be super busy and grow apart. He'll be the big man on campus and he'll have zero time for her. You can be the alternative."

He mimicked a game show buzzer. "Uh, sorry, but I relied on that, right up until she fucked him and rushed to tell me about it."

"Well, you need some polish, I'll admit," Lottie said quietly. "You can't say things like that."

"I got shot!"

"And she knows that. It'll always be at the back of her head. She knows you love her, even now. It's so obvious. But you have to be attractive, too, Wyatt." She took the cigarette from him for a few pulls.

"How?"

"You've got money now. That can make it happen."

"I'm in Boston. She's in Baton Rouge."

"Money can also take care of that."

Wyatt shook his head. "I can't do it. She doesn't want me. I spent all of therapy learning how to accept that she doesn't want me, that my thinking is unhealthy."

Lottie sighed. "Maybe you don't love her as much as I thought you did."

Wyatt recoiled. "What? Why would you even say that?"

"If you're already done fighting—"

"I'm not done fighting. I'm not anything. She. Doesn't. Want. Me. And why should she? I'm a poor, pasty virgin whose dad drinks too much." Even as he said it, he'd heard it. He'd called himself poor. He had millions of dollars to his name, but inside, he was still Wyatt Green.

"Let's go to Baton Rouge," Lottie said. "Let's win her for you."

He wanted to. God, he wanted to. But why would Lottie be keen on helping him?

"What's in it for you?" he said.

"Your happiness?" she tried.

He shook his head slightly. Try again.

She let out an exhale and began to trace a finger on the bed stitching. "My parents threw me out. I don't want to… live here with Granddad if I can help it. I don't know how Sandra has done it."

"With copious amounts of underage drinking, I think," Wyatt said, then nodded. He'd been thinking the same thing. He didn't want to live with his grandfather either. He'd have to wiggle out from under his thumb in the most diplomatic manner possible, but yes, it would be nice just to breathe the same air as Edy Phelps again. Even if said air had Hassan Pradhan filching off it, too.

"Okay," Wyatt said. "Let's figure out how to get to Baton Rouge without raising the old man's ire."

Five

Hassan slipped into Edy's room in the dark of the night when the hotel was at its stillest. He passed his father's room, Nathan's, and what might have been Rebecca's. He couldn't be sure about hers, though, since he hadn't seen either her or Cam, her significant other who was also the father of his friend Kyle, since the plane landed.

Hassan had a key to Edy's room. On using it, he discovered that she was up and waiting for him.

The sight of Edy in a little black dress made his breath trickle away. Barely-there straps near the shoulders held up lacy, plunging cups—cups pushed to overflowing with unbelievably plush cleavage. A swing of loose fabric halted to expose long, lean, impossibly gorgeous legs. Dancer's legs.

Man, he loved that girl.

She grabbed his hands, grinning. "What do you think? I bought it this summer and couldn't wait to surprise you."

Hassan tried to remember that breathing was a necessary part of life. "I'm surprised," he said softly.

Her smile widened in that way it did only for him.

He thought about pocketing that smile, about stealing the sunshine of Edy to hoard for himself.

"You won't believe what I have to tell you," she said. "I have news about your dad."

He raised a brow. That parachuted him back to earth. Well, he had news about her dad, too. "Ditto on that," he told her. "Me first or you?"

She maneuvered to the bed, still holding his hand. He didn't know about her, but he was in no hurry to let her fingers slip from his just now. Maybe not ever.

"Go ahead and spill," he said. "You can't hold water anyway."

She did her best to look indignant. "I can *too* hold water!" She tossed his hand away, making him laugh. So much for forever.

"Look at you," he said, feeling a bit bereft without her hand in his. "You couldn't even keep holding on to me."

Now she grappled for his hand, but he hid both behind his back, laughing as she twisted and turned in desperation to make contact.

God, he'd missed all this. Eventually, he gave in.

"See?" she exclaimed.

"Yeah, sure. Just tell me your news already."

She took a deep breath and sat up. "Your dad's giving us his blessings."

He stared at her, sure his brows had drawn down before collapsing like some concave tent as she rendered him unable to speak. There were words out there, words for him that he could reach out and grab, and finally, eventually, he did.

"Impossible," Hassan said.

Edy blinked. "You *bájjur*. It's not impossible. What kind of future did you expect with me if you thought that?"

"Did you just call me an idiot?"

She waved a hand, like his father did when something was of no consequence. "Your father is so proud of you. He just wants to see you happy."

A flicker of emotion rushed helter-skelter through Hassan: a stutter of hesitancy followed by outright disbelief. Finally, his face pinched into an armor's worth of denial. Because of that, he was already shaking his head.

"No," Hassan said. "He's borrowed a lot of money. He may want to accept us, but he's being pushed constantly not to."

"By the Bathlars," Edy concluded.

"And my mom."

With a forlorn sigh, Edy stood and went over to the window. Once she drew back the curtains, an incredible view emerged of a dark, broad, and imposing Mississippi River. It loomed close enough to reach out and touch, broad and sparkling under a crescent moon.

"Your mom will never give in to us," she said. "It's all so personal for her."

They would never make progress with his mother.

He knew that and wanted only to make peace with it. But not tonight. Tonight, he had different wants. "Cake—"

"How were things with Daddy?" she said.

Right. Dolled up in the sexiest lingerie and his girl wanted to discuss their parents. Still.

"That's what I wanted to talk about," Hassan said, as his brain attempted to shift gears. "I'm, uh, making progress with Nathan. Finally."

Edy turned back to the window and began fidgeting, fumbling first with the lock midway up, then pushing and pulling at various places to force it open. "Well, you held a big place in his heart. So you know."

Hassan stared. "You said 'held.'"

Edy froze. "I did, didn't I?"

He waited for his explanation.

"I—I didn't mean to imply that I knew something, that he told me something—"

"Forget it," it was his turn to wave a hand.

"But—"

Hassan wrapped his arms around her, tight, and kissed her forehead. "I missed you, *duppar*."

She said nothing, snuggling into him instead. The silly, irrational part of him imagined them staying like that forever, in that room, in that moment, wrapped in each other's arms. Before his mother intervened, of course.

"It's always been your mother, I think," Edy said, as if intruding on his thoughts. "If we could persuade *her...*"

He hushed her, his thoughts already far and away, remembering summers on the Cape, wet footprints in the sand, and long, wind-whipped days high up on their rock — the rock carved with their names.

Hassan pulled back. "No mom talk. We're in Louisiana now. So no more worrying about parental disapproval. Not when they're a thousand and a half miles away."

Edy made a little face before breaking their embrace. He could feel the words she wrestled not to say, but he was determined to turn over this new leaf with her. Desperate to finally make things about them instead of about their parents. And anyway, he knew and understood what she never could about his parents — about his *mom*. That she would *never* accept Edy, no matter how perfect her Punjabi and Hindi, nor how intricate her understanding of Hinduism. Yeah, Edy could *respect* and honor their culture 'til she ceased to breathe, but for his mom she was an outsider — a *beloved* outsider — looking in.

He was tired of thinking of this. Feeling bereft without her in his arms, he went for her when she spoke again.

"It's the money they owe the Bathlars. It's not insurmountable, but it's a lot. Your dad says that maybe he can borrow against the house and pay it all back. If they're willing to accept the money instead of you."

Hassan shot her a curious look. "How do you…?"

Edy blushed a bit. "Your father and I talked while you and Dad were fawning under your fan's attentions."

More than he's talked to me, was Hassan's first thought, though he couldn't muster up the anger to be grudging. This was a way out. With enough money to pay the Bathlars and Mala's willingness to reject the engagement, he could be free.

Hassan ignored the sinking feeling in his belly.

"Which reminds me…" She suddenly looked hesitant. "Dad appreciated you acknowledging him a lot. To that guy, I mean."

Hassan fell back onto the bed and kicked off his sneakers. His legs still half dangled off, bent at the knees, even as he grinned. "I know. He told me."

"He told you?"

He nearly laughed at Edy's incredulity.

"Yeah, he actually talked to me afterward. Now get over here. Didn't I tell you that I missed you?"

She scampered over, giggling, and plopped atop him, before burying her hands in his hair for a kiss. "I missed you, too," she said.

She surprised him with the sweetness of her enthusiasm, as fumbling and eager as he was breathless and deliciously desperate.

For the rest of the night, they didn't need words.

❖ ❖ ❖

Sandra stood over Wyatt with her lips pursed, arms folded, and that characteristic left leg cocked out before her. It was her way of saying she was pissed. And she was really pissed.

"What do you think you're doing?" she said, eyes narrowed suspiciously on him.

He opened another drawer and took out the folded shirts, placing them in one of his Louis Vuitton bags. "Packing, I believe."

"For what? And why isn't Geoffrey doing it?"

"Because I don't want Granddad to know yet."

She huffed a sigh. "You don't want Granddad to know what yet?"

Wyatt resisted the overwhelming urge to roll his eyes. Still, his eyes did it on their own. "I'm leaving, Sandra," he finally said.

She said nothing for a while. "Why is Lottie packing, too? She just got here."

It was now or never, he supposed. "Because she's coming with me," he told the wall.

Sandra grabbed a massive bottle of Tylenol from a nearby dresser and hurled it at his head. Wyatt ducked just in time.

"Are you fucking insane?" she cried.

"Are you?" he countered. He cast a cautious glance at the bottle of Tylenol, as if half expecting it to lunge at his face again in sheer determination.

"Look," Sandra said, shifting gears with a tone so

complacent it caused Wyatt to glance at her, "I know Granddad's hard to live with—"

"It's nothing to do with that." He returned to the drawer for another stack of shirts, all of them new enough to still sport tags.

"Then what? Because whatever Lottie told you isn't —"

"I want Edy," Wyatt said. "And Lottie made me realize that maybe I finally have a chance."

Sandra stared. She stared so long that Wyatt was forced to stop his packing.

"You don't get it, do you? Hassan is *it* for her. He's the one."

"And she's *it* for me," Wyatt hissed, whirling on her. "Edy's everything. Have you ever felt that before?" He exhaled shakily and ran a hand through his newly cut and highlighted hair, before deciding he didn't have time to entertain his cousin. "No," he said. "I can't imagine you have."

He'd spent the entirety of his therapy, and even his angry moments before it, shoving away his feelings for Edy and filing every stray thought, every erroneous deed, under the 'inappropriate' category. He had to reject the idea that it was wrong to love her, because loving her was so much a part of who he was. She was his happiest memory. She was his best days. No, Edy wasn't perfect, but she cared for others, did her best to love and protect them, and was so much of what his family wasn't. Kind. Generous. Steadfast. So, his love was unreciprocated. He had come to accept that. Maybe.

"They're happy together, I think," Sandra said softly.

He didn't want to hear this. He had packing to do and a flight to catch. Once in Baton Rouge, he'd bide his time, hanging in the shadows until the moment Edy would want or welcome him. He'd prove how far he'd walk for her, how much he'd give, and how willingly he'd sacrifice if it meant having her. Hell, he'd already been shot.

And sacrifice was his trump card, wasn't it? How many guys could give away an actual fortune to prove his love to one woman? Better still, how many would?

Top that, Hassan fucking Pradhan.

Six

Edy snuggled into the unforgiving mold of Hassan's body and felt his arm pull her tighter even in sleep. Harsh rays of sunlight bore down through curtains they'd forgotten to close, mingling with that godforsaken river to create blindingly stark white rays.

"Ugh," she meant to say, but it garbled in her morning mouth and came out as gibberish.

"You okay?" Hassan murmured, voice thick in his half-roused state. He ran a careless hand up and down her arm, shooting sparks through her soul as he half-dozed.

"The sun's harassing me." Edy shifted from her back to her side... not that there was any getting away from the glare.

"How about I harass you," Hassan murmured. His touch grazed from the base of her spine up, up from beneath the sheets, until his fingers slipped through her thick hair and gripped it.

"Hassan..."

He pressed kisses along the back of her neck, melting whatever protests she'd been about to make.

"I—we..." She trailed off into nothingness. A hand

slipped across her breast now.

"'We' what?" he said with no little amount of mocking.

"Have a long day—both of us."

He rose to his knees and rolled her onto her back before pulling the sheets away. He tossed them off the bed, leaving them stark naked under sunrise. When she reached for them, he stopped her.

"It's just me," he said softly. "Me." A hand touched her cheek. "And you. The way it was meant to be."

Her heart thrummed something horrible to that and she gulped to ignore it. Seeing him still naked from their nighttime escapades sent a shiver through Edy. Hassan, never one to miss a thing, bent quick to pin her down for a kiss, then another.

She hadn't meant to moan like that. But when she did, his hand slid low, then grinned at what he found.

"The lady doth protest too much," he said. And she made to shove him away.

Not really though.

When his fingers brushed over her body a second time, Edy arched with a whimper that she buried in his shoulder. He wouldn't allow her to hide there. He nudged her to him with a semi-smile, before his mouth came down on hers firmly.

Hassan's tongue swept inside in a claiming expedition, even as his fingers glided deftly between her thighs, punishing and pleasing her in the same turn, leaving her wholly at his mercy. She had little to do but look up at those darkening green eyes and hang on, breath coming in little bursts.

Edy made a sound—a new one to her ears—and already began to tremble, to shatter beneath him. Hassan slipped into her then, easy, sure of himself. She bit her bottom lip and whimpered.

"God, that's beautiful," he whispered in her ear. He ran a hand down the side of her thigh. "You're so beautiful."

She smiled shyly before curling up to kiss him.

He grinned and kissed her back. A moment of adjustment followed, a silent few seconds of words without speech. Then he began to move, pushing into her with long, deepening strides that made her gasp and fist the pillows.

He groaned. "You're *incredible*, Cake. You—I—can't even... Oh, *God*."

He slowed, then laughed a little. Edy gripped him by the hair and yanked him down to meet her. That was the beauty of them. They understood each other intrinsically. They could simply *be* and it would always be enough. Always.

"Edy, I—I can't—" He squeezed his eyes shut, shoulders hunching as he gathered up on one arm. The whole of his body shuddered atop her.

"You don't have to hold back for me," she said. Truth told, his hovering on the edge of control had her hovering near completion. She lifted both legs and wrapped them around him, drawing him deeper, speeding his tempo.

He gasped, strokes turning desperate, but it was Edy who gripped him first and cried out when lava-like waves rippled through her body. She buried her face in the sweep of his hair and caught a hint of wonderful citrus. His moan came deep, guttural. He followed it with a stabbing thrust, then another, burrowing before he shuddered and snatched away.

Hassan collapsed next to her on the bed. For several minutes, there was nothing but the roar of her own breathing and her heartbeat to be heard. Eventually, they tapered off to normal.

Beyond their silence, she heard shouting. A woman's voice permeated, a sharp slice of venom slashing in.

"Are you serious? You want to talk to me about responsibility? You've been in your own world for twenty years! Books, lectures, tours? Where do you think that left me and your daughter!"

"I guess your mom's arrived," Hassan said.

Edy sat up and rubbed her arm self-consciously.

"Rebecca, I'm warning you." Her dad came through, muffled but menacing. "I'm no fool. You will not hoist the blame off on me. Do you think anyone believes this relationship with Cam just appeared? You've been in and out of this man's bed since college!"

Holy shit. These were not her parents. Not the affectionate father, squinting at some treatise, pausing long enough to give her an affectionate tug of the ponytail. Or her mom, cool, aloof, demanding, and melding every crumb of their high ideals together. Daddy hardly spoke to Edy now, opting for his office at Harvard or at home. Mom kept a very public life in D.C. and let her new home in Quincy echo in emptiness. Same thing for the old one.

Edy slumped down, reaching for the discarded covers. Maybe she could burrow deep enough to find the hotel basement. Absolutely everything in her life had changed. And God, had her mom always been a cheater? She swallowed a lump of something sour and shoved back angry tears.

"Edy?" He pulled what little covers she'd managed to find off and she realized he was wearing his boxers. "Have you heard a word I said?" Her blank stare must've answered, because he shook his head. "I told you to get dressed. Don't just sit there listening to this. It's shit."

Dressed. Right. That made sense. Edy fumbled around for last night's dress with a blind hand, found it, and pulled it on with Hassan's help for faster work. Then she slipped into a pair of black flats, grabbed her room key, and gave him time enough to finish getting himself together. They left hand in hand.

"My room isn't far enough away," Hassan said. "And I don't think you're in for eating breakfast just yet, though I could maybe do with something."

"We haven't had sex in years!" Edy's mother

hollered. "What surer sign do you need that a marriage is over? Death?"

Hassan cringed. "On second thought, I'm not that hungry."

"Certainly, you could have found the nerve to tell me," Edy's father said. "For a woman who prides herself on being the toughest in Boston, you sure couldn't face an old professor. Or did you think we were only playing house?"

Edy's stomach knotted like lattice work for pie. She didn't need to see Hassan flinch, she felt it in the way he gripped her hand. Neither of them moved, rooted to the spot like two peeping Toms.

"I was with you for my daughter," her mom said, earning a faint gasp from Edy. "You know that a two-parent home is much more stable."

"Yes, Rebecca. A two-parent home, not three."

"You should have told that to the Pradhans. We've been co-parenting with them the whole time. All because you were roommates with the guy in college! And now, now you let them treat our daughter like she's second tier. I've told you before to let me set that Rani straight once and for all."

Hassan glanced at Edy. "Let's take a walk." Without waiting for her reply, he started down the hall, practically dragging her with him. Edy smiled grimly. She had to hustle to keep pace. They made their way down the hall, not looking at anything in particular, stride steady, fast, faster.

Finally, Hassan drew to a halt. "You know everything will be okay, right? Our parents, us?"

She didn't, but she wouldn't say so. Edy nodded, noting her uncertainty mirrored in his eyes. They stared at each other, neither willing to state the thousand worries chipping away at their expressions.

Hassan looked away pointedly. "Okay, so I spy with my little eye…"

"I'm not playing that game with you, because you cheat," Edy said. She yanked her hand away.

Hassan burst out laughing. "What? Come on. Learn to be a gracious loser."

"I said 'no', Hassan. *You* cheat. The stuff you hint at is never really there and it's all outlandish or whatever."

"Give me one example."

"Once when we were kids, the answer was 'ghost'."

"I could have seen a ghost!" His laughter rang deeper than even months ago, as if he'd matured even more. It shot through Edy like a tremble.

"Another time the answer was 'moon', but it was the middle of the day," she said, deciding to ignore the flush of warmth he'd given her.

"It's not like I haven't seen a moon before," Hassan answered sullenly. He crossed his arms and eyed her.

"It needs to be seen at that moment, jerk." She shoved him a little. Of course, his body didn't move.

They strolled for a while up and down the halls, down to the lobby and into the street, all with him attempting to lure her into the game. When that failed, he resorted to tickling her, then chasing her right out the hotel and down the street. He was ridiculous with this distraction, but Hassan's charismatic goofiness was better than listening to her parents or thinking about their next days. In a few hours, everything around them would change. They'd check into their dorms and check in with their respective teams. Their entire identities would change in a matter of hours.

After the silliness, the two ventured upstairs for showers and a change of clothes. Edy's parents, it turned out, were still at it.

"You're in this constant state of overreaction!" her mother shouted. "To the affair, the divorce, and now this. Where was all this passion years ago?"

Hassan looked at Edy. "I'm gonna lose my shit. What about you?"

"Uh yeah. You'd think a sitting senator and a Harvard professor would know not to screech their business at the top of their lungs, but hey."

Hassan sighed.

"Overreaction?" Edy's father said. "What kind of insanity are you courting? I've been the very rock, the —the foundation of our family, while you've *cultivated* your lovemaking skills!"

"Okay," Edy said. "Let's intervene."

Hassan's brows disappeared into the fringe of his hair. "Let's not!" he cried, even as she strode for out. With him on her heels, she powered next door, tried the knob, then banged.

The door unlatched audibly and swung open.

"What?" her dad blurted. He sported shadows under his eyes, graying whiskers, and a severely rumpled button up and pants.

"Can I come in?" She swallowed the urge to flee.

Her father looked from her to Hassan. Seconds of staggering silence lapsed. He wouldn't deny her entry, would he?

Before Edy could open her mouth and regrettably step over the boundaries of their relationship, he opened the door wide and let them in. Her mother stood on the opposite side of the room, back against the sill of a massive, curtained window, arms folded. At the sight of Edy, she smirked.

"Well, good morning, Cinderella," she sneered.

Edy turned just as her father closed the door behind Hassan.

"Mom. Dad. Everyone has been able to hear you," she said. She snuck a glance at Hassan. Maybe he could help her get things civil. Or maybe his presence would make things worse. Maybe they both would.

Her mother laughed. "Little girl, you children should go. Really."

Edy's father searched the floor with his gaze. A thin semblance of pain marred his features, surfacing from some deep and secret place, transforming him into a man she nearly didn't recognize.

"Why are you looking at him?" her mother spat. "Is

he supposed to be your savior yet again? Even now?" Rebecca's quick steps had Edy backing up, then flattening against the door when there was nowhere left. "You two idiots don't even know that I'm the only friend you've ever had! That I've always known what those looks and touches meant—or what they *would* mean." She cast a scowl at Hassan, who had rushed to keep up with the ruckus, only to stand there, arms slack, looking helpless. She turned back to Edy's dad. "They've been curling up to each other for as long as they could. Did you intellectuals really think they'd never figure out which part of their bodies fit together?"

Hassan snickered, then buried it in a horrified, wide-eyed cough behind his fist. Edy gave him her best 'what the hell' look.

Edy's mom looked back long enough to roll her eyes as if she couldn't be bothered with either of them. "They've always been some unstoppable force," she said. "Why we had to make a big deal about it, I'll never know." She shrugged as if she couldn't be bothered with that either. "Through it all, I had one wish: I wanted them safe, to focus on studies, and to realize how unimportant romance is."

Edy's father snorted. The sound made her deeply uncomfortable for some reason.

"Mom, I, uh, only came to make sure everything was all right. I could hear—"

"Could you *hear*?" her father snarled.

Yes, snarled. Like a bobcat cornered in a cavern. Like something hellish and wounded.

Hassan moved closer to Edy. He looked as wary as she felt. Something was off in this room. Mom's confessions, Dad's... everything.

"Daddy—" Edy started and hated the spooked lilt of her voice.

"Go," her mother said. "Just leave."

Edy withered, but resolved to hold her ground. She barely registered Hassan's tug on her arm. "I will. But not until you two promise to quiet down. I could hear you in my room and in the hall and..."

Her father laughed. "Would you like to know what I could hear?"

Hassan's grip felt firm now. "Edy..." he warned, his tug insistent.

"What I could hear was my *daughter* and her boyfriend—the boy who I've had a hand in raising, mind you—having sex through a hotel wall." He took a step closer. "Truly, you two sounded as if this place gets rented by the hour."

"I... What?" God on high, why did she glance at Hassan then? His face flamed scalding red; his Adam's apple bobbed endlessly. There was nothing to say, nothing to do in this trap of her own design. There was no escaping, either. Physical pain washed over her father's expression before he shut his eyes and exhaled.

"Daddy—"

"Shut up," he said softly.

"We should go," Hassan said, speaking at last.

"I agree," her mom said. "Nathan's not himself today."

Hassan grabbed Edy firmly by the arm and dragged her away, out the door and into the hall. She'd barely stumbled away before her mother followed.

"Edith," she said. "We have to say our goodbyes now. I won't be following you up to campus."

A mild sense of panic bloomed, before Edy's mother stepped into her vision and cupped her face with both hands. "You'll be fine. You'll be better than fine." Then, in a bizarre turn of events, her mother blinked rapidly, before brushing away a sudden tear. "Look at you, looking like I did at this age." She grinned. "Try not to break his heart."

Edy didn't return the smile. She was busy trying not to hyperventilate over the lone tear they were pretending hadn't happened. "Why aren't you coming?" she said.

The question melted the shine from her mother's doting smile. Now it looked grim. "I have a meeting. And it's best that your father and I aren't together right now." She hesitated. "He's upset at the whole world, including you. He won't admit how deeply he's hurt by your sneaking around behind his back with Hassan or by your applying to colleges in secret. It's as if you've had a whole life we didn't know about. And the dreams he—we—had for you are gone." She inhaled, squared her shoulders as if going to battle, and scowled. "Things will be rougher for you, at least for a little while. Your father's cancelling your credit cards. Hearing you with Hassan was the last straw. He thinks you're out of control, as opposed to growing up."

Edy gave her mother a puzzled look. "But if he's cancelling the cards, how am I supposed to...live?"

Her mom grimaced. "The American Express you share with both of us should be okay. I don't think he'd cancel that one. Other than that," she shrugged. "I was pretty poor in college. It'll give you character."

Character. Right. It was such a Rebecca Phelps thing to say.

Then she dug into her bra, fished out a few bills, and pressed them into Edy's palm. "It's all I have on me. But you'll be okay. You'll flourish, in fact," she said.

Later, Edy wouldn't be able to tell who hugged who first or fiercest, but her mother shoved her away in the end. "Oh, go get ready," she said with a laugh. "Don't be such a sap."

The ride to LSU that morning stretched on forever, somber, silent, tense, foreboding, until the four of them —Edy, her father, Hassan, and Ali—were swept up by the lush greens and reaching lake. A sick, ominous menace seized Edy, a certainty of imminent failure. Study something practical, her parents insisted, something applicable to life, and devote your life to that. Dance didn't qualify. Now, being this far from home felt impractical. Scary. What if something major happened? She could hurt herself dancing. A third or fourth year injury could devastate her life, leaving her with nothing but a nice participation trophy. She wouldn't even be able to finish her degree because of the physical aspects of her major. She'd be ruined, with no future.

"Breathe," Hassan said, suddenly in her ear. "You look like you're not."

Eh. Turned out she wasn't. Edy exhaled in a gust as they turned onto Louisiana State University's sprawling, rolling mass of emerald greens. Another worry hit. What if she couldn't handle the college curriculum? What if she wasn't smart enough or sturdy enough to keep pace with school and the dance team that paid her tuition? She attempted to beat her fears back with a dose of reason. She had sound DNA as the daughter of two brilliant Ivy League grads; she could do this. She had done so much already. She had the foundation for college. She could keep up. Confidence was key.

Hassan slipped his damp fingers through hers and she squeezed. They'd be absolutely, positively, fine. Damn her nerves, she was an awesome dancer and a top tier student. She —*they* were born for this moment in their lives.

Ali spun the steering wheel for a sharp right turn and the suitcases piled in the front passenger seat went for a slide. He shoved them back with characteristic impatience. Edy glanced down at Hassan's hand, comfortable alongside hers and smiled.

"Look, Edy," Hassan said, voice a whispered awe. "Death Valley." He pointed to a massive uprising of rounded white concrete, LSU's colossal football stadium. It seated more than a hundred thousand, and at least on one occasion housed a crowd so ferocious, so hysterical from an out-of-nowhere win, that their reaction registered on the Richter scale. That was the school Edy chose to attend; that was the stadium and the crowd she'd dance for.

Suddenly, there was very little breathing room in the car.

She focused on the back of Hassan's head as he continued to stare out. Silken black locks, sun-streaked in brown and brushing his neckline, once again he'd let his hair grow wild. Most days she longed to rake her fingers from root to ends. Now, she wanted to put her hands there and curl into him, making the world disappear.

Hassan turned to face her. "We're here," he said in wondrous fashion. "College."

"We're here," she echoed sickly.

"Edy will get out first," Ali said. "We'll ensure her bags make it to the room, then we'll settle you in, Hassan."

'We.' 'We'll ensure her bags make it to the room.' 'We'll settle you in, Hassan.'

Had Hassan heard it, too? Better still, did it mean that Ali and her father were doing things together again? Edy put the question aside for the moment, content with the happiness that hope brought.

Mounds, that she'd read were Indian burial grounds, swelled the landscape, undulating it. Buildings that hinted at some Italian influence dotted here and there with smooth, tan stucco rushing up to brilliantly red rooftops. The oaks were everywhere, bursting with bright green plumage and shading the wayside across wide spans of meadow. Moss-strewn magnolias swept near the ground in a breathtaking version of southern beauty Edy had yet to know.

Hassan glanced back at her, with his warm green eyes, shot through with gold, and they shared a single broadening smile. This was their home; the place they'd chosen to start life together. The story of them would pivot in this place, at this moment.

Maybe she should kiss him.

"You want me to kiss you?" Hassan said slyly, quietly. "You look down when you do."

Edy laughed and discreetly flipped him off. One of these days, her actions would take him completely by surprise.

"Let's get this over with as quickly as possible," Ali announced. He glanced at Edy's dad with clear worry; the latter looked as if he hadn't slept since Rebecca left him. "There's still much to do."

They found her dorm, Laughton, after some

twisting and turning. Once there, the jutting, seven-floor edifice complete with fluttering purple banners welcoming new and returning LSU students stood stark.

Edy's gaze dropped to a cluster of grinning girls, each distinctly slight and lissome, with hair in a bevy of subdued and wild styles: long, black and bone straight, strawberry blonde and endlessly curly, boyishly short, shock purple, and shaved on one side.

"Cake? You okay?" Hassan said.

Edy snapped to attention. They'd parked in front of Laughton. Fear squeezed her heart.

"Yeah," she said.

He gave her an admonishing look, acknowledging the lie, before climbing out the rental car. Edy followed, steps quick, eyes down, pointedly ignoring the girls on the staircase.

They weren't waiting for her, were they? No, that was dumb. Why would they be?

Hassan yanked out first one suitcase then another from the trunk, strong-arming most of it. When Edy moved to help, Ali stayed her with a hand. She suppressed a sigh.

"Good afternoon, fellow LSU dancer!" came a bright voice. "My name's Tamela Carpenter and I'm one of your teammates. Is this your family?"

Oh God, they *were* here for Edy. An impossibly short girl stood before her with boobs that needed to be tied down. She had a square face and blunt mouth, as if her lips perpetually practiced scowling. For whatever reason, those same lips tried out a smile too big for comfort.

Edy winced, then looked around as if she'd forgotten who she'd come with.

"I'm her father," Edy's dad said from behind her. He stood up straighter, commanding more dignity in that single gesture than any she'd seen all day.

"Alas," Ali said. "We're but neighbors." He gestured to himself and Hassan.

"I'm her boyfriend," Hassan said. "Hassan Pradhan."

"Oh wow, I thought that was you," said a girl with blonde pig-tails. Another nudged her roughly in the ribs.

"Well, I'm Tamela," the first girl reiterated. "Your captain." She let the declaration ruminate for a while, as if to ensure Edy understood what that meant.

The warning felt palpable. But when the girl's smile returned, bursting to fullness, it was enough to make Edy wonder if she'd imagined it all.

"Since he's Hassan Pradhan," the captain said, "you must be Edith Phelps. Our only dancer from Boston."

The blonde with the pig-tails broke from the pack and pulled out a rumpled sheet of paper. "Got it, Tamela."

Standing next to him, she could feel Hassan's impatience. He shifted with her bags and tried on a tired smile.

"Great! And you prefer Edy, right?" the captain exclaimed. "We've been expecting you. All those accolades, the Boston Ballet, and New York School of Ballet, too? We are looking forward to seeing what you could... teach us."

And there it was. The bit of cattiness her warning tone had hinted at.

"I'm looking forward to what I can learn here," Edy said carefully.

It was the right thing to say. When the captain smiled this time, it lit with authenticity. "Your roommate, Naomi, is already here. As are these clowns." She jerked a thumb at her entourage. A rolling thunder of names ensued. Edy caught only some of them. Holly, Kaylee-Courtney, Bonnie, Dawn, London. They descended, wrapping her on all sides and launching into some bizarre song about music and motion and sisterhood. Edy resisted the urge to squirm, remembering her lifetime of discomfort with girls and her preference for the all-boys club of Hassan and the Dyson brothers. She'd made up her mind to end that foolishness. What better way to go at that in earnest than with her new teammates?

She forced a smile, but figured it looked peculiar. Luckily, Ali was there to save her.

"Ladies," he said. "We appreciate this warm welcome, but..." He gestured at Hassan.

Tamela withdrew and the girls followed her lead. "Yes, sir. Right."

Edy could feel the eyes on her as they made their getaway. Then, she heard it.

"We'll be back to check on you once you've settled in," Tamela called. "Make sure to leave this evening free." A fresh round of giggles followed.

Edy checked in, signed her dorm contract, and received a key. Three floors up in the elevator had them facing a lengthy narrow hall with doors dotting both sides the whole way down.

"This way, I think," Ali said.

Hassan bumped luggage against everyone's legs, since he had the most, earning curses from his dad the whole way down. Eventually, Edy found her door. She took a deep breath and squared her shoulders to meet her room and roommate.

She opened the door to a miniature sitting room. Purple and gold hit her like a strong drink to the gullet. Cheap pine was strewn throughout the place, but this was her space now. And she loved it.

Edy went for what she assumed was her room, only to crash into a tall, willowy figure with nut brown hair twisted into silken locks and gathering at the back for a massively billowing, awe-inspiring afro.

"Edy?" she said. "Naomi."

Edy grinned like a dork. This was the girl she'd been emailing all summer, once the school confirmed that they'd be roommates. She'd never seen her so why did she have this overwhelming urge to hug her? Naomi yanked Edy into her arms.

Hassan grinned at her stupidly, knowingly, and began moving the luggage into the bedroom.

She hugged Naomi back, smiling weakly while surprised at herself, then followed Hassan into the bedroom where he and Ali piled the luggage up amidst more cheap pine furnishings. Edy's father stood back. When they were done, Hassan turned back to her with what looked like hesitancy. It was then Edy realized that although he'd be within walking distance, she had no idea when she'd see him again.

"Cake," he said. It was time to leave.

She met him with the intention of telling him to go on, that things would be okay, but somehow the words didn't form. His words didn't form either.

Edy wondered how a boy she'd known her entire life could make her breathless. She was breathless now.

"We should go," his father announced. "I'd like to remain on schedule."

Edy closed her eyes. Hesitation followed. Hassan grasped her face with both hands and covered her mouth in a touch of delicious sensation. Cinnamon, sugar, and heat pressed in, then snatched away with his shuddering exhale.

"And you wonder why your mother didn't come," Ali said. With a polite nod at Naomi, he nudged his way out the door, completely forgetting to say goodbye to Edy.

She couldn't help but cringe.

"I'll call around later to see if you need anything," her dad said to the floor and went the way of Ali.

"Right," Hassan said. He smiled first at Naomi, then at Edy. "I better go."

"I'll say," Naomi said and pursed her lips teasingly.

Hassan grinned, devilishly this time, and with both men out the door, swept Edy into a crushing hug. "I missed you this summer."

She laughed and felt stupid when her vision blurred. "I missed you way more," she said. After that, he headed for his own dorm.

Seven

Despite Wyatt's promise to Lottie, he didn't want to sit around waiting to stumble upon Edy. First, she'd never believe it was a coincidence. Second, he couldn't stand the wait. Just breathing the same air as her rushed the blood through his veins and bled the loneliness from his bones. He ached to see her. A glimpse of Edy would ease his need.

"What are you thinking?" Lottie asked, bare legs stretched from the cream couch to the glass coffee table of the Baton Rouge townhouse he now rented. "Seeing Edy?"

Wyatt dropped into a chair. "No."

"Liar." Lottie licked, then bit, into an obscenely long Snickers bar and puckered her lips at him. "You need to stay away from Edy for now," she said for the hundredth time. "Otherwise, she won't buy into you running into her."

"She's not going to anyway."

Lottie gave him an inscrutable stare. "So, what? You're just going to hunt her down?"

Wasn't that what they'd already done? Wyatt looked away, annoyed.

"You'll scare her off."

"Then why am I here?" He cursed. He thought about smashing some shit.

Lottie shrugged. "Winning her over?"

"How?"

She made a point of devouring half the candy bar before answering. "Maybe we should start with Hassan instead of her. There's got to be a weak link in their relationship."

Wyatt threw up both hands. "I've been through *that*, Lottie, and got shot for my trouble."

She snorted out a laugh, then buried it with a hand. Wyatt smiled despite himself. "Yeah, so, I got shot," he said, extra surly. The event only filled him with a little bitterness now. He knew his stupidity had played a part.

"Getting shot gets you extra cool points, at least."

"What?" Wyatt said. "Why?"

"Because it's bad ass. Do you have scars?"

Who the hell got shot and didn't have scars? "Uh, yeah?"

"Well, it gives me an idea," Lottie said.

"I'm not getting shot again."

"No, not that. But it's a better plan than staring at Edy."

He probably wouldn't enjoy it as much though. "Yeah?"

"Yeah." Lottie stood, and her razored blue-jean shorts failed to cover even the whole of her pockets, leaving white fabric to poke out the front on her thighs. "Instead of staring at Edy, you're going to compete with Hassan and be the better man."

Wyatt snorted. "Ha ha."

"I'm serious. You're going to be sexy. We'll clean you up and drop money at her feet."

Wyatt shook his head. "She doesn't need money. She never has."

Lottie dismissed this with a wave. "There's always something to want. A purse, shoes, a vacation—"

"Those are things *you* want," Wyatt said.

"Well, maybe we can all get them together. Rome would be awesome."

He'd take them to the fucking moon if it got him somewhere with Edy at last. Still, Wyatt sighed. It was one thing to talk about rivaling Hassan Pradhan but his cousin had never seen the guy's muscles or heard girls go on about his eyes or the buttery-melt of his smile. He was smooth, easy with people in a way that awkward Wyatt could never manage. Not to mention that he'd never known Edy to want more than a charm bracelet here or song for her iPhone there. He tried to tell Lottie all this, but she waved it away with a hand.

"Let things play out. Something has to work."

But it didn't, right?

He wanted Edy bad enough to hope. He had missed her friendship so desperately it ate away at him in California, even as he nodded and agreed and pretended to understand the "objectification he had subjected her to", as his psychiatrist put it. He had only ever loved her. That could never be wrong. It was why he could never turn off his feelings, even when he shoved back at them and her in anger. Even when he screamed her away and wept, snotting into his pillows, she remained right there in his soul. Edy Phelps was the most intense, overwhelmingly desperate ache of his being. When they were friends she had cared for him. She had showed him more attention and love than anyone ever had. Wyatt had fouled that up; he had pushed too hard, too fast. For his trouble, he'd wound up riddled with bullets.

"Wyatt. Seriously, you have got to stop thinking about that girl all the time. Let's get crushed instead. That'll help," Lottie said.

Wyatt gave her a long look. "Crushed?"

She rolled her eyes like she did when he didn't know who sat on top of the Billboard Charts. "Slammed. Sloshed. Slizzard. Peeled. Drunk."

"Oh." Oddly enough, he didn't have drinking experience. With his father's beer cans littering the house like carpet, he'd certainly had ample opportunity. But the odor always hung in his nose like something dying or dead. "I, uh, don't know if…"

Lottie had another dismissive wave. "This is the way to her. She's pretty and bound to be popular. You know Hassan will be. You have to make friends. As many as possible. It's easier when you're wasted." Then, gentler, she said, "Have you ever had friends,

Wyatt?"

The question shot through him, lodging like yet another bullet. "Friends?" he managed weakly. There was Edy, but he couldn't say her. "I've had…you."

Lottie's lashes fluttered and she dropped to the edge of the couch. "That's it, isn't it? Me and her…we're the only people you've ever had."

Her sympathy curled his insides into nausea. "So?" he said roughly. "I've never been popular. Big deal."

Lottie sighed audibly. "So, I'm rethinking my involvement in this."

Wyatt whirled on her. "You *can't*. You promised you'd help me get her back. You owe me." A flash of dangerous energy coursed through him and he flexed his hands, chest heaving.

"I want a new deal. A new deal in light of all this new evidence." Lottie grinned proudly. "You see that? I sound like a lawyer. Anyway, I want to help you make friends. I'll help you make a thousand new friends and be the most popular guy in any room. You should have your pick of girls, not just Edy. If, after all that, you still want her then…"

Wyatt hesitated. The *fury* in him hesitated. "Any girl?"

Lottie laughed. "Yes!"

"Is there a downside I'm not seeing?"

"You're waiting to go after Edy," Lottie said.

Wyatt bit his lip. That was true. But he'd been thinking, maybe he'd approached the Edy situation all wrong. Could it be that she'd want a guy that people liked or... a more sexually experienced one? One that others found attractive too?

"It's worth a try," Wyatt said. Anything was, really. "What's our first move?"

Lottie frowned. "You throw a party, of course."

"But," Wyatt hesitated, because the next point seemed obvious, "we don't know anyone."

"Let me worry about that," Lottie said and actually kissed his cheek.

❦ ❦ ❦

Hassan checked into his room with his two dads in tow, only to find it already infested with Dysons.

"So," he said, by way of greeting to his new roommate. "What has two teeth, is black and red, and a hundred feet long?"

"Don't," Lawrence said. He glanced sideways at his dad. Lawrence and his parents were still barely on speaking terms after his defection to LSU.

"The front row at a Georgia game!" Hassan smiled big for Tess and Steve, Lawrence's parents.

"Hassan," Tess said and the scowl melted from her mouth. "How nice to see you out your cage."

Hassan cringed as the Dyson twins fist-bumped over their mom. "Ouch, Tess. That one gave me heartburn."

The old Georgia cheerleader smiled prettily for him.

"I would like to settle you in quickly, then pay a visit some time tomorrow. I have an engagement later on that I have to prepare for. I didn't expect this morning to…" Ali trailed off, red-faced.

He didn't expect Nathan and Rebecca to spend the morning emptying their lungs of much-needed oxygen.

Nathan cleared his throat. "I, too, have an engagement. Though why Ali speaks of sightseeing and grabbing a beer in such formal terms, I'll never know." He glanced at Ali and received a barely discernible smile.

Tessa stepped up smoothly. "We'll take care of Hassan, like always." She brushed aside a lock of too-long hair that had flopped in his eye. He kept meaning to get a haircut.

"By 'take care' she means 'kick his ass'," Matt murmured.

"Here, here," Mason said. "We owe him one for forcing us onto this parasite of a campus."

"Language, Matthew!" Hassan's dad cried. "Your mother is present; you must show respect." And smacked him upside the head like he would his own son.

Matt grinned. "You're right. I'm Mason though."

Ali rolled his eyes. "Nathan? Are you quite ready?"

"A moment alone with Hassan first, please," Nathan said.

Oh boy.

Nathan and Hassan stepped outside. Once there,

Hassan reminded himself that the other man would notice if he suddenly started panting.

"Do you know why I wanted to speak with you?" Nathan said.

The tiles of the floor were once white, but now resembled beige or white smoke. The particular one Hassan stood on had an aggressive crack down the middle that threatened to bloom into two others. Tiles. His breathing. Steady. Nathan. Edy. He could do this, could do anything for Edy. Even talk to a Nathan that had morphed into a werewolf overnight.

Hassan shrugged at his earlier question.

Nathan said nothing, forcing Hassan to give him a cautious look.

"You're using protection with my daughter?"

No.

"Yeah—yes."

"Hassan!" Nathan cried.

Bile formed at the back of Hassan's throat. His hands wouldn't keep still, so he shoved them in his pocket. Nathan inhaled visibly. He paced back and forth as if on some impossibly short and tight high wire. When he stopped to look at Hassan, his jaw worked and his nostrils flared. Nathan resumed his pace, faster now, then turned and drilled a fist into the slab of wall near Hassan's head.

What. The. Fuck.

"Damnit, Hassan! What don't you get? You and Edy are all I have now. You can't... throw your life away on foolish impulses. You're worth more than that. And I—can't stand it."

Hassan stared at him. His mind had so much to process at once. "Is your hand okay?"

Nathan blinked, as if attempting to catch up cognitively to the moment. "I'm sure it's fine." He held up his fattening hand between them, looking at it as if it were a foreign entity, an offender capable of terrible deeds.

Hassan swallowed. "You said, 'you and Edy'."

Nathan looked up. "What?" He seemed disoriented.

"You said, 'you and Edy are all I have now'." Maybe it had been automated, old talk from old days. Surely, this was about protecting his daughter.

Nathan sighed. "Hassan, you know how I feel about you. At least, I hope you do. All this discord has taught me that nothing will change that."

Hassan's eyes misted over for one horrible second. With brute force, he shoved back unwelcome emotions.

"I need to have this talk with Edy, I know. But I'm sure I've been too distant, erratic and unsympathetic for her to welcome parenting from me," Nathan said. "Then my wife's leaving me and I've been quarreling with my best friend. I'm getting everything wrong."

It was then that the door to Hassan's room opened and his father emerged. He looked from Nathan gripping his wrist—Hassan supposed his hand hurt more than he let on—to Hassan's repentant expression. Then he roared with laughter.

"They'll be the death of us, my friend! I've told you this before," Ali said.

Nathan muttered a reluctant, "Maybe."

Not to be put off, Hassan's dad threw an arm around Nathan—something Hassan hadn't seen in at least a year and continued to grin. "Tonight, my friend, drinks are on me."

At the team's designated meeting time, they reported to a grand room with stark white, reaching walls. Brassy LSU letters trimmed in purple jutted from one side. Guys the size of grizzlies gathered around a white-clothed buffet table and crowded in clusters.

"I hate buffets," Lawrence said. "I'll bet this food's been fondled and spit on ten times already."

Hassan cringed. He hadn't the heart to break it to him. They had nothing but school lunch lines ahead of them for the next four years. Why did he think the upperclassmen gathered around greedily? They knew this was as good as it got.

"And I told him, 'what happens in Baton Rouge makes first page news'!" a guy at the buffet said and a solid wall of listeners roared in laughter.

"Seriously, X," said a too-close voice just behind them, "I don't know what it means when you dream you're naked in public, but you like it. Why would you even think I'd know?"

"Cause you're a Psych major!"

"They haven't covered that, yet," said the first.

Guys everywhere were tremendous. Like steel trap, colossal, Incredible Hulk tremendous. Bigger than anyone on his high school team. And worse, the buffet table encouraged them to crowd up, muscles atop muscles, and jostling for food.

"Let's just post up in the corner," Lawrence said. "We'll stay low-key and—"

"Oho!" The guy who'd been shouting about what happened in Baton Rouge stepped out of the fray. "*No one told me the pageant queen had arrived! Boys! Boys! Give it up for number one, the prettiest girl at the freshman ball!*"

To Hassan's horror, people began to step back and turn to him as the dark and enormous figure started a thunderous, slow clap. Others joined in, whistling, catcalling, and shouting out compliments about his pretty face and bare legs.

"You have got to be kidding me," Hassan muttered between gritted teeth, mouth trapped between a grimace and a smile.

"And what's a queen without her first attendant?" the big guy shouted. "You better give these girls their due!"

"He's talking about me, isn't he?" Lawrence said. He took a tentative step back as if there was somewhere he could go.

"Yeah," Hassan said. "He is."

A slim, pale player comprised of ropey muscles that

came together for that tough country look gave Hassan a nudge.

"That's Freight," he explained. "Real name's Jackson DePaul. Team loudmouth, official busybody, gossip, harasser, know-it-all." He dragged every word he spoke through his mouth, losing consonants along the way. He wasn't grinning obscenely, at least. So, when he shoved a hand toward Hassan for a shake, it was accepted.

"And what should I call you?" Hassan said.

"Paul," came the answer. "Paul Metcalf."

Hassan's arm turned to lead.

"Yeah." Paul said. "The guy you've come to replace. Maybe."

A whistle sounded, followed by the collective groan of the group. Like well-trained sheep, their path became clear: out of the room and into the auditorium next door.

"Listen," Lawrence said amidst their sluggish progression. "Let's grab a seat at the back and stay low-key."

Because that plan had worked so well a moment ago. "Absolutely," Hassan said.

The auditorium seating staggered upward from front to back, so that the seats in the rear were the highest and each one before it required a step down to access. The podium down front was without a stage; instead, purple carpeted flooring and a massive projection screen rounded out the dais.

Immediately, Hassan realized Plan A was a bust. The back rows grew thick with knuckleheads laughing and jostling, shoving each other. He exchanged a tentative look with Lawrence and moved down a few rows. He'd create the best buffer he could so that—

"Hereeeeee she is, *Miss America*," Freight crooned in a deep and booming tenor. "I said, 'Here she is, Miss America'," and swept an arm out in mock reverence. When Hassan cast him a wary glance before taking a seat, Freight hustled to the next row and dropped down on one knee, engagement style.

Bodies continued to file in as Freight placed a hand over his heart and became solemn. His singing continued, voice dropping through the basement in a ridiculous, irksome bass.

Hassan's face heated blow torch quick as the roars of laughter took over. Was this really what they thought of him? That he was a fussed-over pageant queen? The wild laughter said 'yes, hell yes'.

He sighed. "You about finished?"

Freight grinned and squeezed into the row behind Hassan. So much for buffers. Soon a tall and leathery brown guy with swaggering confidence in strides came down to join him. One even leaner and more towering with skin like the night rounded out their group. Hassan recognized Mr. Swagger as Caiden Cash, team quarterback. The last guy was Xavier Wright, the team's star wide receiver, who, rumor had it, had bitched so much for a second wide receiver that

Lawrence likely owed his scholarship to him. Still, Hassan pretended to not know one from the other, especially when they congratulated Freight on a serenade well done.

"So, tell us, Pradhan," Cash said, practically leaning over into Hassan's row and therefore his seat. "What the hell took you so long to commit?"

Yikes. He should have seen that coming. Now, Hassan felt like his pants had dropped and he'd forgotten to wear underwear. There was no way in hell that he'd utter a word about his girlfriend. Not when they were already calling him a damned queen. So, he glanced at Lawrence for help, found him already looking at him, and immediately realized his mistake.

"The couple had to discuss things. You know how this can be," Freight said.

Hassan's mouth flew open and Lawrence kicked him. *Play this cool,* Lawrence seemed to be saying. *We're pros at this. Think of the twins.*

"I don't know," Hassan said finally. "I had a lot of offers. I had to pick the best school."

A moment of silence followed, where he could see this answer settle into their bones, gaining approval.

Caiden Cash clapped him on the shoulder and chuckled. "I'm just giving you shit, man. I swear. I don't care why you're here, so long as you're half as good as the hype. Cause the position's been empty."

The guys snickered just as an image of Paul flashed into Hassan's mind. No sooner had he had the thought than did he look up to find Paul glaring at them—glaring at him.

It must've been a special kind of torture to watch the ticker tape parade come through for the guy slated to replace you.

Eight

Edy and her roommate spent the next few hours unpacking, with Naomi pausing here and there to fiddle with the iPod and the speakers she brought along. Their taste in music coalesced in some places and crashed in others, but for the most part both girls liked just about everything. With the sun having set and half Edy's clothes put away, she and Naomi took a breather and contemplated what to do about dinner.

Naomi had suggested the cafeteria, but honestly, the idea didn't appeal to Edy just yet.

"We could order a pizza," she suggested.

Naomi shook her head. "I came down on a discount Greyhound ticket. I don't have money to waste, kiddo. What little I do have, I plan to make last."

A thunder of banging rattled their front door. Naomi raised a brow. "Hassan?"

"Not Hassan," Edy said, as her boyfriend had both a team meeting and the good sense not to knock as if he had warrants.

Naomi, who must have been from some small and trusting town, went to the door and opened it immediately. A rush of girls spilled in.

"Naomi! Edith!" Tamela bellowed as the gang flooded every possible open space. She was a force, this girl, Edy could see that already, with her boisterous bounce and wide, arresting eyes. She had command in her voice. Edy wondered how she backed it all up.

As Naomi emerged, the introductions ensued rapid fire. These were some of the girls from earlier, plus more. Lana the Blue-Haired with ruddy cheeks and dark eyeshadow, Cecily Call-Me-Cici, who had hair like burning embers and an aggressive swath of freckles, and London Wu, back again, and grinning like she wanted the center of attention.

"We mingle tonight," Tamela said as she pushed her way into the room. "Everyone goes to Lure. It's a team tradition and an LSU tradition. It's also a great way for us to begin bonding."

Edy almost said that she didn't recall mingling from the official schedule of events. She was hungry and tired and drained and not up to hanging with people she'd have plenty of time to get to know. But she held her tongue. She held her tongue because this was the first time she'd ever been part of a team and she didn't want to spoil it. Also, she didn't know this girl and the Rebecca side of her warned to keep silent and study her surroundings in unfamiliar territory.

So, Edy smiled like a dork. "I'd love to," she said. "But I'm starving."

Tamela's blinding grin faded. She shoved past Edy

and Naomi, leaving them to stare dumbfounded. Once in their room, she yanked open first Edy's closet, shut it, then attacked the nearest suitcase. Muttering to herself in open disgust, she turned to Naomi's closet, which apparently had much richer fare. She snatched down two dresses and hurled a black, skin tight bandeau wrap at Edy. It made her blush to even *look* at it. "Get dressed, Phelps. I'll tell you a second time because you're new and don't understand how things work around here, but I run the show."

Edy didn't bother with protests. She simply slinked off to the bathroom, wondering just what the hell she'd gotten herself into. She needed this scholarship, wasn't a quitter, and refused to be intimidated. No need to alienate her captain on the first day.

London Wu stuck around to fuss over her makeup when it became apparent that Edy didn't know the application side of a kabuki brush. The girl tutted, rolled her eyes, and sent minions to retrieve various shades of fierce from Naomi. She couldn't believe Edy didn't have makeup.

For the ride out to Lure they divvied up into three cars, piling so that they squashed, stacked like dishes heaped with no regard for safety.

Tamela drove like the Devil on wings of retribution, slicing from one lane to the next, slashing out at anyone who dared get in her way and cursing for good measure. Edy wondered what her dad would say to see this, then put him out of her mind. Her fingers toyed with the hem of her dress, inching somewhere near her bottom, and resisted the urge to demand out, and now. They had Uber in Baton Rouge, didn't they? Or yellow cabs, at least.

Tamela whipped into the parking lot of a blighted, black-windowed, double story with its name in glowing script. Edy could gather nothing from the car-swollen parking lot or the building's face. Was this a restaurant? Bowling alley? Sports bar?

She looked down at her clothes.

Strip club?

"Let's party, girls," Tamela said. "Because the grind begins tomorrow."

They spilled out into the parking lot, with the upperclassmen whooping and howling like hyenas. They broke into a run.

Shit.

The older ones had no problem bolting in heels. The freshmen squeaked and shouted after them, some stumbling like Edy in their determination not to be separated from the group. Everyone made it to the door, however, without snapping an ankle.

"Hey! The party has begun. The Lady Tigers are here!" shouted a muscle-swollen guy at the door.

Tamela pressed a familiar kiss on his cheek and his smile grew monstrously wide. He snapped a glowing bracelet on her wrist and went down the line, treating them each to the same. "Go in. Honored to have you, as always," he murmured.

As each girl passed, she suffered a grunt of appreciation, whistle of recognition, and, in a few instances, a murmur of, "My God."

Thick, dense hip-hop poured from the single open door as the girls slipped inside. Bodies already crowded the dance floor, entranced in lazy sways. A few scattered tables and chairs stood on the far sides of the club, with stairs tucked away in each corner. A bar lined the back.

The girls' hyena shrieks returned. Edy tugged on the hem of her dress again, snatched Naomi by the wrist, and went straight for the bar, praying the credit card she'd shoved in the broadside of her bra work had managed to stay lodged. They both needed to eat.

The mozzarella sticks were good. The jalapeno poppers even better. Edy had just processed her bartender's suggestion that she try something stronger than the kid's fare when the music shifted from one pulsing tempo to the next funky, syncopating one. London Wu screeched and kidnapped Naomi for the dance floor. More pairs broke off, and somehow, Edy wound up with Tamela's cleavage too close for comfort.

"Me and you, freshman!" she shouted over the foot stomping shouts of a crowd who apparently knew what dance routine went along with the song.

The hardest part, it turned out, was keeping her chest in check as Edy two-stepped, sashayed hips, and swung round to change partners, first to Dawn, then to a dark-haired guy with a 'V' of eyebrow and polite tip of his head. When Edy stomped his toe with her heel, he grimaced, causing her to attempt an apology at the same moment he hurled her back to Dawn.

A commotion at the entrance caught Edy's attention where a swell of gargantuan muscle—two, three guys, maybe more—all attempted to get through the door *together*. Jostling, shoving and yelling ensued before the D.J. slammed the music to a halt. Some sort of truce must have been reached in the blink of Edy's lashes as one colossal, dark guy emerged. He dropped to one knee. Then...

"Is he singing Lou Rawls?" Naomi said, back at Edy's side.

"It's... pageant music," Dawn said. "Right?"

Just as Edy gave up on figuring out why the big guy was singing the *Miss America* theme song, Hassan entered.

She literally squeaked her surprise, before sprinting like an upperclassman in heels straight for him. Only later would she remember the arm that tried to stop her and missed.

"Cake!" he said and scooped her up like they hadn't seen each other in eons.

"Aww," came the chorus of males, with one guy placing a hand over his heart.

Lawrence stumbled in. "I'm not telling you again: don't put *flowers* in my hair!"

Hassan moved as if to help Lawrence, but a hand on

his shoulder stayed him.

"This is rude, Queen. Introduce us to your pretty little friend." Edy knew this guy, at least: he was the team quarterback Caiden Cash.

Hassan grimaced, dropped a hand between her shoulder blades and allowed it to drift to the small of her back. "This is Edy." He stopped short at the open leers and crawling gazes.

"Edy, huh?" one guy said breathlessly.

Hassan scowled. "She's my girlfriend." As if to emphasize the point, Edy wrapped her arms around one of Hassan's without thinking. Just then, the music kicked in. "Cake, this is Cash, Freight, Titan, X, Tennessee, and... you know Lawrence."

Edy grinned at Lawrence and waved. She supposed that was a smile he returned.

"Alright, *Hassan*, we'll give you a few minutes," Cash said. "After that, we need you at the bar for a round."

Hassan visibly exhaled as Edy pulled him off to the dance floor.

"That going okay?" she said with a jerk of her head towards his teammates.

He laced fingers with her and drew her in. "Forget them," he said, with a lean into her ear. The music had become one obnoxious autotune hit that had grown on both of them. Edy was ready to dance to it.

"I don't know this dress," Hassan said, eyes drinking, swimming in greed, "but man do I like it."

He pulled her in so that his mouth brushed her ear. "I'd like it on the floor, too." He flicked his tongue into her ear discreetly, causing her to squeal and jerk away, but only a bit as he was still holding her hand. The result was that she wound up looking like an utter fool.

"Hassan!" Edy cried.

"You're getting forgetful, *duppar*" he said. "I asked a question."

"The dress is my roommate's," Edy said. "Let's dance while we can. Something tells me we're both on borrowed time."

Hassan laughed, but it held no humor. "Yeah, I know. Me and Lawrence and a couple of the other freshmen have to treat our teammates to a few rounds. My dad's gonna shit when he sees the credit card bill."

That reminded her of her fellow dancers. Her gaze swept the landscape and landed on a few cold glares: upperclassmen watching without moving. Most of the others were dancing in pairs, though.

Yeah, Ali would shit for about a dozen reasons if he could take in the totality of their night.

Edy threw her arms around Hassan's neck and together they began to sway to the beat. His hands slid in easy, familiar, at her waist, and for a moment only they existed in their world.

"Let's find you a dozen of these dresses," he said. "Seeing one wrap those curves makes me crazy." He flashed one of his devilish grins and her pulse skittered wildly. Their bodies pressed close, moving tight together, and somewhere in the distance, Edy vaguely registered some sort of techno.

"I'm in love with you," he said, breathless in her ear. She closed her eyes to his words and tried to breathe again. God, how did he still have that power over her?

"I've... always been in with love you," she said up into his ear.

"Always?" he said, with a trace of confusion.

They were definitely slow dancing to the wrong music now. Her eyes closed as Edy considered what she'd said. Was that possible? Could she have always loved him, even as a little girl?

Thinking back, her devotion to him had always been infallible, unshakeable. They were indivisible, as her mom used to say. And when it came time to notice boys, Edy had something of a breakdown on realizing how overwhelmingly attracted she was to him.

"They're coming for you," Hassan said. "Kiss me."

Edy's eyes widened and she instinctively turned. Hassan anticipated and grabbed her chin to guide her to his mouth. When velvet brushed her tongue, she heard them and knew her time with him was up.

An all-female chant swelled in size, matching the music and growing closer. "Shots! Shots! Shots! Shots!" A hand darted out of the dark and pulled her away.

"Freshmen don't get boyfriends!" someone shrilled in a sing-song voice. "Freshmeat thinks it's prom!"

another shouted, while someone actually slapped Edy's ass. She yelped, then clapped a hand over her mouth.

Tamela grabbed hold of her wrist and her grip was absolute. Around them, bass-laden trap music thudded as her captain glared with eyes of iron. "You'll learn how we do things around here, freshman. Quickly." Not for a second did Edy doubt her.

Edy's teammates lined up from dance floor to bar with most girls clustered on the floor. They passed drinks hand to hand, dancer to dancer, like some bucket brigade until they arrived at the huddling mass of whooping girls. Somehow, Edy wound up in the middle. She didn't think it an accident. Tamela downed the first drink and got a hollering, foot-stomping roar of approval. She shook it off and joined the girls in chanting for more shots until the next drink arrived.

"Freshman?" Tamela said. "This one's for you." She held it out to Edy.

For a long time, nothing happened. Edy could see the other girl swallow under the strobe lights. What would happen if she didn't take this drink? What was the worst that would happen if she did? She heard her father's worries and fears, the thousand academic journals he'd cited to her and Hassan, and for a moment she hesitated. Then she felt a yearning to bond with these girls and be liked. If swallowing one drink could do that, then what was the big deal?

Edy reached out with both hands, tossed it into her

mouth, and felt her cheeks fill like a chipmunk. A pungent aroma filled her mouth and nostrils; she took it down in two hard gulps to be rid of it.

The girls whooped and crowded in on her.

Edy danced with her roommate a bit, laughing at an ugly limp and shuffle that her old boyfriend swore would be the next hot dance. When Tamela brought around another shot, Edy hesitated only briefly before drinking it. The crawl down her throat went smoother and she shook it off a tad faster.

Hassan showed up right after she'd been handed the third shot.

"Can we talk really quick?" he said and looked over his shoulder.

Edy stepped away with him. "I'm gonna get flayed for this," she said.

"Me too." Again, he looked around. "What's with the shots? Maybe you should ride back with me?"

She squeezed his hand and hoped it alleviated that black, heavy look. "I'm okay. I promise that if I start feeling sick I'll call or text you."

He studied her, opened his mouth, then buried whatever he'd been about to say with a bite of his lip. "Fine." He swept her into the tightest embrace. "As long as you remember your promise and stay safe."

Nine

Wyatt couldn't see past his own arm because of the horde crushed into his apartment. Beer splashed on furniture and people shouted over cranked-high hiphop as weed smoke like fog threatened to choke him. Shots flew. A six-way bong funneled beer into waiting mouths. He had no idea where Lottie was, had only seen glimpses of her fleeting form in a fluttering, ruffled skirt that barely covered her hindquarters and a sheer top revealing a close to concave stomach. When she did scurry to him again and again as the night wore on, she held his hand and introduced him to people she'd met, smiling profusely and acknowledging that it was Wyatt's party and Wyatt's beer and Wyatt's weed (which he hadn't known about). This got him a handshake or fist bump of acknowledgment that always felt unexpected. Some of the girls that he met even lingered in their looks at him. One bit her lip and smiled. Each time his stomach warmed in a chaotic bramble of nerves that let him know something was happening *to him*.

He ordered ten boxes of pizza and got cornered by a guy who wanted to talk nothing but local brewed beer.

His dad had a brewery in the city. Would Wyatt be interested in buying a few kegs for his next party? Yeah, sure. They exchanged numbers and made plans for Wyatt to check out the microbrewery.

Then two girls started making out. Hard and heavy, right there on Wyatt's couch. The brewery guy, whose name was Solomon, started nudging him, repeatedly and hard enough to bruise the ribs. Cheers erupted from a sweat-laced crowd. One guy leapt up on the coffee table and began cheering them on, giving them instructions, that, unbelievably, they followed. When the tops came off Wyatt forgot how to blink. When the bras followed, he managed a few hard swallows, as his hands opened and closed in tight fists. He'd never seen breasts before, in person, that is. He'd never seen two women making out open-mouthed. He felt his manhood respond like a thump and he turned away from them, desperate for control.

"God, to be in that sandwich," Solomon said. "Two years and my last girlfriend never kissed me like that."

Wyatt wondered if Edy kissed Hassan like that, open-mouthed and ravenous, starving for more and taking it no matter the consequences. He bet she did.

Lottie appeared before Wyatt. "There's a girl that wants to meet you."

Between the two on the couch and his thoughts of Edy, Wyatt was in no condition to meet girls. He shook his head. "Maybe some other time."

Lottie pursed her lips in disapproval and grabbed

him by the wrists, tugging Wyatt before he knew what was happening.

"Lot, stop—"

She whirled on him in a rare show of impatience. "Look, I know she's not Edy, but there's more than one way to pass the time without her. Maybe you could learn how to make yourself a better option in the meantime."

There were so many ways to take that.

It was a short distance from here to there, from where he stood to where this person was.

"Wyatt, Kennedy. Kennedy, Wyatt." Lottie made herself scarce.

Kennedy brushed back brilliantly copper hair. "Hi, Wyatt. I saw you over there and, uh…" Briefly, she looked unsure of herself. "Want to dance?"

Wyatt stared. It was the last question he expected, even at his own party. His mouth flapped. His tongue lolled. Fabulously, he embarrassed himself.

"It's okay if you don't," Kennedy said.

He could feel her withdrawing and nearly reached for her. At the same time, a wild shout went up from the crowd. Wyatt didn't dare look behind him, at the girls.

"I'm not much of a dancer," he admitted. He would have made an attempt for Edy, but for this girl… she wasn't worth the laughter he'd earn.

She lifted a slender shoulder. "That's cool." Kennedy took a shot of dark liquid and grinned. "Shit. You've got the good stuff."

Now, it was Wyatt's turn to shrug. He'd only provided the money and given Lottie free rein. He didn't even know how she bought the alcohol when she wasn't old enough.

"We could talk," Kennedy said gently.

Wyatt hesitated. The friendliness all felt so alien that he had to bury his innate defense mechanism. Did she know he was Wyatt Green? Did she know what he'd been accused of? If she knew Roland Green, she'd be curling a lip in mockery.

"Talk about what?" was what Wyatt said.

Kennedy looked around, as if she'd uncover a topic. She wasn't an unattractive girl, with skin the color of savannah gold and a burst of frenetic freckles across the nose. He liked her hair, though, which was wild and so much like Edy's, tumbling on and on, though not the same shade of midnight. This girl had heavy-lidded almond eyes and the ripe sort of mouth guys went on about.

She stepped close, so close that he felt the roundness of her breasts as she jammed her hands in the back pockets of her jeans. "Maybe you do want to dance, after all."

Wyatt rolled his eyes. "I'm not trying to dislocate anything tonight."

She smiled grandly. "That accent is absolutely adorable."

He smiled a little at her, shyly because he didn't

want her to see his dental work—or lack thereof. Both the race of his pulse and the sweat on his brow were problems, too. "Yours is cute, too."

This was the closest anyone had ever come to flirting with him, and it meant nothing, of course. Her, in his room, meant nothing, of course. He wasn't crazy enough to think anyone wanted him that way.

"Wanna make out?" Kennedy said.

Wyatt choked, most likely on his own tongue. "I—I —" His stomach ground down and his fists balled tight. He gave her a closer look. Was she serious?

She watched him intently, hazel eyes following his minute movements.

Maybe. Maybe not.

"You—you wouldn't want to," he said, almost to himself. "I've never kissed before." He wasn't even sure if he'd actually said that part.

"You're kidding." Her eyes crinkled at the corners. Yep. He'd said it.

Wyatt took a step back and hit the wall, as his fingers toyed with the button of his shirt. He'd had a bit of beer, but not much. After all, Roland Green was his father. He wasn't interested in pissing on the furniture.

"You're not kidding," Kennedy said. "You've never kissed before."

For some reason, he couldn't bring himself to look away from those eyes, doubtful though they were. He shook his head and tasted his beer, before remembering that he didn't really like it.

Kennedy licked her lips and his gaze flickered down to them. They were lush and full, wet from the licking, and he thought of those girls on his couch, of the guys cheering them on, and of how he wished this was Edy with him right now.

But did this girl really want to make out with him?

"Well, can we?" Kennedy said. She leaned in, looking naughty as a kid tearing into presents on Christmas Eve. "I'll be your first."

At the moment she said, 'I'll be your first,' a distinct moan rung from the couch. Wyatt gasped in surprise, lips parting, as every part of him flashed alive.

He was thinking of another type of first, of course, one that he and Edy could no longer share. She'd given herself to Hassan and taken his word that he — the star athlete — had been a virgin.

Yeah, right.

It was all wrong. There were rumors of Hassan and any number of girls back at South End, including Sandra. Why couldn't he have settled for them and left Edy to Wyatt? It was an old complaint, yes, but one that still irked him, even as this plain girl offered her mouth up to him. Wyatt took another drink of beer, felt the earlier bit slosh in his stomach, then shut his eyes.

"Yes," Wyatt said.

The first touch of lips to lips was far more gentle than he would have anticipated. It stirred something deep and primal and left him flexing, reaching so that he ended up hand-in-hand with Kennedy. He pressed, warming to the heat and friction of the kiss, thrilling at the dip of her tongue in his mouth and the collide of curves against him.

They broke, smiled a little, then began again. Wyatt found sureness in his footing, and grounded himself in bits of reality. Yes, he was kissing a girl. They both had beer and cigarettes on their breath, and God, the slopes of her body were like sweet teases against him. She had to feel the beat of his heart, like a knock on the chest, or his hardness, straining in its own silent plea. But it was her that left a whimper in his mouth as her arms wrapped his neck. He was back against the wall when she rocked her hips hard against his, earning a hiss from Wyatt.

He squeezed her breast through the shirt and no one said or did anything to protest. As a matter of fact, she moaned. Kennedy's kiss was raw and open now, leaving Wyatt to hold on as they grinded together, music thumping in his ear, his own gasps the loudest sound in existence. He worked a hand under Kennedy's polo and shoved up her bra. His thumb found her nipple and caressed. She laughed breathlessly in his ear.

"I can't believe I'm doing this," Kennedy said between the unschooled nips Wyatt had taken of her mouth. His hands had begun a free roam once he realized he could do what he wanted, and both now were under her shirt and working hard.

He didn't know the right moment to take things further with her. Touching the other girl, kissing and squeezing her like this all felt so outrageously thrilling, but Edy was his heart and there could be no forgetting it.

What would he do if she walked in right now?

Wyatt pulled away, horrified at the thought, only to hear a shout for Kennedy at the exact same time.

"Kennedy, what the hell are you doing?" A girl with the same spray of freckles and sensuous mouth snatched Kennedy back as if it were a rescue. She turned to Wyatt with an upturned nose of disgust, before pulling Kennedy even further away. Two other girls, both with mounds of straight hair and wide hips, stood behind as additional backup for the rescue effort.

Wyatt inhaled, waiting for the fallout, the accusations, the fleeing from town.

But Kennedy snatched away from them. "Jesus Christ, Merissa, at least let me get his number."

"Like you shouldn't have done that before!"

Kennedy giggled and returned to Wyatt. The moment came when they exchanged cell numbers. He couldn't believe it.

"I'll wait for you to call," Kennedy said and winked at him. God, the wink made every bit of his blood rush to the groin. Wyatt nodded dumbly, tucking his phone away. He still couldn't stop thinking about the feel of her rocking against him or the swell of her breast in his hand.

If only that had been Edy.

Edy was at the back of his head, of course. Where she always lived.

When Wyatt went to the bathroom, he stumbled on a pair screwing roughly on his sink. Startled, he stumbled back out, cheeks flushing red, apologies on his lips. Then he went outside to take a leak and started in on the clean up early. He was at a loss for what else to do.

"You're so silly," Lottie told him, grabbing him as he went for a mess of Budweiser cans littering the hall. She had her blouse misbuttoned. "Let the hired help clean that up," she said.

Wyatt stared at her. "There isn't any hired help."

Lottie smiled prettily. "There is now."

When he flinched, she merely patted his chest. "We'll need it with all the parties."

Parties with Cîroc vodka, pounds of marijuana, and Ecstasy floating around the place. He didn't ask who provided what and how. But now, with her talk of more parties already, it worried him.

Wyatt swallowed hard several times as he thought things through. As chances stood, he might not get his mother's portion of the inheritance. That meant he had to make his two million last.

"Lottie, maybe we should talk about what's being spent. This place is expensive. So were those first-class flights. Maybe we don't have to have... so much at the parties?"

She narrowed her gaze at him. "You want people, don't you?"

He shrugged. "I don't care about them, only Edy."

"Not even Kennedy?"

Did she even have to ask?

"Every freaking thing is for Edy! You don't think you owe me something, Wyatt? You weren't the only one affected by what people *think* happened. How do you think people look at a cousin fucker?"

Wyatt started. A couple of passers-by glanced their way, curious, drunk, giggling. One guy made the shape of a hole with one hand and penetrated it over and over with his glow stick. Another shouted that there was no shame in getting it how they could. When he disappeared with a towering brunette into Lottie's room, she barely gave them a glance.

"It was your idea—" Wyatt started, loud and sharp, as he grabbed her arm, then caught himself, wondering just what in the hell he was doing. "You needed me to take the blame for your boyfriend," he insisted. "And I did."

Lottie's gaze narrowed. "Do I not say 'thank you' enough?"

He shook his head. Exhaled. Took a step back. Lottie and her boyfriend had always fought a lot. That fight wasn't the first time things had gone too far, only it was the worst. Wyatt had made the mistake of showing up during one of those brawls. He'd called the police and kept his mouth shut about her asshole boyfriend tearing out the front door a few minutes earlier. Wyatt hadn't needed to be told. Between the guy's dad being his father's boss at the factory and his instinctive need to protect Lottie, he hadn't been willing to cooperate much with the police before talking to her. He knew she wouldn't want him in trouble. Besides, he knew those officers and didn't like their superior looks. It wasn't like they didn't know Wyatt. They brought his dad home from the bar when he drank too much and fought, or when he strutted around in pissed clothes and ranted. His town had been a small one and the asshole town drunk was known. So was his kid.

Lottie softened. "I didn't know it would go so bad for you. I didn't know my dad, or the other people, would go insane like that."

Wyatt choked on his breath. What had she thought would happen? What had *he* thought? He'd been so young and stupid, wanting so desperately to be worth something to someone. He'd thought his loyalty to her would do it. He still didn't know if it had, or even if he wanted it now.

Lottie sighed. "Let's just party and have fun. I've always wanted the life of zero worries. And you deserve it. Let me give it to you."

As if she could.

"Are you listening?" Lottie said. "There's this guy

here tonight that I really like. I think you'll see more of him in the future."

What did it matter who she liked? It wouldn't work out. First loves were so passé. Divorce was common. He had a lifetime to wait for Edy while Hassan needed only one screw up to be gone. Wyatt was barely listening with the first optimistic cogs in his head turning since that first night when Hassan kissed Edy.

With that calming thought, he later drifted into sleep with a smile on his face. He dreamt of his parents. His dream-self had woken up across the street from Edy, stomach cramping with the smell of eggs in the air. Unable to believe it, he swept out of bed and hit broken glass, cursing as a shard dug deep into the softness of his arch. Oh, but those eggs. When was the last time Mom cooked? Or Dad? They'd never been able to afford takeout, and anyway, Dad complained that it was all run by foreigners.

Glass out, he hobbled to the bathroom for a bit of tissue, staved off the bleeding, and cursed when he swore bacon joined the smell of eggs. And coffee? Get the fuck out of here.

He practically skidded down the stairs, stumbling on his too-long pajama bottoms, before realizing at the last possible moment that he was supposed to meet Edy. He couldn't miss that. Not even for bacon and eggs.

There was time to shove a few slivers in his mouth —delicious they were—thank his mom for cooking, swallow a bit of her coffee and rush upstairs to get dressed.

He couldn't get ready fast enough. Somewhere in the back of his mind, he remembered falling out with Edy, remembered vowing to never speak again, and yet somehow here they were drawn to each other. Agreeing to meet anyway.

Wyatt stopped short at the sight of her in the street. For all his fantasies, for all his absolute worship of this girl, his mind never did her any justice. It never managed to capture those dark, soft eyes, that pretty little pert nose, or a mouth so soft and sensual it dried his throat. And her body. *God.* Her lithe and petite dancer's body had bloomed into jutting curves and shapely thighs.

She hugged him like she always did and a shiver of want electrocuted him. She seemed to notice, but didn't care, in that weird Edy way of hers, chalking it up to the biomechanics of some such forgivable nonsense.

They walked arm in arm, strolling, as if it weren't deathly freezing outside. Wyatt thought, not for the world would he speed this walk up. They laughed and teased and tickled and more than once he chased her, happier than he could ever remember.

He caught her near an old building that once belonged to Boston City Hospital. Somehow, Edy knew history about this building, both about how it had been part of the mental health wing, and before, when it had a darker past.

The wind cut through, furious, and on its heels came the first snowflakes.

"You're not dressed for a blizzard," Edy said softly.

He wasn't dressed for the cold weather they'd been running in either.

Wyatt shrugged. "Want to explore inside?"

He never expected her to agree, or to grab his hand, rushing inside first.

Brick walls and a low ceiling brought the temperature up in a bit. The hurried scurrying they heard was dismaying, as were the layers of dirt and grime caked on the windows that made it impossible to see out. Dirt packed the floor, making puffs whenever they took a step. Still, Edy turned to him with those eyes that always glinted.

"Want to make out?" she said in a bawdy, southern accent.

"What?" He hadn't heard that. Still, he looked at her with so much longing.

"Make out. I thought you...?"

"Yes. *Yes.*" Wyatt couldn't think beyond the word.

She smiled shyly, and his heart turned over.

He found her with his mouth, fumbling and uncertain but eager to please. She tasted like licorice and smiles. When she did smile at him, he kissed that, unable to believe his luck. He pulled her in by the elbows, reaching down around her waist, finding her hips and finally gripping those as the kiss changed, as he changed. He wanted to slow down, but he couldn't stand her changing her mind. Not now. He wanted her too bad and he'd waited too long.

His mouth punished her for that, for the waiting and humiliation, making her take his tongue, backing her into the wall, until the fight in her became clear — then *he* became clear, using his body to pin her, unbuttoning his jeans with a hand, reaching up and under her coat until he became the Wyatt he'd always been accused of being.

She cuffed him in the ear, making it ring, and he staggered back, cursing and pissed. Edy sobbed in earnest now, swearing at him in Punjabi or Hindi or something. It pissed him off, making him think of that bastard Hassan and how *he'd* never get hit for kissing her. No, she'd treasure a guy like that, open her pants for him, all while treating Wyatt like shit.

He hit her back. She looked at him, wide-eyed and startled, gaze full of accusations and Wyatt awoke with a start. He hurled over the side of the bed, sending a spray of fetid alcohol and stomach acid from his nose and mouth, lurching and heaving his vomit on the floor. He began to sob along the way, even as he threw up, that image of hitting Edy foremost in his mind. He would *never*…

Eventually, he stumbled towards the bathroom.

"Dude, you look like shit. Let me help you." Halfway there, a spare, tallish guy with a smile bright as lightning held out a hand. Wyatt may or may not have recognized him from the night before.

"Whatever," was what he muttered.

Twenty minutes later, Mateo had fixed Wyatt some chicken bouillon, sent Lincoln in the rental for some Gatorade and V8, and had Tristan making him tea. Still unsure of what these people were doing in his house, he figured one of them must be attached to Lottie.

But when Lottie came out the room a few minutes later, she had a shirtless meathead following her, laughing before he slapped her on the ass.

Wyatt thought about Edy again. That dream had been so real. His anger at her had been so palpable, so honest, and he could feel her body yielding to his kicks. She was at mercy to him and he'd *enjoyed* it.

He resisted the urge to vomit again.

Ten

A call came at a quarter to eight in the morning. A flash of Rani caught in open-mouthed laughter, followed by the chiming roll of *Shabdkosh, Shabdkosh,* the Bollywood musical, let Edy know that Hassan's mother wanted to talk. With her backpack on, Edy stared at her cell, eyes enlarging as the ring continued. What could Rani Pradhan want with her?

Especially when they hadn't spoken in months.

Maybe that's what this call was about. Maybe after all this time, with memories nipping at her heels, bouts of maternal guilt had finally given her an about face.

Edy snatched up the phone. "Hello?" she said, way too loud.

"Where is he?" Rani demanded.

"I don't know."

She scoffed. "I hardly believe that to be the case."

Edy glanced at Naomi's Mike the Tiger clock hoisted on the wall. "He's probably on his way to Accounting. I think that's his eight o'clock."

"And yet he isn't answering his phone. Is this because of you? Have you turned my own son against me?"

"I've barely seen your son!" It wasn't as if Rani needed help turning her son against her. When she wasn't pestering him about the arranged marriage, she was guilting him about his disobedience and inability to be like other, more respectful sons. No, any ignoring that Hassan was doing was being carried out for his own sanity.

"I cannot find my son."

"Right. So would you like me to, er, go to his room and—"

"No! That's absolutely inappropriate!"

It didn't even matter. Edy couldn't be caught socializing with Hassan. The upperclassmen dancers would roast her on a spigot.

Mike the Tiger ticked loudly, reminding her that in a few short minutes she had a class in a building she'd never been to.

"Can we talk later, Rani? I have History of Dance soon." And she was really, really looking forward to it.

"There's no reason to talk. Just let Hassan know that his mother is looking for him, if he concerns himself with these things anymore."

Edy sighed audibly. Rani's guilt trips could get a bit tiresome. But instead of saying that, she said, "Of course he concerns himself with these things. You're his mother. He loves you."

"Not as much as you, it would seem." It was early for this.

"It's a different kind of love," Edy said. "Both are

special. Don't deny him one when both make him so happy."

In the silence, Edy started walking for class. If she generally headed in the right direction, then it would shave a few minutes off the route, at least.

"You should have sisterly love for Hassan. You should have rejected his advances for my sake."

Edy said nothing. She wasn't sure what she was meant to say.

"It repulses me, you know," Rani continued. "The way you two look at each other. You've been raised as siblings."

"We were neighbors," Edy said. "Our fathers were roommates in college. Our families were close." She hesitated before adding the finishing touch. "I don't think you'd be raising this objection if I were Punjabi."

Rani made a noise in her throat that sounded like trapped chicken bones were there. The last time Edy had heard something like that, Hassan and the twins had smashed out his bedroom window with a baseball and nearly tumbled out trying to catch it, drawing the attention of gawking neighbors.

"You are neither Punjabi nor Hindu, Edy. Don't pretend to misunderstand."

"My parents are Christian. That means I can't *date* your son? We haven't taken wedding vows. We just enjoy each other's company."

Again with the sound.

"He loves you deeply," Hassan's mother said. "I

cannot imagine him turning away from you, once you have opened your arms to him. You bear the blame for what's happened between you two. You are the stronger; he is more emotional, impulsive. You can calculate, Edith. You know the weight of his heart and the power you hold."

"You think I manipulated his feelings?" Edy said as she made her way down the hall. "You think I caused him to reciprocate some emotion only I had?" She'd never considered it, but was it possible? Was it possible that she'd misconstrued Hassan's protective nature, assigning it some deeper meaning? Had she romanticized what was practical and convinced him that this behavior was evidence of love? She didn't think so, but it was a new thought.

"No," Rani said, "I do not think you willfully manipulated him." She paused. "However, I think you are more responsible for the mess you've made. I think as a young lady certain things should have been explained to you... better. Perhaps it was my job to do so and I did not."

Edy descended the stairs when she saw the crowd for the elevator and made it out to the street. She continued to head in the general direction of class. "What is it you wish would have been explained?" she said softly. It had taken a while for her to gather enough courage to pose the question. She could feel a unique sort of wounding coming on and she shied away, even as she pressed forward, willing to take any contact at all with Rani.

"Boys are... driven by their urges. Impossibly so. It is incumbent upon you, as a girl, not to give in to such urges and sully your reputation. It humiliates the entire family, not just the girl who has debased herself."

Debasement. Is that what Edy did with Hassan? It felt anything but. She swallowed, wondering how she could deliver a sufficient reply without further inflaming her relationship with Rani. Or whatever it was they had.

"You're being completely ridiculous. Not to mention outdated in this country by about fifty years. My 'reputation', as you put it, is not sullied by your son. We do nothing but complement each other. And what happens between us is... no one else's business, really."

She hadn't meant that last part. Well, she meant it, but she hadn't meant it like that.

"You want me to mind my business when it comes to you and Hassan?"

Edy groaned. She stood on a sidewalk as students streamed past, purposeful in their strides. She could feel the impatience coursing through her veins. "Yes. I am what Hassan wants. He is what I want. My parents accept it. Ali has said he only wants our happiness. It's only you now, Rani. All alone and making everyone miserable." She flexed her hands, stretching her fingers then making a fist.

"My husband said that he no longer opposes you?" Rani

was on the verge of yelling, reverting to her native Punjabi in another rarity Edy could file away: yelling. But Edy had also run out of patience.

"Yes. Like you say, he practically raised me. He actually loves me. I make his son happy and his son makes me happy. What else is there?"

"Spoken like a selfish child. Whatever makes you happy, whatever whim, is what should be done. Utterly ridiculous."

"Why?" Edy demanded and her legs powered forward, angry, irrational, only sort of maybe going the right way. At least she was moving. "Why is my happiness utterly ridiculous? Or Hassan's? Why should we even listen to you when you don't try to understand what anyone else wants? When every word out your mouth is just... *bakchodiyān!*"

Edy gasped and clapped a hand over her mouth, horrified at the way she'd insulted the other woman. *Bullshit.* She'd said that everything that came out of Rani's mouth was bullshit.

Her heart beat a cadence of fear as she waited for a response. When it didn't come, Edy glanced at her cell phone and realized she'd been hung up on.

Oh God. That was so bad.

Before her conversation with Rani, Edy had attempted to memorize the location of her class. She didn't want to look like a freshman dork, wandering around in search of where to go. Now, she used her cell phone's GPS to navigate the campus, cutting across lush grass and ducking beneath the swing-low branches of lush magnolia foliage. Despite the GPS, she didn't seem to be finding the building.

"Music and Dramatic Arts?" One student walked past her, rocking to oversized Beats headphones. "Music and Dramatic Arts?" People swarmed around her. "Music and Dramatic Arts!" Eventually one person slowed down enough to point. Trouble was, he pointed in the opposite direction of where GPS said she should go. Three steps along, she asked another person, whose point coincided more with her phone's directions. Breathless, Edy took off at a trot, knowing she looked like an idiotic freshman but unable to help it.

When she burst into the tiny classroom adjacent to a much larger theater it was like bursting into a bubble: sudden and shocking for the bubble itself. Every head turned, including that of the slight, smallish woman at the front, who froze mid-speech. Even so, she did manage to turn one hellish scowl on Edy. That alone would've made a lesser girl shrink back. Maybe one who had a normal mother, instead of the bulldog that was Rebecca Phelps.

"Get in, set your bag down, and come back for a syllabus." She jutted a finger at her desk.

Edy frowned. Certainly she'd pass the teacher's desk and the stack of syllabi atop it as she headed for a seat. Wouldn't it make more sense to get whatever paperwork on her way to the seat?

"Well?" the woman barked.

"Sorry," Edy muttered, but not loud enough for anyone to hear, before actually stepping into the room.

"Shut the door the way you found it!" The professor's body rattled with each word.

Edy mumbled more apologies, closed the door as quietly as tense muscles would allow, and headed for the stack of paperwork up front.

"Learn to follow directions! Place your possessions down, then return for your syllabus!"

Edy's jaw shut tight enough to snap. Her nerves rattled and zipped through her body. First day. First class. Now this.

Edy took a deep breath, turned away from her teacher's desk, and tripped over her own shoelaces. Two stumbles in, both her arms flung out and the point of her chin slammed against an occupied desk.

The bang was deafening, right through her skull.

"Holy shit. You okay?" The sound of one male voice came in crisp, alongside a chittering of laughter and a few snorts.

"What an idiot," a distant, female said.

"Let me help you," said a male, mildly amused voice, before Edy felt a hand on the tender flesh of her arm. Tanned warm skin, a narrow face, crisp harsh brows, and cool gray eyes turned down to her.

They were laughing. Everyone. Instinctively, her cheeks heated. Edy had to remind herself that she was fine and yet another guy thought she needed rescuing or protecting.

"I'm fine," Edy snapped and snatched from his grip.

His features turned cold, harsh, instantly forbidding.

"Then get off the floor," he hissed, looming like a Titan.

Edy inhaled at the harshness in his voice, certain there'd been a temperature drop in the room. Then she remembered her awkward position on the floor of her first college class and began to carefully pick herself up. She'd lost a book and a few notebooks in the process of falling, she realized, and the other guy had stepped on them, leaving a massive imprint on her binder.

"Queen Elizabeth," their professor said with false sweetness, "you are disrupting my class. *Still*."

The other guy groaned, gave her a massive eye roll, then scooped up her possessions and dumped them on a desk. The laughter continued, unbidden.

Edy inhaled. She was a freaking idiot, but she would not apologize for falling. Hell, if this woman hadn't been so rigid in her instructions, then she would not have fallen. Right? Except, she *had* been riled up by that conversation with Rani.

Edy managed to gather herself without further struggles and went for the seat her rude ass knight had picked out for her. She could practically feel the heat coming off him, the anger at her for Lord knew what, and she didn't want to engage him any further. For one, she wasn't even supposed to be talking to guys.

For two, he was an asshole, obviously. Still, that was the only seat. So, she sauntered past the would-be-savior and dropped down behind him.

"Through making your entrance?" he said.

Edy snorted out a laugh, then couldn't believe herself.

"And I thought they said all dancers had grace," a girl at the back of the room said. Though she got a few laughs from the wisecrack, none laughed as loud and long as she did at her own joke.

Edy scowled Rebecca Phelps-style at her.

"Here," the professor said, after returning from her desk. She slammed the syllabus in front of Edy and went to the front of the room. "Because I don't plan to spend half the class getting you settled in."

Despite her best efforts, Edy flushed all over and slumped down in her seat. What a way to start college. If only she hadn't answered the phone when Rani called.

"Back to introductions," the professor prompted. "Sierra from London went last, right?" she said and gestured to a girl at the back of the room.

"Yes," the girl said. Edy recognized her as the one commenting on her grace. But she didn't sound very British. Instead, she strong-armed that southern accent as much as anyone.

"Well, wow, London," Edy whispered, thinking of The Royal Ballet and all the opportunities a girl like that must have had.

"Calm down. It's London, Texas," said the rescuer.

Edy shot him a look. What was with this guy?

The professor prompted the next person to speak up. It turned out to be him.

"I'm Silas," he said. "Silas Swain from… Baton Rouge, by way of New Orleans."

"Dance background?" their professor prompted.

Edy wanted to dig out her schedule to find the woman's name, but she dared not make too much motion and draw her attention yet again.

"Lots of stuff," Silas said. "I'm into all-purpose performance."

Edy rolled her eyes. What the hell did that even mean? Certainly, their professor wouldn't stand for it. Not when she'd lost her shit over Edy's entrance into the classroom. But the corners of the instructor's mouth twitched as if unsure whether to laugh or scowl.

"Schools of instruction?" she said finally.

Silas sighed. "Nederlands Dans and, uh, the School of American Ballet."

Ballet? Really? "Wow," Edy whispered, leaning forward. "In New York?"

"No, in Chattanooga," Silas snapped.

Edy's features wrenched into a scowl.

"Aspirations?" the professor prompted.

"I don't know," he said sullenly. "Whatever."

"Then why are you here?" their teacher snapped. "Why not go and join a company? School is expensive.

You have competitive credentials. Or is it that you have no talent to match?"

Silas lifted his head. "I'd like a degree. It was important to my parents... It's... important to me." An awkward silence followed.

"Was?" the teacher probed harshly.

"They're dead," he said. "Nothing's important to them now, obviously."

Edy cringed. She could feel the stares on him, could feel the gaping maw of morbid curiosity, and wanted to erect a wall of protection. She blurted her next words so as to divert attention to her. She was next anyway.

"I'm Edy — Edith Phelps — from Boston, Massachusetts," she said too loudly. "I'm a dance major and a Lady Tiger. I began classical ballet around my fifth birthday so I have twelve years of training, mostly at Boston Ballet. I had intensives there and at the School of American Ballet. I've also competed competitively a number of times and placed every time —local, regional, even national. Ballet aside, I'm interested in contemporary and modern dance. I love street dancing and improvisation." She blushed, realizing she'd said more than she'd been asked and talked more than anyone so far. Now she didn't know how to end it. Edy dropped her gaze. "I don't know what's in my future. That's why I'm here."

"They say that's not the only reason she's here," Sierra from London said and snickered.

Edy flushed hot, then cold. Did she mean Hassan? She must've meant Hassan. But how could she possibly know that? *Wait.* She vaguely remembered Hassan being interviewed for puff pieces and blogs after he'd made his college selection known. He hadn't made Edy a secret then; in fact, he'd said that she had been part of his decision process. But had people actually read those things? She guessed so. And if they had, had they somehow discredited the minor footnote about her helping to select their college? She supposed the fact that she and Hassan had wound up at a major football college meant to some people that whatever input Edy purported to have was minor at best. She was seen as following Hassan like a lapdog. She was seen as tethering her future to his. The implication was that dance came second to football and that she'd dance anywhere just to be near him. Edy resisted the weak urge to turn on Sierra and blurt out how LSU had been just as much her choice as Hassan's. But why bother? No one would believe her. Her parents did. Maybe, deep down, Edy didn't believe herself either.

"Thank you, Edith from Boston," the professor said disapprovingly. As she did so, she raised a brow in much the same way Edy's dad did before consulting the Internet for which drug he thought she might be abusing.

A girl with a narrow hammer of a face introduced herself next. She was Bridgette from Biloxi, in to modern dance.

The introductions continued. Edy's instructor finally revealed herself as Anya Martin, daughter of the somewhat celebrated French choreographer, Michel Martin. Though she talked her dad up quite a bit, Edy ignored it mostly because she'd heard of her father, the elder Bouche, and his reputation preceded him. Back in Boston, she'd met another dancer claiming to be the daughter of Martin. Then another. It turned out that Martin was a serial philanderer known to favor his current love interest when casting—irrespective of talent or lack thereof. As a result, Martin left a string of disgruntled talent in his rear-view mirror. Still, his choreography transformed classical ballet into the breathtakingly modern, and for that he was remembered.

Class began with an open discussion about dance and when it might have started. The slender redhead to the left of Edy, with a great burst of freckles on both her cheeks, had quite a bit of speculation to offer up.

"I'll bet dance was, like, the first thing ever," she said. "Because sound makes you wanna move, you know?" If Edy hadn't been in Louisiana, she would have guessed that the girl exaggerated her broad southern accent as a joke. It seemed to swell with every word. "Also my mom, who would have liked to have been a dancer back in her day, says the same thing. She has a dancer's body, you know. It's what my daddy first noticed about her. Anyway, she says that dancing is the one art that don't have to be taught. But whenever she says that, her and daddy get in a big argument about how much my lessons cost and whether he ought to try and get his money back. But you know what I think?"

Edy resisted the urge to slam her head on the desk. Lord, this girl could talk. She could practically see Hassan's vacant stare if he had happened to be subjected to this, followed by the single sidestep of a man planning his getaway. The way this girl carried on, Edy hardly thought she'd notice anyone escaping.

More people threw in their opinions as to when people began to dance. Silas said nothing, as did Edy. They spent the hour discussing dance in its various functions, including celebratory, funerary, communicative, and educational, before the professor held up the class textbook, *The Evolution of Dance*, and gave them a massive reading assignment to be done before the next meeting.

Damn. As if time wasn't already a thin commodity.

After class, Edy could feel eyes on her as she packed up her belongings.

"So, you were at SAB," Silas said appraisingly, blocking the aisle and her exit. "I never saw you."

The halls were filling. The door was opened. Edy couldn't take the risk that Tamela or one of the other dancers might pass and see this guy talking to her. It wouldn't matter that she hadn't opened her mouth at all or that she only opened it to pass by. She'd be made to swallow the blame for this interaction and every other. Edy had to get rid of this guy.

"I didn't know you took attendance for the school," she muttered as the last of her possessions were packed up. She didn't bother to lift her head just in case one of the girls did pass by. Maybe they wouldn't recognize her. Or maybe they wouldn't see her talking to a guy.

Silas snorted. "Fucking *Lady* Tigers. Don't expect everyone to scrape and bow. You're a joke, after all."

Edy snapped up at that, body tense, hands flexing without her permission. She worked hard for that team and already sacrificed so much. What did he know about it, anyway?

"Get out my way," she said instead. "I have class."

He laughed and stepped aside. "Of course, Your Highness. Anything you say, Your Highness."

Edy mimicked his laugh in a bout of pettiness, unhappy with her need to do so, but feeling immature in the moment. With a sneer she stormed from the classroom, as unhappy with Silas Swain as with herself.

Eleven

Silas Swain swept onto his motorcycle, pulled the clutch lever, and flipped the kill switch. His mouth pulled down in what had to be a characteristic scowl before he pulled out and nearly collided with a pickup.

"Watch it, pretty boy," shouted Caiden Cash from the window of a grimy pickup. The doors flew open and that freshman running back, whose name Silas made a point of not remembering, jumped out and fed him a scowl.

"Fuck both of you," Silas said and eyed them for good measure. The football team may run the school, but they didn't run him. He refused to look up to a bunch of D minus assholes who took a pummeling for a living. They were probably suffering from concussions now. The sunlight probably tortured them.

The quarterback, then the freshman, came over and stood in front of his bike. Both looked him over as if he was supposed to be intimidated.

"Don't you have some dancing to do? Or maybe you've decided to save that for the girls?" Cash said.

For some reason, the running back looked over at

him with a look of dismay.

Silas rolled his eyes. His kid brother, Levi, had dreams of professional football. But why? The boy was smart enough to do and be anything.

"I wonder how that second-string option is looking, Cash. He'll need to be strong since I'm about to run you over." *And your asshole sidekick,* he almost said. Who had time for people who followed blindly, anyway?

Cash glared at him another minute, tall, strong, and solid enough to blot a bit of sun from where Silas sat.

"You don't want to go making enemies you can't unmake," Cash said.

"Ditto goes for you. Now as much as I'm enjoying that battered mug of yours, some of us have got to earn a living. It would please me if you got the fuck outta my way."

The freshman stepped back first. He'd looked uncomfortable since the moment Cash had said Silas danced. Maybe his little brain had been shattered by that. Maybe he thought only cheerleaders danced. *Ugh.*

Cash moved and Silas peeled off. He'd been pissed since the moment in class that he'd mentioned his parents. He didn't talk about them. He didn't think about them, if he could help it. These days, it was Silas and Levi. That was the beginning and end of his family.

As Silas turned onto Dalrymple and followed the winding drive alongside the lake and off campus, his thoughts turned to the twit who'd stumbled in class and rambled on and on about herself. Typical that she'd be a Lady Tiger. She'd probably been one of those self-centered airheads who had an entire high school of admirers just last year. He could picture Edith Phelps looking down that pert little nose at everyone she passed. No doubt she dated some football player who was equal parts asshole.

If she was looking for a coalition of devotees, she wouldn't find a taker in him. No, as a matter of fact, he was willing to bet she was shallow and disgusting.

Silas couldn't be bothered with that.

Twelve

The guy was a friggin *dancer.* Why did that unnerve Hassan so? He had the look of an athlete. And Jesus —wasn't dance where he and Edy had always diverged? He used to drag his feet to her recitals, complain about time served at her practice sessions, and zone out when she got technical on him. But this guy, this Silas, could connect, could understand her. They'd share passions. They'd click. Hell, just how many Silases were there at LSU?

Hassan pushed back at the queasiness that snaked through him and reminded himself how firmly his girl loved him and how inseparable they were. Hadn't that been what the fuss was all about between their families? Hassan stood up a little straighter at the thought. Really, why was he even wasting his time on this asshole? He was being stupid.

And he had a class to get to.

The second he took off for English class, Hassan's thoughts turned from the asshole on the bike to the last time he'd seen Edy.

"It's just the dance team, pageant queen. Gorgeous, but crazy as hell. Better to admire them from afar." That had

been what Freight said to Hassan on the practice field on the lone occasion Hassan had seen Edy since their arrival at LSU. Since then, Hassan had gone through weigh-ins and measurements, followed by meetings, early morning practices and evening ones too, all with the same demanding tempo. After their night at the club, she had early morning jogs with her team. Freight said that it was purposely done as a way to torment the girls after drinking. Edy, who definitely was getting tormented, had stopped in a nearby bush to vomit with two girls hovering and rubbing her back. She'd broken her promise to come to him if she drank too much or otherwise felt sick. Hassan watched her, perplexed about why she hadn't reached out to him, and unsure of what to do next. His last glimpse of Edy had included glancing in his direction before she wiped her mouth with the short towel tucked at her waist, smiled weakly, and took off.

It was that weak smile that haunted him, and all the possibilities it conveyed. What was happening? What was she going through? Why hadn't she reached out to him?

What was she going through? Because she was going through something—he could feel that much. They hadn't spoken in days because of his and her maddening lives, but if she could speak to him without actually speaking what would she be saying?

Was she happy, at least?

He'd heard things about the dance team. Odd

things. Weird whispers about dens and helpmates and walking the walk. Hassan had problems of his own though, what with clear tape constantly placed all over his locker so he'd look like a jackass, or his third Jansport backpack now stolen and switched out for a Dora the Explorer one (the other two had been Pikachu and a Disney Princesses tote). Plus, there were the half dozen times he'd already worn Gatorade, got Gatorade for the veterans, or had his cell phone ransacked so a bunch of numbers were rearranged. These were pranks though and his teammates' way of ensuring he understood his place. He was a rookie, and likely to catch a little more hell than the rest, given that he'd come with so much fanfare.

Hassan and Edy were able to text, but truly, by the time he finished with his daily schedule, showered, and returned to his room it was almost always close to curfew time and the ache in his muscles fought with fatigue for which would get the most attention.

Even their messages were clipped. Brisk hellos. A few I love yous. More often than not, night after night consisted of the same loop-the-loops where he mentioned a long day and she mentioned a long day before the two promised to talk tomorrow.

But talking wasn't what they did. Texting was what they did. He felt crazy for being irritated by it, but otherwise couldn't shake the feeling that something, somehow was happening to the two of them without his permission.

And how the hell was she? For the first time, he didn't know.

Hassan and Edy had exchanged schedules and discovered they had the same freshman English class together. It gave him the idea to hustle there early, hauling ass from Accounting over at the Business Complex through campus and over where his GPS said English classes were being held. He earned a handful of hoots and cheers as others recognized him on his sprint, but Edy was his only thought.

He made it to class before her and stood outside the door like he used to in high school. Despite the crowd, he saw Edy, with her head down and ponytail up, rushing through the swarm as if she was about to be late. She had another girl with her that helped run interference, a willowy, undersized girl who blocked so cleanly they could have made a spot for her on his team. They were at the door in no time. Edy looked at him, silently pleading in some way he couldn't decipher, and went past without a word.

Hassan blinked, pretty sure that hadn't happened.

But when he turned, there was Edy taking a seat towards the back of the auditorium, then making slow work of unpacking her belongings as the girl who'd come with her shot off into the hall.

Hassan's eyes narrowed to nothing. He inhaled. He exhaled. Still, the image stirred more fury than he could control. His gaze snapped to her. He watched, but almost immediately decided that he couldn't play her game. He didn't do ignoring people. He didn't do watching and waiting. He marched over and grabbed the problem by the collar.

Hassan dropped into the seat next to her.

"That... did not just happen, right? You didn't just pretend not to know me," he said.

Edy looked at him with unmistakable alarm in her eyes. Whatever organizing she'd been doing of her books and supplies came to a halt as Hassan finally, finally had her undivided attention.

"No," she said weakly, her voice a broken whisper.

"Then what?" he demanded, a little louder than he'd meant to. "Was your greeting so low, I missed it? Were you saving it for the class? Or was that something else no one can see?"

Her face crumpled and her shoulders came up in that way that meant she was embarrassed, incredibly so, but the idea of anyone being able to make her pretend not to know him did horrible things to him. Things he had to back away from.

"Just tell me what that was," he said quietly.

Edy studied him for another quiet moment, pretty eyes sweeping his face in vulnerability, shoulders drifting down little by little.

She was still his Cake and he still wanted to help. He knew offering her money outright would get him told off, even if she needed it. He'd come prepared to do battle with her pride, but then she'd pretended not to know him and he'd lost it.

A few of the people ushering in glanced their way, some in their seats outright turned to watch.

"You have a fucking nose problem, brother. Let me fix it for you," Hassan said.

Edy's hand dropped onto his arm and it felt like a burst of warm water. He wanted to drown in it.

"Don't," she said softly.

Not this shit again. "Why are you whispering?" he said.

Edy glanced around, as if the walls had ears and tongues to wag.

"I can't talk to you," she said. "I can't talk to any guy. You know this. I just got in trouble for talking to a guy. I can't..." She trailed off, shaking her head.

"That's bullshit," Hassan said. But just as soon as he'd uttered it, he remembered his own circumstances and how he'd become the water boy for the vets. He looked around, as if he were suddenly in on this madness. "For how long?"

She shrugged. Then switched over to Punjabi. *"Until I get out of the den."*

"The den?" Hassan echoed.

"It's where we sleep at night," Edy said.

Hold on. What?

"Cake," Hassan said. But then he wasn't sure which way to go. Part of him forever needed to protect her and wanted to drag her from this place. They could start all over somewhere else, doing football and dance. But then he looked at her, really looked at her.

This was the girl who had saved him from getting shot. She'd grown up with four football players, and jostled rough and tumble through the years. She'd stared down a gunman and saved his life, instead of vice versa. She'd told their parents who they were and what their intentions were towards each other. This girl could take whatever the den was, plus more. This girl was truly fierce and he owed it to her to treat her as such.

But then he remembered something. *"You just got in trouble for speaking to another guy... But you can't talk to me?"*

She shot him a single desperate look. When she opened her mouth, nothing came out.

A squat, slump-shouldered man with a shining bald spot at the center of his head entered the classroom and rushed to the front as if someone was chasing him. He proceeded to rattle off a long list of things and people he didn't care about: the Kardashians, summer vacations, weather, pets, pop music, incendiary devices, or feelings, apparently. Writing about any of them would earn them an 'F' on their paper.

"Incendiary devices?" muttered one guy to the left of Edy.

Hassan pulled a sheet of paper from his notebook and a pen, making a great effort to stay calm. Whoever the guy was, he wasn't important. He decided to focus on what was.

WHEN CAN I SEE YOU? he wrote and handed it

to her.

She hesitated. Stared at the sheet. For one wild moment, he thought she wouldn't answer. AFTER A GAME, MAYBE TWO.

Okay. Okay, fine. He was busy, too. Real busy. Classes, practice, school work, more school work. He had plenty to focus on right now. He'd miss her, but it wasn't as if he didn't have a ridiculous amount of options for keeping busy.

He began to draw mindlessly on the paper. After a moment, he realized it was a sketch of that goddamned Pikachu he was creating. He took out another sheet of paper, ignoring her questioning stare, and started up another conversation.

ARE YOU OKAY? DO YOU NEED CASH OR ANYTHING?

She stared at his question so long he sighed. Before she handed over her response, he knew what it would be.

I'LL BE FINE.

Hassan wanted to argue with her. But he knew he wouldn't win with a few scribbles on the paper as both of them pretended to listen in on the never-ending assortment of rules for their class.

He had another thought, and so pivoted to that.

IS THERE A WAY TO CHEAT? SO THEY WON'T KNOW THAT YOU'RE WITH ME? he wrote and slipped her the note.

Yeah, so he really did want to see her, so what? He

missed her closeness, but he missed her friendship, too. That was as much her fault as his, he supposed. His practices had dropped from two-a-day to one with the approaching of school, but now he had mandatory study sessions, team meetings, position meetings, and intermittent changes to the playbook that required studying. On the off-chance that Hassan found a moment of freedom, he spent it with his teammates or in the gym shoring up on deficiencies, studying NFL running backs, or improving overall. He didn't care what compliments he got. Good was never enough.

On their first day of practice, their coach had surprised Hassan by giving Paul an open chance to compete for his position. Hassan took that as a showing of uncertainty in what he could do, as a call for him to prove himself. By the end of the first day's practice, the team had begun calling Paul 'Slowpoke.' Hassan felt confident he'd start. Judging by the anger and anguish coming from Paul's direction, the other running back felt sure, too.

He knew that hanging with Edy before he'd ever even set foot in Death Valley would earn him shit from the guys. 'He hadn't earned the privilege of girls,' was what team wide receiver, Xavier Wright said. He usually didn't make much fuss over Hassan though, as tormenting Lawrence was his main course.

Hassan was willing to put up with Xavier and Cash and Freight and whoever else they threw at him if it earned him some time with his girl. Wasn't that the point of being there in Baton Rouge? Surely she felt the same.

"Edy," Hassan said and hated the uncertainty in his voice.

"Yes," she answered quietly in Punjabi.

Hassan sighed. "Just... text me when you can."

She nodded quickly, as if glad to be rid of him.

Most of the week passed without a word about when they could meet. Hassan's pride wouldn't allow him to bring it up again, but every minute, every second he allowed his mind to roam, an irritation settled in that he neither wanted nor could displace.

Edy had things to do. Fine. He was on the top collegiate football team in the nation. Who had more things to do than him? Truly, he didn't have time to see her anyway. If she wanted to see him, he'd be busy. And he certainly wouldn't break curfew for her like he had been thinking.

No, he certainly wouldn't do that.

Edy texted him at two o'clock Thursday morning and asked if he was awake and could meet her. He hadn't been awake before her text, but swallowed at the sight of it, already knowing he would break curfew for her. He would do this stupid thing right before his very first goddamned game and what a game it was. Virginia Tech. Edy. Virginia Tech.

His pulse skittered as he stared at his cell phone. When he crept from his bed, it was with an eye on Lawrence, knowing he woke at the slightest provocation. He didn't disappoint when the mattress squeaked.

"Where are you going?" he asked when he saw Hassan throw on a pair of black gym shorts, silently cursing that his Mustang hadn't arrived from Boston yet. What was taking his parents so long?

"Downstairs to get a soda."

"You need to change for that?" Lawrence said.

Hassan exhaled. It wasn't that he expected to trick his best friend and slip out undetected. It was that he expected to at least try.

"Give me a break, Lawrence, okay? Edy just wrote me and—"

He was up in an instant. "No. Hell no."

"I haven't spent time with her in weeks—"

"Sawn, we're playing *Virginia Tech* on Saturday. Have you lost your mind?"

A little bit. Maybe. Yeah. He just needed to make sure that Edy was okay. He also needed... her steady hand? It was more than nervousness about the upcoming game though. It was about just wanting her near. That was their life. Always.

"Go back to sleep. I won't involve you," Hassan said and reached under the bed for a random pair of Jordans.

"Okay. You won't involve me. Just the whole fucking team." Lawrence sat up.

Hassan stared at him. He was right and he knew it. "Yet, the text message from Edy..."

Lawrence sighed. "Look, I know you didn't get to see her much during the summer —"

"At all."

"At all then." Lawrence said. "And I know you aren't always levelheaded, you don't have much patience, and you're impulsive as shit. But what good is coming here if you don't allow yourself to get on the field? Give yourself a chance. Girls can wait. *Edy* can wait."

Hassan scowled. "Fine," he said. "I'll tell her no."

Lawrence rolled his eyes. "For the first time in your life. She might explode from the shock."

Thirteen

Edy cast a fretful glance at her roommate. She made sure her iPhone's vibrate option was on and tucked the device under her pillow. That way, if it went off and she was too sleepy to hear it, the vibrations through her skull might carry some resonance. Maybe.

"He said he couldn't break curfew," Edy said. "I know he would have been here if there was any other way, but for him, it wasn't an option."

Naomi looked as disappointed as she felt. "Maybe you should tell him that you have no idea when you'll get another time."

After all, it was the first night they'd been allowed to sleep in their own rooms. Tamela told them that they'd be permitted personal time in preparation for the game and they should use it wisely. The second they could bolt from the imposing upperclassman's presence, Edy texted her boyfriend. When she did so, it was with shaking hands, knowing the older girl would be absolutely disappointed. After all, she was the most promising freshman, the most solid on technique, the most insistent on applying exacting artistry. Even Tamela gave her grudging compliments, though they came with a thoughtful frown. Just that night, Edy found out why.

"You really are talented, Boston," she'd said while they were still crowded into the one bedroom apartment, otherwise known as the den, that they slept in each and every night. "Don't fuck yourself over with that Pradhan."

It was as if she'd been wedged in the airplane bathroom with them or rolling in the sheets at the hotel. It was as if she knew about the little worry niggling in the back of Edy's brain: the little worry that threatened to become a big one.

"You're as good at dancing as he is at football. You owe yourself to seeing it through," she'd said. It was something that Rani would have said in Edy's old life and she choked unexpectedly at the captain's words.

Seeing it through. What did that mean for Edy? Four years of college and a dance major, followed by endless auditions and the hope of joining a company? What if she could join one now, would she?

Naomi looked at her with wide, doleful, sympathetic eyes. "We should probably just get some sleep," she said. "Lord knows rest is hard to come by."

She was right, of course. So, Edy shut off the light, snuggled into bed, and tried to drift away. Exhaustion eeked through her limbs, tangling with a melancholy of ache and homesickness. She saw dance and missed Boston, Dunberry Street, and her family with every breath she took. She missed Hassan and realized that, for the first time, they were disconnected. But they were adjusting, adjusting to whatever it was that Baton Rouge promised, all while hoping whatever that happened to be was enough to make up for what they'd lost.

When the tears came, Edy credited them to exhaustion and loneliness. All summer, their parents had kept her and Hassan apart. A thousand miles away, others conspired to do the same. How long would it last? Worst still, why did the silence of their separation echo so harshly? Frightened to think of what it meant, Edy squeezed her eyes shut and reviewed Saturday's halftime show in her mind in the hope sleep would soon claim her, but she couldn't keep her thoughts off Hassan or off the arranged marriage he tried his damnedest to ignore, but which his parents —mother especially—refused to let him escape. A big part of him just wanted the freedom to make decisions for himself, but another part, she supposed, expected to marry her one day.

Then what? Children? Lots of them? She knew from their childhood talks that he wanted a brood of his own, like the Dysons. What concessions would she have to make to give him that wish? What part of herself and her dreams would she have to give up in order to help him meet his? And while she was busy cutting years off of her dancing career becoming a wife and a mother, what would he sacrifice?

He wasn't even willing to break curfew for her.

Fourteen

Friday afternoon, just before the team boarded their bus for the local hotel that would house them until after the game, Coach named his starters with Hassan among them. Paul choked a sob in his throat that no one missed. When Freight tried to clap him on the back in encouragement, he shoved at him and muttered something about being part of the Pradhan entourage.

While the other starting freshmen were beyond elated, Lawrence going so far as to brandish a rare smile, a sullenness settled into Hassan. He couldn't stop thinking of Paul and that sound he'd made. Of how disappointed he must've been, of what this all meant for the other boy's future in football.

Hassan checked into his room all brooding and silent, but determined not to spoil Lawrence's debut elation. Under normal circumstances, he would have been running plays through his head endlessly, but now he couldn't. Hadn't he heard that the other boy had a baby on the way? Maybe this year could have been a breakout for him if Hassan hadn't come along. Maybe he would've been able to support a family by entering the draft and getting picked up. He couldn't stop the maybes. It was only when Lawrence told him that he had a call on the bedroom's phone that the merry-go-round ceased in his head.

No one should have known where they were, or who was in which room, for that matter.

"Yeah?" croaked Hassan, certain some media asshole had found him to unleash some further torment.

He was met with silence.

"Hello?" Hassan said. "Last time."

"Don't hang up. I, uh, wanted to wish you luck," said the familiar voice, "and tell you to watch out for Thornton on defense. He's large and quicker than most his size."

Hassan couldn't stop the smile. "Nathan."

"Yes?"

"I—" There was so much to say about responsibilities and expectations and how Paul may or may not be having a baby. But he needed Nathan to know that he didn't want to disappoint him anymore, that he loved him like a father, and loved his daughter endlessly. She was the most beautiful, awe-inspiring, perfect creation. He was sorry he'd allowed so much to come between him and Nathan. He wanted to say it all, but when he opened his mouth, there was only silence.

"I owe you and Edy an apology," Nathan said. "I haven't worked up the courage to call her, but I am sorry for not supporting her decisions and yours. Also for being so impulsive as of late."

Hassan paused. "Is everything alright?" While he assumed Edy's dad referred to their hotel fiasco, there was no way he'd ask for clarification.

"Well, if she hasn't mentioned anything, I suppose..." Nathan trailed into a dramatic sigh. "I've handled things badly. If Edy asks, let her know that replacement credit cards will take some time getting to her. They need to be mailed to Boston before I can mail them to Baton Rouge."

Right. Hassan filed it away.

"I do have a question, son," Nathan said. "My behavior when I was in Louisiana... has Edy mentioned it?"

"Not since you were here."

"And has she forgiven me?"

"That's for her to say."

"She's a good girl. And she's sacrificed exceptionally for you. An Ivy League education, the opportunity to join a ballet company, even the counsel and companionship of your mother, whom she adores. Edy has forgone all this for you, Hassan. She loves you deeply."

Hassan's breathing slowed. They'd chosen Baton Rouge together, hadn't they? This was the place where both their dreams would be realized. Wasn't it?

But what if it wasn't? What if Nathan was right, and Edy had given up some future, some opportunity, just to be near him now? He hadn't wanted that. He hadn't wanted her to sacrifice any more than he'd had to. And yet, according to Nathan, she'd done just that.

Long after their phone call had ended, Hassan wrestled with whether he'd pushed Edy towards her dreams or dragged her into his own.

After his talk with Nathan, Hassan had a night in the hotel, followed by breakfast and lunch, before the trek back to campus for the March Down Hill. Though he'd heard about the tradition, and read about it, nothing had prepared him for the clamber of shouting fans, pressed shoulder-to-shoulder and one-on-top-another, for the outright screaming as his team went to the beat of a cheerful LSU band down the road to Tiger Stadium. Down towards the front was Edy. Hassan knew that, and the thought made him feel a bit more grounded. It was Saturday, the first Saturday in September, and finally time for football.

A few narrow turns brought them to the locker room. A gleaming gold helmet trimmed in purple and white hung from a hook in each, while neatly folded towels took a corner on private shelves. Each locker had a black folded chair before it, and an LSU jersey propped up with padding. White with purple letters.

PRADHAN. 27

Was he breathing? Hassan wasn't sure. It all seemed so surreal. Like a dream he could never work hard enough to make reality.

27 was his number in high school. When he tried

out for JV football in middle school, he didn't make the first cut. He'd gone straight to Edy's house and cried like a baby. Literally, he fell apart and wound up sobbing into her pillows.

Hassan felt like a fool, he'd said, running around behind the Dysons, begging Nathan for every scrap of information he could use. He didn't have the pedigree to be out there, couldn't stand the setbacks and uncertainty: everyone said he was too emotional. And when was the last time she'd seen an NFL player named 'Gupta' or 'Patel'? Who the hell was he kidding exactly? He knew he never should have tried out.

Edy had pulled him into an embrace tighter than any he'd ever known, then whispered in his ear that one day he would be the most incredible football player *ever*. He still heard that little girl voice on his bad days, on his worst days. On that day, she had held him, squeezing until he hugged her back. It was then that the tears had started. He only had a general idea of how much time had passed by how dark her room grew. Finally, when he thought she had fallen asleep against him, Edy said, "Don't give up. Please." Even then he hadn't been able to say 'no' to her.

When he made the team the following year, he was second string and given 72 as a number, usually reserved for lineman. He worked hard and moved up to starting, then varsity by the eighth grade. When he got to high school, he was able to make varsity and prove he deserved the starting role a lot quicker. He kept the digits 7 and 2, but inverted them, to remind himself of the nobody he'd once been. Each time, each school, he'd begun anew, having to prove who he was one more time. This time, he decided, no one would forget again.

Fifteen

Their season opener was fabulous. Edy marched with her teammates in a parade that weaved through campus, through throngs of screaming fans, reaching children and little girls who clamored to take pictures with her. Some were even dressed like her. She paused for photos where she could and found she couldn't keep the smile off her face. Along the way, nestled between the throngs of LSU devotees, stood Silas Swain, like a rock in rippling waves. With both hands in his pockets and a twist of the mouth, a single eyebrow rose at the sight of Edy. She had no idea why, but his expression irked the hell out of her. She scowled without meaning to, earned a flat out grin from him, and then turned away as a pair of pigtailed twins pulled on her arm. With a smile as bright as the sun and Silas Swain's annoying ass out her thoughts, Edy paused for a picture with the grade school girls. She could hardly believe the way people clamored to her, shouting with excitement. Would this really be how she spent her weekends? The idea shot equal parts intimidation and thrill right through her.

Once at the stadium, she had a problem of a

different kind. Never. In her life. Had she seen a crowd so enormous. They packed in with their banners and screaming, ready to see her, to see Hassan, to see their teammates. This was their new life. This was what they'd signed up for. She'd had the quivers something fierce. Amazingly, Tamela gathered them, first in the bathroom, then in a snug corner near the field, for a quiet moment, some reflection, encouragement, and finally prayer. She squeezed hands and hugged with them, surprised that she'd been calmed by talking to God.

What a massive crowd. What a beautiful football team. Though Edy stood in the stands, twisting, turning, leaping with her teammates, there was only one player she could see. She gasped when he took to the field, solid and ready and in an actual freaking LSU uniform with *Pradhan* on the back. It was all Edy could do not to squeal and shove her fist in her mouth, she was so excited. They were there. This was college. It was real.

They were in for a helluva good game. Even before starting, Edy knew that Virginia Tech had picked up a monster of a defensive tackle on a transfer from Georgia. They also had a linebacker made of pure muscle and viciousness. That guy would break up a mother and her child for a football on the other end.

The game began. Edy watched, fists balled, breath coming in shallow jaunts, as she silently prayed for Hassan. Somehow, she knew he needed something big, some jolt of confidence, to solidify his belief that he belonged on this field. Three minutes in, it came. A snap of a ball, followed by a handoff to Hassan, exploded when he burst past, no, *through* defenders and flashed towards the end zone. Edy screamed his name, leapt into the air, and forgot the studied poise she was expected to exude. So, when Tamela hissed her name and Edy caught a glimpse of those meanly narrowed eyes, she remembered that that was *not* how Lady Tigers behaved.

"You're a freshman," Tamela said when the crowd had settled down. "So, you need time to learn. But it's a lesson I'll make sure you remember."

Edy grimaced, thinking of the lessons she'd already learned and the punishments that followed the stubborn ones. Eyes down and off guys, precision before flare, and never question authority were the favorite warnings of Tamela and the other upperclassmen. Should anyone of the freshman be caught so much as grinning enthusiastically, the lot of them paid for it with shouts to the face, late night exercise, and endless hours of standing. Edy had no idea what ordeal she'd inflicted on the others with her ridiculous screaming, her irrepressible need to cheer. It wasn't even like at South End, where Hassan could hear her, sense her, where they were connected despite her distance from the field. At LSU, she was one in a sea of thousands, indistinguishable, insignificant.

More than once, Edy swallowed his name and

cautioned a glance at Tamela as the game wore on. Oh, he was doing so good and it had been so long since she'd seen him... He must've been about to burst; she knew she was.

When half time approached, Tamela led Edy and her teammates in a sashaying march to the football field. During this, Edy suppressed the urge to giggle in what had to be a bout of bad nerves. She kept her eyes on the back in front of her, Cassie's back, in an effort to block out the throngs of fans who would soon be staring at her.

She was ready for this, right? Edy stole a glance up into the stands.

"Face forward, freshman," she heard from behind her.

Edy's head snapped front.

They eased onto the sidelines and huddled in a corner, mostly away from the danger of the field. Edy's gaze swept the football team, skipping over Lawrence, before resting on number 27 again. She had a stupid grin on her face. She was sure of it.

Half time had arrived. With wide eyes, Edy watched LSU's football team approach before she realized that the dancers practically stood in the way of the locker room.

He noticed her at the same time that she noticed him. And there was nothing in the world that could have stopped that stupid grin.

Hassan had jogged off the field, but now he slowed

to a stop in front of her. He paused long enough to take off his helmet. When he looked her over, one side of his mouth jerked up in a smirk of a smile, he touched her face, just barely, before ghosting fingers down her arm. Before Edy could properly respond, he took off again, catching up with his teammates for the locker room.

"Jesus. Don't be quite so easy." The male voice startled Edy and she turned to see Silas Swain just behind her. He came around to the front of their cluster like he belonged there.

Edy grimaced. Thankfully, Tamela and her co-captain, London Wu, were seething in the throes of some hushed argument. So she narrowed her eyes at Silas.

"Easy?" she echoed. "He's my boyfriend." And the only guy she'd ever be with.

Silas laughed. "Yeah. You and every other girl."

What? Edy opened her mouth for a vicious retort, only to be disappointed when he promptly walked off. He seemed to hush Tamela's argument with a word, interject something, then disappeared.

"Ladies," Tamela said and the flutters raged in Edy's stomach. "It's time."

Sixteen

The rain began right after the game. It gushed in torrents, steaming up from the heat of the night. Dirt-stained and sore, Hassan broke into something of a run alongside half a dozen other guys who straggled from the locker room. It was a hard win against Virginia Tech and Hassan had played his part. They ducked into random cars, swung onto the back of pickups, and encouraged stragglers to squeeze in so they wouldn't, according to Freight, ruin their perms, melt the sugar in their tanks, or whatever. Just about everyone went in the same direction, to the 'football' dorm where they occupied two floors.

As he took the short ride from the stadium, Hassan stared out at the storm, thoughts whisked away by the rain. He couldn't help the smile that rushed to his lips as he remembered summer storms on the Cape and dashing in the rain—him and Edy—always him and Edy. She'd squeal and hoot and splash into the ocean in an absolutely idiotic bid to get away from his tickling fingers. She could be ridiculously ticklish in the right places. And, of course, he knew the right places. He thought now of how irresistible she'd looked at the game and how he couldn't help but touch her, even there, in front of everyone. God, that girl was everything to him.

"Get that stupid look off your face, Pradhan," Freight said as he maneuvered Cash's pickup. Freight had snatched the keys in the locker room—without permission—and now sat behind the wheel. Since he'd given Hassan a head's up, he'd been able to get the passenger seat. They'd locked the team quarterback out so that he'd been forced to ride flatbed in the rain in his own vehicle. Hassan had zero guilt. In fact, it was partial payback for a shitload of shampoo squirted into his shower and into his hair a few days ago. Not only had it taken forever to get out, but it reinforced the narrative that he was, in fact, like some pageant queen who needed special amenities. Those special amenities included long showers with a pissed locker room attendant waiting for him to finish.

"You were thinking about that girl again," Freight said. "The dancer chick you came down here with."

Hassan glanced at him in surprise.

Okay. So, Freight knew more than Hassan thought. That was the way of this team. Somehow, everyone seemed to know everyone else's business. Because of that, it was common knowledge that Edy the Dancer was Hassan's girl and they were some kind of sappy sweet couple who had had their first kiss in diapers.

Hey. So, the guys weren't much for accuracy. But they got the gist of things. Anyway, it wasn't as if he'd made efforts to hide it—especially not caressing her arm in full view of spectators.

"What makes you think I'm thinking about Edy?" Hassan said. They hit a speed bump at full throttle and, even with the windows up, Hassan could hear the flurry of cursing that erupted from Cash.

"First off, you are thinking about her. Second, you always get this stupid look on your face, like you're not here with us," Freight said.

Hassan glanced at him. "I was thinking about plays."

He wasn't interested in becoming the team joke, and if everyone thought all he did was spend his time obsessing over a girl, he quickly would be.

"I had a girl that made me think about plays a lot, too," Freight said conversationally. "She was a dancer, too, if you can believe that. And an asshole." He peeled a corner as if it surprised him, yanking the steering wheel at the last minute and ejecting another volley of swears from Cash.

Hassan almost felt sorry for him, back there in the bowels of his own vehicle, wet, and being thrown all over the place.

Almost.

"Did you hear me?" Freight said.

Hassan snapped to attention. "Yeah, sure, of course." Freight hated not to be heard. It was usually better to at least pretend to have heard him than to let him find out you hadn't been listening. While he'd say it wasn't a big deal, Hassan knew that he hadn't gotten his shampoo bath until he'd ignored Freight for something trivial.

The rain fell wild now. The smile returned to Hassan and the warmth with it. Edy was so close. He didn't have curfew on game night and he wondered if Edy had the same break.

He could go to her, he realized. Go to her, kiss her, tell her he had to see her. She wouldn't turn him down, nor would she slam the door in his face, no matter what rules applied. He missed her. He just wanted her close. Half a campus away, tethered by a text here and a text there, he could admit that he wanted more. He wanted to hold her, kiss her, to be inside her, please.

He made up his mind to do it. He'd see her tonight, no matter what. He'd had enough of this shit. A thousand players wanted to micromanage, to control their lives. Hassan refused to put up with it. Not tonight. Maybe not ever again.

At the dorm, Cash leapt from the bed of the truck and went lunging for Freight, a monumental tower he couldn't possibly topple. Still he tried, and the two grappled in the drenched grass as a few others hooted and cheered. Hassan went inside, out of the rain. He wanted to see Edy. He wanted to love her.

Xavier, Lawrence, and two linebackers caught him in the hall. They were celebrating the Tech win at some frat house down the road. He was coming, wasn't he? They wouldn't even have won if it wasn't for the early touchdown Hassan had scored. He had to be there. Half the school would be looking for him. All his teammates would.

Hassan sighed. Edy was what he wanted. But maybe he could see her, then attend the party? A plan began to form in his head. So he agreed, then headed up to his room to call her. She'd have to flat out reject him for him to stay away that night.

❈ ❈ ❈

"Hang on," Naomi said and tipped out the room. They were supposed to be getting ready for a series of frat parties nearby. They were as mandatory as practice right now, according to Tamela. Since part of the team's fundraising efforts included selling calendars in the spring, it was important for the girls to be seen, out in public, looking attractive. Their captain said that parties were the best way to accomplish this. Still, the idea of prettying herself up so that other people could gawk made Edy's nerves crawl.

"Did you tell her I wasn't feeling well?" Edy resisted the urge to twist her hands together and instead balled them so that her nails dug into her flesh.

Naomi nodded. "She said for you to remain in the room. Don't leave for any reason."

A flash of hope shot through Edy. "And you think we can get away with sneaking him in now? He wants to come now."

Naomi cringed. "It's not the best idea. But I think we can pull it off. If Tamela or London show up, we can always stuff him in the bathroom."

Edy's cheeks heated at that. They were going all in for her, risking their own necks because she missed her boyfriend. "Are you sure about this? I mean, you don't have to help me." Her heart pounded at the thought of crossing their captain so openly. Still, Hassan had said he needed her and her heart had nearly pulled apart at the words.

Naomi squeezed her hand. "I know you miss him. You've been down about it since you got here. Let's cheer you up."

Edy had the sudden, rushing impulse to hug her roommate. So she did. When had the girl began to mean something to her? When had she gained these friends that would go all in with her, risking obscene punishments like running suicide laps and standing endlessly? But she would do it for them, Edy realized.

"Let's get to work," Naomi said. "The faster we get him in, the faster we can breathe easier."

The operation to sneak Hassan into Edy's room was embarrassingly elaborate. A girl at each end of the hall: Willow and Naomi. Cassie posted up in front of Captain Napoleon's door just in case it opened, then she would raise her hand as if she'd been about to knock. Her job would be to block Napoleon's view. Edy, meanwhile, stood in her doorway to usher

Hassan in. The whole arrangement went off beautifully, flawlessly, even with Hassan's bewildered expression. There hadn't been time enough in the two weeks they'd been in Baton Rouge to explain the fist-tight rule the upperclassmen held over them. So, Edy swung him in and leapt to embrace him, only to find those strong, sure, solid arms wrapping her and melting her into the warmth of his body.

"You," Edy said against the flex of his chest.

"You," Hassan said and brushed his lips across her forehead.

"I missed—"

He cut her off with a kiss, a kiss hard and insistent, yet somehow tenderly wanting, too. His hands dropped from the small of her back, lower, to grip her backside, then kneading it, before racing up underneath her tee to lift it off all at once.

His touch seared, incinerating, burning her from within. He was greedy for her, he said. He needed her, he said, and her mouth moved without need of thought. "Yes, please," she said and wondered how it was that she said it again, and again, 'Yes please,' until she came to beg.

Both his hands slid down the side of her body, gliding over her hips and looping her pants and panties in one go. No sooner had he dropped them than did she lift her mouth to kiss him, to taste the intensity of him just a second after they'd parted. She found her fingers in his hair, gripping, pulling, saying his name, and her forgetting how to breathe.

He lifted her onto her dresser and shoved aside a few toiletries and pictures of them. A moment of their fumbled kisses passed, with him unbuckling his jeans and her blindly helping, then him reaching around for something. She exhaled at the sound of crumpling foil and caught a laugh from him in the middle of their kiss.

He kissed her deep enough to curl her toes, then her legs, tight around him. His tongue slipped deep in her mouth, then deeper, sliding to a rhythm she knew and wanted, to the rhythm of him loving her.

And with a lift of her leg so that she curved back and open for him, he shoved into her with such intensity that an earthquake avalanched inside her.

She gripped his shoulder and bit down on a moan as her whole body went rigid.

He filled her to capacity, stretched her a bit beyond, and settled, finally, into a fit he'd molded himself.

"Hassan," she said.

"Yeah, Cake?" he said, voice raw.

But she had no words for him, only a name, his name, whispered like a last wish, a dying word. Soon he grunted, snatched her tight to him, and pressed into her with unrelenting pressure. She trembled against him, whimpered what might have been a word, and ruptured.

He'd been holding back on her. She knew that now as he plowed into her over and again, knocking lotions, perfume, and a bottle of vitamins from their rocking dresser. He didn't care. He was on fire. He burned and wanted extinguishing. He wanted everything she had to give.

Hassan fell still, breathing ragged, as he gripped Edy's dresser. She wrapped her arms around his neck and felt it dampened now with his sweat.

"God, you feel incredible," Edy murmured. "So incredible."

She opened her eyes when he didn't answer, only to find him looking down at her. Searching her face for... something.

"I love you," he said and drove in again.

Edy ate a moan. She felt her body curling against him, racing to the finish line, and she buried her face in the thick, corded muscle of his shoulder.

He rammed. Rammed until she jabbered, until she clawed at his slickened back, until her own forehead pricked with sweat amidst an anguished stream of begging.

And then they were done. Skin-against-skin wet and pulsing against each other, both of them struggled for breath.

"I have to go," Hassan said and pulled away from her.

"What?" Edy said and blinked blankly.

Hassan eased off his condom and disappeared for the bathroom, where a flush sounded a few seconds later. He returned to grab his jeans, pull them up, and zipper them.

"It's a thing—a tradition," Hassan said, "with the football team and us having won our first game. I—I have to go," he said.

Edy's lips screwed up tight. She had traditions she'd blown off for him. She'd stuck her neck out—twice now—to be with him and all they'd done was have sex and text. In fact, they hadn't had a single detailed conversation since they'd arrived in Baton Rouge. She'd been looking forward to changing that.

"Night, Cake," he said and kissed her on the forehead. When he took a step, Edy grabbed him by the wrist.

"No," she said.

He looked at a loss. "I want to stay. But I have to—"

"Go after you hear me out," she said. "Because we came here together. But not for what just happened. We came *to be together.* That means more than a quick physical connection and a run out the door. You may not understand it, but there's a price I pay anytime I'm with you right now. The least you could do is..."

She failed. She didn't know what the least he could do was. But it wasn't run straight out the door.

He stopped. Seemed to consider it. "I'm sorry, Edy. I'll be in a hurry sometimes. But have faith in me, okay? Have faith in us. It doesn't mean anything when I rush. I just try to get the most of what little time we have and I..." He looked around, as if the room might suddenly help him. "You mean everything to me. You believe that, don't you?" He reached up to brush a lock of her hair behind her ear. Sweaty, it clung to her skin.

She nodded, because she still did.

Less than a minute later, he was gone.

Sunday night they had the den. Edy had been through enough nights with the upperclassmen to know that something was amiss. They said little as they blindfolded each freshman and shoved them into cars. During their eerily silent drive, Edy stressed in anticipation. The darkness was the worst, with its blind need for trust and its sense of disorientation.

They were meant not to know where the den was so they could never pass the information on. Since Edy still didn't know her way around Baton Rouge, there was no chance of her recognizing her whereabouts anyway, when they climbed out the car, removed the blindfolds and entered the apartment complex.

They were in someone's apartment again. Someone's cheaply-carpeted, white-walled, possibly just-fumigated apartment. Dust layered the sparsely furnished place. One maroon couch, which Edy had never had the luxury of sitting on, sat against a wall nearly close enough to touch the moment she entered. In one corner, a roach the size of Edy's palm lay on its back, legs bent. She couldn't stop staring at it.

Tamela and London lined the freshmen up, creating a miniature arc because of space restrictions. Afterwards, they would likely have to recite team history, noting famous dancers that had come from the squad, or some other such mundane task. After that, there would be an excruciating amount of exercise, some alcohol for the upperclassmen, and whatever other humiliating tasks they could think up.

"Tonight, ladies," Tamela said, "you are here because one of you has decided to disobey. The rules and the den are here to help you shed all presumption, pride, and naivety. Where are your priorities? With the future of this team and your career or with whims of the moment?" She cast a meaningful glance at Edy. "You will decide once and for all where your priorities lie. And if those priorities lie with your boyfriend, then by all means, we wish the two of you happiness. Understand that, Phelps?"

Oh God. Every pair of eyes turned on Edy. She nodded weakly, anticipation cranking up enough to make her stomach cramp.

"Good then. Step out to receive your punishment. Meanwhile, I have something special for the rest of you, as I know you helped her sneak that goddamned boy in her room."

Faye Richardson's mouth fell open. "I've been meaning to ask whether all this is sanctioned?" she said. "Because I don't think —"

Tamela stepped into her space, so close that they could've kissed. She folded her arms and looked up at Faye like the bulldog she was. "Thinking of reporting me, are you? And just who do you think is ready to listen? Our coach, who just happens to be my mom? Or will you take something down to the Athletic Department? Maybe we can go together. I haven't visited Aunt Violet and Uncle Ray in a while. They're always getting on their favorite niece about neglecting them. Oh! I have a suggestion. Why don't you take your complaint straight to the Dean of Students? Dr. Beck is Mummy's first cousin, once removed. Or something like that. I keep meaning to ask her how that works. Guess I'll ask at the next family reunion."

Edy stared at her.

"Shit," Naomi said.

"Uh, what is it you want me to do?" Edy asked loudly. She had Rebecca Phelps for a mother and knew not to screw around with people who had connections.

"Step forward," Tamela said.

Edy glanced at her, wondering about the wisdom of doing anything they said, before she moved, her feet deciding for her that she would comply.

"Rat," London said.

"Rat! Rat! Rat!" the older girls began to chant, falling together in some sort of monstrous chorus. Edy's eyes swept wide as she took them in, angry faces, balled fists, shouts all around.

"We make examples of rats," Tamela said, "and you have been marked as a rat."

"But… I don't know what that means," Edy said softly.

A bottle of tequila started around the room. Each girl took a swig straight from the source. When it came to Edy, she knew to do the same.

"You questioned my authority," Tamela said to her. "As did this one." She gestured to Faye Richardson. "Step forward or find your own way home."

Edy lifted her chin. She forced air down and into her lungs. The urge to pant swung in and Edy clamped down hard. For some reason, meeting their abuse fearlessly was important to her.

"On your knees, please," Tamela said. "Both of you."

Every fiber in Edy resisted the notion of dropping to her knees before this girl. But the gauntlet had been thrown. Disobey and get tossed from the apartment and the team, of course. Edy didn't doubt that the coach's daughter could persuade her mom that one or two teammates had violated core rules. There would be no recourse for a stranger with no connections. And it didn't matter anyway. She'd crawl through fire to keep on dancing.

Without looking at Faye, Edy dropped to her knees, careful to keep her head up. She would not bow unnecessarily. She was not afraid.

Several girls down, Faye took a step back. "We were told in orientation that we were not to be subjected to any physical or mental activity meant to cause intimidation, threat—"

"On your knees, Richardson," Tamela said softly,

the warning in her voice subtle as the wind.

"Physical or mental stress, humiliation or anguish —" Faye continued, voice approaching a shout.

Edy leapt to her feet, panicking. "Just get on your goddamn knees," she said and yanked Faye down. The girl was a brilliant dancer. She couldn't let a couple of assholes keep her from what she loved. She could do this. So could Edy.

Tamela smiled. "Beautiful. Now crawl to the window and smile at *la cucaracha.*"

Edy's eyes flew wide. Did she mean that fucking roach? A roach would be part of her punishment for seeing Hassan?

The grinning faces looking down on her told Edy her answer. Face the roach. Smile at him. Her skin crawled in response.

Edy began the crawl, knee by careful knee, eyes averted, willing herself not to think as the space to her destination withered away. But then she looked.

God help her, the thing was ugly — ugly and unforgivably repulsive. With its rigid brown body and curled, pinched legs revealed, Edy found herself cringing, her body stiff and desperate.

She looked away again. She couldn't help it. Having crawled so far that her head stood above the roach, Edy opted for the wall. She conjugated Spanish verbs in her head so as not to think about the carcass mere inches below her chin, sprawled so close to her hands. *Voy, vas, va, vamos, vais, van.* She organized possible

NFL picks in order of her anticipated draft: Leonard Cummings, Brad Daniels, Wayne Chestnut, Xavier Wright, Andre Theobald... Finally, she glanced down and pressed a fist to her mouth.

She absolutely hated bugs.

The rest of the freshmen were standing on one leg. They stretched the other skyward, so that it was parallel with their body. They were expected to stay that way indefinitely. Faye, now on her knees, came to a stop near Edy.

"Faye Richardson, you are not quite close enough to our friend," Tamela said cheerfully. "Do us a favor and lean forward."

Edy shot a glance at her fellow freshman. She'd craned her neck back as if she'd hoped to sever it from her head via stretching. With Tamela's words, the girl started panting. A tear streamed down her face. It made a lonely procession over her pale, rounded cheeks, before the rivers began. Edy couldn't shake the notion that she was responsible for this. If she hadn't caved and agreed to see Hassan, then they wouldn't be facing the roach. Maybe they wouldn't even be in the den that night.

"Faye," Edy said, "please don't cry. I know it's my fault and all, but I'm sorry. Just... try to be strong. It might go harder for us if you cry." Somehow, Edy had thought that would do the trick, but then Faye shuddered. She opened her mouth and a whimper emerged, as her bottom lip trembled.

"Don't look at him," Edy said. Then she messed up and looked herself, failing to follow her own advice. It was still there and still dead.

"Closer, ladies. You need to admire him," Tamela said sweetly.

Christ.

Faye's sobs broke like a dam. Then she began to gag.

Edy side-saddled over and grabbed her by the arm. She tilted her head so that her view of *la cucaracha* all but disappeared.

"You can do it," Edy said, quietly, between them. "You're a dancer. You fall and get hurt and get back up again. Your body gets battered and you persevere. You're unbelievably talented. Do what it takes to have influence on this team, then change the way things operate."

Faye peeked at her. "You think we could do that?" she whispered.

Edy nodded, then dropped back to her hands and knees when she noticed London looking. Faye followed her example.

"Phelps," Tamela said. "You may rejoin the team. This evening you will regale us with stories of you and Hassan, since you are so unable to stay away. We want to know everything. How you met, when you first kissed, when you knew it was true love."

Edy drew up slow and cast a backwards worried glance at Faye, who was still on the floor. She wondered how long the girl would have to stay and whether she'd crack from the roach.

Edy didn't want to tell the upperclassmen anything about her relationship with Hassan. It made her nervous as she tried to contemplate ways they could use the info against her. But how could they? She and Hassan were rock solid. They always had been. And she didn't think they'd do something as malicious as spread rumors or otherwise meddle in her personal life. Tamela, in her own crazy way, wanted each of them to show that they would do anything for the team, that their commitment to LSU's dance squad was real. As far as Edy was concerned, it didn't matter whether she had to stand on one leg, stare at cockroaches, or confess her sins. She would do that and more to be a dancer.

It was that simple.

She knew Hassan would understand.

Seventeen

Hassan had smashed the first game, putting up massive yards and even scoring a touchdown in the first half. Granted, the single touchdown he'd scored had been the roughest one he'd ever earned given the strength of the guys he'd faced, but hell, he'd done it and had only a sore body plus a few bruises for his trouble.

He wasn't a baby, he could handle the pain. Already, he looked forward to their second game against a cupcake opponent. The stats racked up there could be massive.

After his performance, Hassan's teammates transformed overnight. He was still the newbie freshman subjected to the occasional prank, but they seemed to be slowing to a trickle and carried out more for the principle of the matter rather than reminding him that he was not yet one of them. Because he did feel part of the team and it had happened in an instance.

After the Virginia Tech game and visiting Edy, he and a bunch of guys headed over to the Zeta Kappa house where they got smashed and made a ruckus.

Hassan got more fist bumps, slaps on the back, and cups of beer shoved into his hands than he'd ever had before. Through it all, he had a niggling sense of needing to talk to Edy again. He didn't like the way they'd parted, with her all stiff and eyes downcast. Shortly after, he'd called her cell and got sent to voicemail While at the party, he texted her and got no response. He had no idea what was up with her, but he told himself it was nothing. She hardly ever answered the phone anyway. Her teammates demanded all of her time, all of her attention, and all of her energy, it seemed. Why would she answer the phone just because her boyfriend called? There were teammates to think of, he thought bitterly. Their wants had to come first.

After the party, some of Hassan's teammates headed out to the club. He decided to kick up his legs and stew in bitterness back at the dorm. In the dead of the night when his teammates returned, Freight told him about spotting the dance girls at a club. It was late enough for Edy to have been there, since it would've been after he'd departed. As Freight and Cash regaled him with tales of the girls throwing back shots of liquor, squealing, and dancing counter top, and of the two so all over each other they needed a room, Hassan tried not to imagine Edy amongst them and failed. Was this what she did when she never answered the phone? Danced counter top and threw back shots? When the hell had she learned to party like that, anyway? Was it what she preferred instead of time with him?

Hassan was too embarrassed to ask if they'd seen Edy. Since they didn't say they had, he told himself it meant she wasn't there.

But still, he wondered.

By the time Hassan's phone rang on Sunday afternoon, he was too pissed to answer it and rejected the call without looking at the screen. He didn't care if it was Edy. He wasn't calm enough to talk to her just yet. He'd been busy being jealous of imaginary men slow grinding on his girl in the dark. He'd been jealous of the time other people got with her, day and night. Hell, he had obligations too. But it didn't make sense that he could never see her. What was the point of them coming together? Would she really let someone —anyone—take away what they'd so carefully put together?

Hassan's phone rang again. It was his mother. He hissed before rejecting it.

"Why don't you just block whoever it is?" Cash asked as they got in line for lunch.

"Because him and his baby mama have got the drama," Freight said. "Don't you pay attention?"

"I don't have any damned kids," Hassan said. He took another step towards the hot lunch display.

"Right," Freight said. "You deadbeat dad."

"Fuck off," Hassan muttered, more to himself than anything. Freight grinned and regaled him with a bright smile in response.

A broad woman with rough red cheeks, dinner plate lips, and a broad mouth waved Hassan up. "What will you have?" she said in a child's voice.

He couldn't think straight. He didn't know why he was being so petulant. So, he and Edy had barely touched, or spoken to, or seen each other since their arrival weeks ago. And before that, they'd been separated for the summer. It could have been worse, he told himself. She could have decided to go to Harvard, like her parents wanted. He'd have no hope of seeing her then.

Sufficiently cheered by the thought, Hassan tried on a smile. "Give me anything," he told the lunch lady. She had the soft, simpering voice of Marilyn Monroe and the face of a pulverized linebacker.

She spooned what looked like stew onto a plate.

"Is that beef?" Hassan said.

She looked up with a roll of her eyes. "Yes." Her voice was still sweet, still childlike. But her shoulders were as broad as his.

"I can't eat beef," Hassan said. "Anything else."

She let out a huff of a sigh before shoveling the food back into its bin. Then she went to the chicken without changing his plate.

"Hey, don't even —"

A laugh caught his attention. A laugh he knew and recognized as out of place. But it was a silly thought.

"'Don't' what?" the lunch lady said, surly now. She

still had the dirty plate in her hand.

"Listen, give him the stew and we'll trade. Otherwise, we'll be here all day," Freight said.

Hassan shrugged before extending his arm to take it. The soreness in his shoulder bloomed.

"Get chicken for me, Freight," Hassan said and got through the line. When he paid, he thought of Edy and the craziness with her credit cards. He hadn't had much use for money since being at school, but that didn't mean she couldn't use some. After his meal, he'd text her and offer, though he was pretty sure she'd refuse out of pride.

Hassan sought out a table big enough to hold the handful of teammates with him, then claimed it. Freight, Lawrence, and Cash followed in a steady stream. They shuffled around and pulled up more chairs when Xavier, the wide receiver, and a few linebackers joined them.

With school having started, Lawrence switched from carrying his playbook everywhere to carrying his textbooks instead. Now, as their small group of football players sat at a single round table, Lawrence pulled out a nutrition textbook and eased it open next to his lunch.

"Put that away and study your playbook. I saw you screw up a play yesterday," Cash said.

"That's because there are a thousand of them," Lawrence said. "And anyway, I have time penciled in for the playbook. I can't devote all my time to dreams of the NFL like you bunch of losers. If football doesn't work, I'll go into the family business."

"The family business is the NFL, isn't it?" Freight said.

Their laughter echoed through the cafeteria, a roar amidst murmuring conversations.

Then it came again. That laugh he knew but denied because it didn't make sense. Not here, not now.

Hassan jerked around in his chair and saw him.

He saw Wyatt.

Half an inch taller, with hair that played at being some new color, he was leaner, slightly more fit and tanned. He was different. He held himself different, with his shoulders back and his head tilted to one side, relaxed nonetheless.

He had people around him. They were listening. Laughing. Buying whatever shit he was shoving down their throats.

Wyatt Green was in Baton Rouge.

Hassan shoved back from the table. He'd balled his fists without realizing it, as images of his smile, his grin, collided with that damned police report and every sick thing he imagined the bastard had done to his own cousin. Was he here for Edy? Did he think he could get within fifty feet of her?

Of course he did. The asshole was nothing if not persistent.

"Shit!" Lawrence cried from somewhere behind Hassan. Furniture squeaked in those tight seconds when Hassan strode across the room, ready to confront his nemesis.

"What the hell are you doing here, Wyatt?" Hassan said.

The boy turned on him, paled, then offered a watery smile.

"Hassan," Wyatt said. "Didn't expect to see you."

"Bullshit. The whole world knows I'm here," Hassan said. "You followed me."

Wyatt crossed his arms. "Did Edy follow you? And Lawrence? Because they're here too." He lifted his chin. "Maybe everyone follows Hassan Pradhan around. He's that important, you know."

That earned a measure of snickers from his new friends.

Hassan's jaw worked and his knuckles cracked. He had no memory of doing either.

Wyatt looked from one guy to the next at his table of new friends. "You'll have to forgive us. Athletes—Hassan especially—seem to think everything's about them."

"That's because it is," Cash interjected brashly. Behind Hassan, a few of his teammates chuckled.

"Don't play games with me, Wyatt. You know I'll put you through a goddamned wall."

Wyatt stood and slammed his hand on the table. "And I'll sue the shit out of you and every Pradhan I can find. You stay out of my way, Hassan, and I'll stay out of yours."

Sue? Oh, right. He was rich now. Momentarily, Hassan thought of his family's financial troubles, being as how they were the reason he couldn't extricate himself cleanly from the Mala Bathlar engagement. His father wouldn't take well to being sued. Or would it just be Hassan getting sued? He was a broke ass college kid and didn't appreciate this line of thought.

"Stay away from Edy. I don't trust you," Hassan said, less certain of himself now. The suing bit had thrown him off his train of thought. But he didn't trust Wyatt not to hurt her. He'd hurt his cousin, after all. "I know what you're capable of."

Wyatt blushed, but recovered too quickly for Hassan's comfort. After all, was he really making peace with what he'd done? Should he be allowed to make peace with what he'd done? Or sit amidst civilized society either?

His friends had caught something though, judging by the way they shifted, murmured to each other, and cast Wyatt the stray questioning look. But Hassan didn't care. There were girls there too. They deserved to know that this guy could snap, kick their ass, and try to get his rocks off in an instant.

"Whatever, Hassan. So, is her number still the same? I think I'll call later," Wyatt said and actually fucking smiled.

Hassan dove, only to get locked in a flock of arms, a steel trap of teammates holding him back.

"Sawn," Lawrence kept saying. "Sawn. C'mon. Be

cool." It was his mantra in these situations, as a worthless voice of calm.

But Wyatt was here. *Here.* He'd set his eyes on Edy when they were in the ninth grade. He'd obsessed over her, got shot trying to break them up, and chased her a thousand miles south. And he'd committed a real crime when he attacked his cousin.

It didn't matter that he wasn't prosecuted for it.

Lawrence's hand wrapped one of Hassan's forearms. "Be cool," he said again, voice quiet at his shoulder. "You know we can't afford—"

Fuck *that.*

"Does Edy know you're here?" Hassan said. He tried to jerk forward, only to be yanked back with brute force. He ignored the teammates that tried to soothe him with words.

He didn't want this. He didn't want this shit to have followed them to Louisiana. He didn't want to have to worry about Edy and what Wyatt might do.

But there was the question of what Wyatt was doing in the cafeteria. Was he a student? How could he be, when the secret of their commitment to LSU had been made public the same year as their attendance? They'd waited until spring, late spring, which was far too late to start an admissions process. Yet, here he was. Hassan could think of only one explanation for it.

He thought back to when he and Edy had visited Wyatt in the hospital. She'd been worried about him, naturally, but had a hard time separating herself from him when it became clear that he didn't want her there. Hassan swallowed. Had he been a fool in thinking that the Edy-Wyatt-Hassan triangle was all in Wyatt's head? Was it possible that she even... felt something for him? He was in Baton Rouge, and if he was a student there was only one way he would have known to enroll in time.

Edy.

Suddenly, Hassan had an irrepressible urge to smack the smugness from Wyatt's face. He didn't like what it implied or the sudden fear boiling inside him.

Wyatt cocked his head to one side, as if considering Hassan's question. "Well, I saw her on Saturday. She was beautiful."

Hassan lunged, but got nowhere for his trouble. He wanted to be let go. He wanted to handle this. These guys had no idea who Wyatt was or what he was capable of. If they knew, they'd be helping Hassan pound him.

"Sorry about that," Freight said sympathetically. "Team rules."

Hassan suppressed the urge to spit. To think that this guy had seen Edy on Saturday... was it at the club? He couldn't think of any reason why Edy would allow this. And yet, his heart and mind went back to high school and the rumors that used to surround them. They'd been inseparable in the beginning, Edy and Wyatt, and lots of people swore she was with him behind Hassan's back. But even if she was... attracted to him, she knew what he'd done to his cousin. Edy would never tolerate someone like that.

"Listen, lover boy. You've had your confrontation. It's time to go eat." Freight used one of his Christmas ham fists to start pulling Hassan in the direction of their table. Soon others joined in. It was only then that Hassan noticed the sea of peering faces, watching, waiting.

"I'm not hungry," Hassan said once they'd made it back to the table. He stared at his food sullenly, seeing Wyatt's grin instead.

"Eat or leave, freshman. Cause if you fight, I'll kick your ass myself, you idiot." Cash dropped down in front of his baked chicken and stabbed it with a fork.

Leaving sounded like a damned good idea, because there was no way he could choke down food in sight of Wyatt. Not without answers first. Hassan snatched up his book bag and bolted, making sure that he kept his eyes straight on the path before him.

Not long after hitting the grass, he heard his name.

"You know it's all bullshit, don't you?" Lawrence said and caught up to him. "What Wyatt said? What you're thinking?"

It felt like bullshit. Only… "What's he doing here? How could he even have got here in time?"

Lawrence shrugged. "Maybe he's a poser. He could not even be a student. Who knows with Wyatt?"

And yeah. That was exactly the problem: who knew with Wyatt?

Shewanda Pugh

❀ ❀ ❀

Edy's head thumped as she rounded the bend. Didn't these people know that they kept the lights too bright? She pushed through the cafeteria line in 459 Commons. Milk. Chicken Caesar salad. Red grapes. When London suggested they party again tonight, Edy's stomach lurched. Had she even cleared her system of last night's alcohol? Nausea roiled in threatening bursts, here again, gone the next. She only hoped she didn't vomit in public. Twice in one day would be ridiculous.

"Your total is $7.92," said a bored-faced woman in white uniform. Purple trimmed the edges of her name tag: Nichole Gates. Geaux Tigers.

Her financial aid situation was still a tad iffy. Any time she left messages with her dad about the credit cards, they weren't answered. She had the scholarship, of course, but the processing would take a few more days. In the meantime, she had to pay her bills another way.

One swipe later, the woman frowned.

"It's been declined." She held up the card and squinted as if it suddenly sported hieroglyphs. "Let me try again. It's probably the machine."

Heat warmed Edy's cheeks. This had been happening lately.

"It's okay," she said, all too aware of the line forming

behind her. "Let me give you a different card. I think maybe it's expired."

The woman turned the card over for a closer look.

Edy snatched it. "Hold on a second." She unzipped the keychain pouch affixed to her waist and pulled out a gold MasterCard. Her last place of refuge.

Please God. Don't forsake me.

"Declined." Behind Edy a few titters erupted as the woman swiped again. "Still declined. I'll bet it's the machine though. Let's move to a different one and—"

"No!" Edy blurted. "I'll—I'll just get the milk." She grabbed her carton and thrust it toward the woman as she tried on her best politician's smile.

"Okay." The woman appeared genuinely baffled as she set Edy's milk aside, cancelled out the previous order, and rung up the beverage. "A dollar nine," she said.

Edy held her breath. It was okay. She'd be okay. After all, milk was fortified with essential nutrients, right? And babies lived on milk. No, not cow's milk, of course, but milk just the same. This was just a temporary fix, after all, until—

"It's been declined."

Fuck! Her third and last credit card cancelled like all the others. Her parents meant to starve her out.

"Okay," Edy said, "just, okay." Then, because manners had been drilled into her with her earliest memories, "Thank you for your time."

She wandered off into a suddenly blurring cafeteria,

eyes stinging with anguish. But she was reasonable: a reasonable adult knew crying wouldn't solve her problems. Except she was seventeen and not eighteen. She still had a few weeks to go until her birthday. So even the part about her being an adult wasn't entirely true.

She had no money. Nothing. Standing there, so many hundreds of miles from home and from the safety of her parents, brought into sharp contrast what she'd left behind. She and Hassan had vowed to be together, no matter the consequences. So they'd forged ahead with what they thought was caution and conviction, with what now looked like naivety and stupidity. Edy had been especially stupid; that was what her stomach now proclaimed. How long could she live without food?

"This seat taken?" a male voice spoke softly.

Edy didn't even remember wandering to a seat, let alone taking it. There was no one else with her because she ventured to the cafeteria impulsively, never inviting a teammate to see how dire her money situation was. Before Edy could answer whoever had intruded on her misery, a tray nudged her arm. A glance toward it showed chicken Caesar salad, red grapes, and milk.

Her abandoned meal. Brought by some random Steve who had taken pity on her and meant well. A flood of humiliation filled her eyes with tears and she shoved the tray back the way it came.

"Listen, I —" *Am going to pass out if I don't eat soon.*

"You?" he prompted from where he stood.

Wait. *Wait.* This wasn't possible. *That voice wasn't possible.* And yet…

Edy lifted her head. "Wyatt?" she whispered.

He flashed impossibly white teeth, and his cheeks flushed with a hint of color. "Hey, Edy."

"Wyatt!" She upended her chair in a rush to him. "Oh my God!" And once more because there was nothing else to say. "Oh my God."

She stepped back and examined him. Tall. Taller than she remembered and tanned now. Lean muscles gave his body definition. Were those highlights in his hair?

He took a seat. Two trays of an identical meal waited on the table. Suddenly remembering how hungry she was and how much studying she needed to do, Edy dug in.

A full minute of lip smacking silence ensued, with her pausing only to chug milk or shovel grapes down her throat. Bit by bit, the unrelenting shakes that accompanied her hunger began to retreat, until at last ease weaseled its way in.

"What happened with your money?" Wyatt said. He reached for his milk and tore the carton open, making Edy realize that he hadn't even begun to eat.

"I don't have any, that's what. My credit cards have been cancelled and financial aid is waiting on some documentation from my mother."

Wyatt stared at her. "So, call them. I'm sure they don't know your situation. They wouldn't have you wanting for food or anything else."

Edy almost smiled. In a topsy-turvy world, they'd pivoted positions. He'd become the naively optimistic one with casual designer wear, while she looked on in hunger.

Life, it seemed, stayed fueled by ironies.

"Listen," Wyatt said and shoved a hunk of chicken in his mouth. "I meant to grab food to go because my friends are expecting me."

Edy followed his gesture to a clustering group of guys smattered with two girls. One girl, with platinum streaked in her hair, stared intently.

"I saw you," Wyatt said, "and I had to speak. I had to help."

Speak. Speaking! Oh shit, he was a guy and Edy was so not supposed to be talking to guys right now. Not after Tamela tore her a new one for letting Hassan run his hands all over her.

But she couldn't escape this conversation if she wanted to. And she didn't want to. There was so much to say. So many questions. Edy would ask at least one. "What are you doing here, Wyatt? Here in Louisiana?"

How did you find me?

Wyatt picked at his grapes with a fork.

"That's a fair question," he said finally.

Edy waited.

"I finished treatment," he admitted. "And when I did, I knew I couldn't go back to living with my dad. I couldn't live with my grandfather for long, either. We weren't getting along and neither place felt like home. Boston wasn't home for me anymore. It was all misery." He hesitated, stealing a glimpse at Edy. "Eventually, I realized that all my good memories were with you or of you. They were memories of our friendship, a friendship that I spoiled. So I decided that I had to be near you, if only for that reason. Even if we never spoke or ran into each other again. Our friendship felt like home to me.

"When I saw you in line, I decided not to speak. I figured that things were probably best that way. But when I saw you couldn't get your meal," he shook his head, "I couldn't stay away. You know I could never not be there for you, Edy."

Edy dropped her gaze, unsettled by the warmth in her belly and the certainty that Wyatt put it there.

He swallowed the last of his milk. In the silence, she stole a look at him, only to find him appraising her frankly. "I have to go. There's so much I want to tell you. About how I've changed, about the work I've done on myself." He jerked a thumb in the direction of the platinum blonde and her friends. "I have friends, Edy. Me. And they're waiting. But if you need me, need anything at all… Please find me. You know I'd do anything for you."

He reached over and brushed a thumb against her

Shewanda Pugh

cheek, causing Edy to flinch. Before she could form an answer—a sensible, intelligent answer—Wyatt had swept his tray away and gone.

Not long after, Edy lifted her milk for a sip and found two damp twenties had been wedged underneath.

Eighteen

Edy didn't keep Wyatt's money. Instead, she slipped it in the Red Cross box sitting in her dorm lobby. For the rest of the evening and as she got ready for class the next morning, she wondered why Wyatt was at LSU and for how long he'd be there. Had he really come just to be near her? And if he had, why hadn't he tried to contact her? Would she have talked to him if he'd called? She really had no idea. It all felt so bizarre —she felt bizarre just seeing him.

She would have to tell Hassan that Wyatt was in town. He'd lose his shit, of course, but what choice did they have? America, and Baton Rouge within it, remained a free country. The boy could come and go as he pleased, even if it made others uncomfortable.

Edy really had nothing she could complain about. He had only spoken to her in a moment and at a time of obvious distress. Maybe he had been in Baton Rouge for as long as her. Maybe he had arrived before. So long as he didn't make a point of being in contact with her, what could she object to?

Hassan wouldn't see it that way. He had always seen Wyatt as creepy. Eventually, through deliberate purpose, Wyatt set out to prove him right. Edy hadn't been the best friend for him, yet he hadn't been the best friend for her. Neither had been honest with the other about their true intentions. Maybe neither could have or even knew how.

The more Edy puzzled over the best way to tell Hassan that Wyatt was in town, the more her brows drew together and her heart pounded. He would not be civil about this. He would not accept it at face value. Even face value sucked, because Wyatt's story of lurking nearby because Edy felt like home just wouldn't play for Hassan. Edy worried that he'd do something stupid and drastic. He'd lash out as he did whenever he got super pissed. Except there wouldn't be a wall, but a Wyatt.

Maybe she shouldn't say a word. If she kept silent and Hassan never ran into him, then they could go on with their lives uninterrupted. With more than thirty thousand students at LSU, it seemed possible that Wyatt could slip by. And was he even a student? It seemed unlikely. How could he have completed an application, been accepted, and enrolled all over the course of a few months? Then there was the issue of him in a psychiatric facility. Surely, he wasn't tracking her down while getting treatment for…

What was he getting treatment for anyway?

It didn't matter. They were no longer friends. Edy wished him well; she wished him great health and tons of happiness, but a friendship with him proved too problematic.

It was exactly this thought she'd had when she cavorted quickly around a parked motorcycle only to trip over the sidewalk instead. Edy slammed into the worst possible person she could think of at that moment.

"Idiot," Silas said. He had her in his arms as if he'd caught a baby, but he'd snarled the insult just the same.

Edy righted herself in an instant. "Asshole," she snapped.

They were just outside History of Dance and glaring as if a knife fight would follow.

"You have a serious problem with walking, don't you?" He looked more than a little amused. "First you trip in class, now you trip out here. Are you sure you can even dance?"

"I can dance better than you, I'm sure!" she cried, halfway past appalled and thinking that knife fight might be possible after all.

Silas rolled his eyes. "You're a Lady Tiger. I'm sure half of what you do is shaking that massive rack of yours." He pointed at her breast with a finger, nearly close enough to touch one. Edy slapped his hand away and thought of slapping him too for good measure.

"You're a nasty little thing, aren't you?" she said.

Silas jerked a brow, then leaned forward from his bike. "There is nothing little about me, Edith Phelps. Get to know me and you'd find that out for yourself."

She blushed like Vegas lights. "I don't want to get to know you!"

His lips curled in disbelief. She supposed with his height and powerful frame, plus those ice gray eyes, plenty of girls wanted to get to know him. But not her. She didn't even want to be near him.

"I have class," Edy announced when he kept right on looking her over. She swept past him, knowing he'd be headed the same way.

At the door, she realized that everyone had fallen into the habit of taking their seats from the first day. With a sigh, she reluctantly slid into hers, knowing that meant Silas would sit before her.

"Miss me?" he said intimately and dropped into his seat.

Edy had been watching for him, but only because she dreaded him. He couldn't possibly know she'd been on the lookout, could he? She looked away, breathless with embarrassment and anger.

Once class began, they went into a discussion about dance in ceremonies and rituals. The discussion was based, in part, on their assigned readings. Edy hadn't done the assigned reading yet.

She'd spent too much time in the den.

Still, she was able to ad-lib a bit when she was called on, as she knew a bit about Shastriya Nritya, a type of Hindu classical dance done in the temples. After that, they were told that part of their semester end project would be to perform a short piece from some point in history. The professor paired partners up and down the class lazily. With dawning horror, Edy realized what was happening.

"Swain and Phelps," their professor said as if she'd done nothing of consequence. "Adams and... Nesme, is it?"

Silas turned to Edy and scowled. "Try not to fall, if you can."

"Try not to be an asshole, if you can," Edy snapped back. She realized she was asking too much.

He lifted a shoulder and in that gesture said that she shouldn't hope for much and Edy couldn't help but roll her eyes.

The second class ended, and Edy gave him a reluctant stare. They'd have to communicate now and civilly would be best. Otherwise, this project would turn into a nightmare for both. Still, she couldn't believe she'd actually have to tolerate this jerk.

"So," she said, in an attempt to push the negative thoughts away, "I'm thinking we could get away with ballet. It's about six centuries old and we both have tons of experience with it. Or even —"

"We're not doing *ballet*," Silas said, mocking her as he slung his backpack on. "Or whatever else you dream up. I know you're used to guys falling at your feet and doing what you say, but you're crazy if you think I'll do the same."

Edy's eyes flew wide before she exhaled in disbelief. She was *not* used to guys falling at her feet. Though she had the arsenal of boys she'd grown up with, who were all but sworn to protect her. Then there was Wyatt who, she realized, in hindsight, had strong feelings for her and could fawn. And she'd always been a daddy's girl—she made no apologies for that. She'd always been her father's girl, and Ali's too.

Wait. Did that mean there was some merit in what Silas was saying?

He smirked at her as if having read her mind before starting off for the hall.

This was ridiculous. They had a project to do and it had nothing to do with her personal life. She told him as much when she caught up.

Silas sighed. "Fine. Then give me a call when your social calendar frees up. I'm sure it's chock full of admirers."

It wasn't, of course, because she was an ordinary girl with ordinary looks who just happened to be talented in a more obvious way. There were girls prettier than her in that hall at that moment, girls prettier than her on her team. But again, none of this had a thing to do with their assignment and Edy had tired of Silas running off course.

She took down his number, gave him hers, and exhaled in relief when he disappeared. The guy was intense, she'd give him that.

With Silas out of the way, Edy's thoughts turned to Wyatt as she headed over to English class. His presence felt... forced. He had disappeared from school after the shooting, going through hospitalization and an extended recovery period. He had disappeared from life after that. Word was that he'd been forced into a treatment facility to deal with outstanding mental health issues. His grandfather, who turned out to be a well-known benefactor of five Harvard degree programs and known to both Edy and Ali, was said to have insisted on Wyatt's treatment before recognizing him as an heir. While others at South End High could only speculate as to what mental health concerns Wyatt had—and speculate they did—only Edy and Hassan knew about Wyatt attacking his cousin. But what had her old friend done to his cousin exactly? What was he capable of doing? Whatever it was—however complete the attack—Edy knew that he could have done the same to her. Maybe Hassan and the Dyson boys' overprotective streak had worked in her favor, after all.

And now he was there at LSU.

Back when he was hospitalized, Wyatt had told her, had convinced her, that he had nothing but hatred for Edy. She'd ruined him in ways she couldn't understand. Loving her had ruined him. Now he was back in their midst. She only wished she knew why.

Edy made it to class first and slipped into her seat. Hardly a minute passed before Hassan dropped into the seat next to her. When he looked at her, his glare made her recoil.

He had nerve. Especially after screwing her and

hopping off to do better, more important things. She'd done just what he asked. She'd shoved aside her obligations for him and oh, how she'd paid for it. Other people paid for it too. What in the world did he have to be mad about?

She decided she didn't care. After all the stress of figuring out how to spend time with him, only to have him not appreciate her efforts, she couldn't give a ripe damn about whatever had him pissed. *She* was pissed. He didn't have a monopoly on temper tantrums.

"Well?" Hassan snapped. "Have you got anything to say to me?"

Oh, she could smack him just now.

When she didn't answer, Hassan's mouth pressed to a crease and the bits of his ears that peeked out from overflowing hair turned red around the edges. "Cool," he said as if absolutely nothing was cool. "I'll remember this."

It sounded like a threat.

"You'll remember what?" Edy snapped and turned to face him. Her blood practically gushed through her veins, boiling and burning and threatening to rupture her fury.

He flipped to Punjabi. *"That I tried to talk this over with you and you…"* He shook his head, trailing off.

"We're in class!" Edy cried. Now she couldn't ignore the eyes turned in their direction. Sure, they couldn't understand what was being said, but they felt the fury vaulting between the two.

Wrecked

"Fine," Hassan said. *"After class, then? I've got an hour to spare."*

Edy looked away. *"Well, I don't. I had more than an hour to spare when me and my teammates went to the trouble of sneaking you into my room. Had I known it was all for you to get off, I wouldn't have bothered."*

His face blotched red. *"What? You weren't into that? If not, you should have told your body."*

"You left!"

"And you're busy!"

"Like you aren't!"

"And where the hell do you even sleep? In some new boyfriend's room?"

Edy's fist curled around her pen as if she might use it to gouge something. *"Be serious."*

"As much as we're enjoying this passionate Bollywood cinema, you've forgotten to provide us with subtitles. So, if you don't mind, I'd like to start class," their professor said from the front of the room.

"I have an hour after class," Hassan said in English.

"I can't." And she really had no business talking to him. There was still the Iowa game to look forward to. If she could get through that without issue, then the den would be a thing of the past and she could really spend time with Hassan. Just a little more time, she wanted to tell him. Couldn't he make that sacrifice for her?

Then low, so low she nearly didn't hear it, Hassan said, "You play games. You'd better believe that I'm

203

getting tired of it."

She shot him a look of puzzled disbelief, then made a point of ignoring Hassan for the rest of class. Afterwards, she swept past him without a word.

Iowa came. Hassan managed to start and put up impressive numbers. Edy put in a flawless appearance that Saturday, and afterwards she and her teammates were rewarded with Tamela's declaration that they were full-fledged members of the team and would no longer be submitted to the den. It was Faye who screamed first, followed by Cassie, then Naomi, and eventually they were shrieking and clinging to each other and falling in a single tumble to the stadium parking lot's pavement. Older dancers who Edy had never met wandered up to them with congratulations; they had been in attendance at the game. Strange girls and familiar ones hugged Edy and, for the first time in her life, she not only didn't care—she welcomed it.

She had done it. She was part of something. Truly, part of something. There was no one she wanted to tell more than Hassan.

And this meant that she'd have more time for him. Briefly, she thought of the argument they'd had in English class. But that had been nothing. They were Hassan and Edy, after all. They forgave each other endlessly.

"We're celebrating tonight, girls!" London cried and threw an arm around Edy and Naomi. "Get cute and ready to party!"

"Too late on both counts!" a middle-aged guy cupped his mouth and called as he passed. More than a few of Edy's teammates giggled. Cassie waved until Edy reached around Naomi and smacked her arm down.

They had two hours to get dressed for some off campus party that promised to be stellar. London swore a guy with a ton of cash to blow and way too many friends had invited them. She'd promised they'd make an appearance. And so they did.

Nineteen

The dance music flowed tonight, courtesy of a DJ who had become Wyatt's friend. Already his bit of living room had turned into a dance floor, crowded though it was as more and more poured in. He'd relied on liquor more so than beer for this all-nighter, though he hadn't been able to toss the kegs because, well, there were girls who did keg stands. Their shirts would fly up as they got plastered, and hell, Wyatt couldn't have been the only guy who ogled them desperately.

He was a modest guy and didn't always feel comfortable in the crowds he created with night after night of parties. These days, he kept company round the clock, and someone was always plastered—himself included. There were his constant friends: Solomon, Mateo, Lincoln, Tristan, and of course, Kennedy. Wyatt hadn't gotten any further with the tallish, copper-haired girl, but she had thrown hints that she might be interested in rounding the bases with him. So far, Wyatt had feigned ignorance after every brush of the hand and flirt that came this way.

Now Kennedy was on the dance floor. While she

wasn't much of dancer, she did feel the music, all close-eyed and swaying with a beer hoisted high in the air. She had an okay face. A prettier body. But she didn't talk about much and she was certainly no Edy Phelps. She didn't pump his blood or hijack his dreams. Still, he considered her willingness to join his bed. Was this what other guys did? Take what they could get? He could do worse. Roland would certainly be proud of him.

He needed... no, wanted a beer. It was his father who needed beer. Wyatt only needed something in his hand, something to sip and appear busy with. Something that would help him not look so awkward in his own house.

A few fist pounds and claps on the back came his way as he tapped the keg to refill his empty plastic cup. Mateo, who was homeless and sleeping with Lottie (which Wyatt supposed meant that he technically lived there with them), threw an arm around Wyatt and called for some of the strong stuff.

Wyatt didn't want the strong stuff. But he didn't say 'no' either. Instead, he threw back the bit of beer he'd managed to get, winced at its harsh, awful, pungent taste, and watched Lincoln weave through the mass of bodies.

"Cîroc, baby! The best for the best!" he cried.

Wyatt wondered if Lincoln knew who he was calling the best. He wondered what Lincoln would do if he saw an old picture of Wyatt, from not so long ago, when he wore faded polos, mom jeans, and thick, dingy sneakers with names that rhymed with more famous brands. Would he still be 'the best' if Lincoln saw that? Would he be 'the best' if he met Roland Green? Or Wyatt's mother, who had run off with a South End senior?

Wyatt shook his head. "Don't call me that," he said quietly. But Lincoln didn't seem to hear.

The door opened, and one of those lean, brawny types came in. He had a motorcycle helmet that he hung on the coat rack before heading straight for the keg, shouldering people along the way. Wyatt stepped back before he got stepped on, sure that this guy had to be one of Hassan's nasty little teammates.

"Good to see you've finally learned southern manners, Silas," Lincoln said dryly.

Silas looked at the much shorter Lincoln as if he were a common bug. Then he downed his full cup of beer and went for a refill. Only then did he wander off.

He had the looks of a James Bond, Wyatt realized, and the grace of Hassan. How did some guys luck out like that?

"What an asshole," Wyatt muttered.

Lincoln shrugged non-committedly. He was a good-natured kind of guy and seemed to genuinely like everyone. Soon he turned back to Wyatt with a grin. "More alcohol!"

Of course. Alcohol was the answer to everything

with this crowd.

Obligingly, he drank. And drank. When Kennedy pulled him to the dance floor, he relented, laughing, knowing he was going to make an absolute fool of himself. For the first time, he honestly didn't give a damn. This was his house. His music. His friends. He could do what he wanted.

Wyatt jerked to the music. Kennedy didn't mind. Around him, a few of those who knew him cheered him on, as it was rare for him to dance at these things. In those moments, he could see why Edy loved dancing. He could feel the rush through his soul, like happiness set to music, and he wanted more of it, he realized. When Kennedy bowed out for the next song, a cute and chubby girl took him up. Then another girl and another. Lincoln brought him Cîroc and, much to Wyatt's disbelief, he was actually having fun.

Then she came. Huddled in a cluster of girls who hooted and cheered and got a wild cry in response, Edy slipped into Wyatt's house as sure as Lottie had predicted. She was there and he couldn't bear to tear his eyes away.

God, what was she wearing? He'd never seen her dress like that, unless he counted the skimpiness of her dance uniforms, which he didn't. This was somehow different. Those hadn't been her choice, but this outfit... God, she had *chosen* to wear this.

Cleavage. Cleavage for days in a top that cut so wide and low that bending over was an impossible feat for Edy. A deep V-neck scooped down to nearly meet the fluttering fabric that swept up to expose her abdomen. It wrapped from the left and right, careful to leave her belly button exposed. In that moment, Wyatt realized that he had absolutely never seen her belly button. He exhaled nosily.

She wore short shorts with it. They halted high on her thighs. While he had seen that much of her legs before, he had never seen them while she stood in high heels. Wyatt bit down hard on his lip and looked away. He opted to concentrate on his breathing.

The music switched up to a heated, brash hip-hop song—something rough and serrated around the edges. But Edy whooped and scurried to the center of the room at a time when the slower tempo cleared the way for her. She didn't care. The girl was bold as hell and doing something Wyatt had never seen before. And she looked absolutely bad ass strutting around and popping various parts of her body, each of which seemed to snap of its own volition, before bringing them together in a brilliant succession of moves he hadn't even known she was capable of.

Another girl she'd arrived with, dark with a massive spray of natural hair that fell to her shoulders, threw herself out there in the fray with Edy, and together they began jerking, laughing, fully aware that they had the attention of everyone.

When a shot came Edy's way, she paused, threw it back with a wince, and snapped right back into her routine, as if drinking had been part of it all along.

How long had she been drinking alcohol exactly?

A short, slender guy appeared next to Wyatt. He had what looked like a mixed drink of his own creation in his hand. Or maybe Mateo had created it. He liked to play the bartender at these parties.

"I'm not into the sisters, but I'd do those two, you know?" the guy said and nodded towards Edy and her friend.

Wyatt scowled at him. It took all he had not to snatch the cup from this asshole and frog march him out the door. "'The sisters?'" was what he echoed instead with a faint tone of disapproval.

The guy grinned unapologetically.

The music picked up, a more familiar dance beat that drew braver souls to the floor. Wyatt shifted enough so that he could still see Edy. It was in time to see an Asian girl hand toss back a shot and hand Edy yet another. She laughed and threw that one back too. Then she climbed up on his coffee table, got a round of cheers, and slid into an array of slides, picking up momentum until she became a feat of acrobatic motion, with the music and more aggressive than it, seizing every sound as if it were made for her to dance to.

Even the other dance girls she'd come with stopped to watch this wild, free, gorgeous version of Edy. And how sexy was she now? With a quick scan around the room, Wyatt saw he wasn't the only guy with his eyes married to her. When another drink came her way, she took it. Half a shot, followed by a shudder, a brief hesitation, before the rest went down in a hard swallow.

Edy climbed off the table with the willing hand of some strange guy. When he didn't let go, she snatched back and whipped around to dance with the first willing person. She found a grinning guy who had moves to match Wyatt's. Briefly, Wyatt wondered what she would do if he cut in, if he asked for the next dance. Would she take him up? If not, would any amount of alcohol make her take him up on that offer?

He didn't think so. With that thought, he retreated to his bedroom.

At least there was no one screwing in it. He was amazed at how many times people had done that during the dozen or so parties he'd already thrown.

Wyatt locked his bedroom door and flung himself across the mattress, face down, breathing hard.

He was an absolute idiot. No girl would want him, least of all Edy Phelps. Even with money, he was nothing. He wasn't charming or funny or good looking. He wasn't fooling anyone. Edy wasn't the sort of girl who would care about his cash. What else did he have to offer?

He had love. Mountains and mountains of love. But she wasn't exactly starving for that, either.

A tap at the door startled him. When he tried to ignore it, it grew more insistent.

"Wyatt, it's Lottie. Open up."

Wyatt groaned. This was someone he couldn't get away with ignoring.

"Yeah?" he said once he'd thrown open the door.

She pushed her way inside and locked it behind her.

"Why did you leave?" she said.

"Edy's out there," he said sullenly.

Lottie's eyes widened. "She was the girl on the table, right? I thought so." She grabbed him by the wrist and pulled, but Wyatt snatched back.

"It's no good," he said. "This plan won't work. Just…" He looked around, as if the furniture might help. "The last time I saw her in Boston, I'd treated her so bad. I can't expect her to fall into my arms now." Not when she could have her choice of any guy who'd just seen her dance.

"You're nervous, Wyatt. C'mon. I'll—" She reached for him again.

"No!" He had no idea why, but seeing Edy like that ripped panic right through his soul. He didn't want to try and talk to her. He wasn't ready to convince her that he was the guy for her. He wasn't ready to hear her inevitable rejection. After all, there was no point in these parties and extravagant lifestyle, was there? She'd known him before. She'd known him in the faded polos and mom jeans. She knew the worst parts of him.

"Fine, Wyatt. Don't talk to her. But if you don't come out, I'll bring her back here."

His eyes gaped. "You wouldn't."

Lottie folded her arms. "You know I would."

Wyatt gauged her, trying to determine if she could possibly be bluffing. When he saw nothing to indicate as much, he cringed. "Alright. I'll… come out. But I can't talk to her. I haven't thought about what I'd say." That was a lie. It was all he thought about. But he had never settled on anything that would be good enough.

Lottie unlocked the door and he followed her out. A few guys in the hall raised their drinks to him, and hooted stupidly, obviously thinking that they'd been up to something.

Wyatt froze the second he entered the living room. He'd spotted Edy, not far from where he stood, wrapped up in conversation with Silas.

She didn't look happy.

Twenty

Fingers wrapped Edy's wrist before sliding down to grip her hand. She made to pull away until she saw who they belonged to.

"Wanna dance?" It was Silas.

His hair fanned in a shocking, messy, yet stylish array that gave him an absolutely brazen look, while his gray eyes peered down at her as if he'd laugh at any second. He stood close, body lean and hard and imposing in the small space.

Edy shrugged nonchalantly. "If you want." After all, they'd have to dance together for class. There was really no difference.

He released her hand, slowly, then shifted back and forth in place as if warming up to the music. His eyes were closed. Edy raised a brow.

The moves came quick and in time with the beat, sharp, snapping power plays from a strong dancer looking to show his dominance from the start. When his legs scissored and he tapped Edy's cheek playfully, she grinned and jumped in.

So, this Silas really was a dancer like her. Interested and able to do it all.

But he was bold, rude even, braggadocios, though he wouldn't intimidate Edy. That's what he wanted.

But we can't always have what we want.

She didn't know how long she danced with Silas, only that the music changed and they changed, and something like anger and grudging respect brewed between them somewhere between song after song. There were cheers occasionally and someone—she had no idea who but suspected it was one of their teammates—laughed and sprayed them with a rush of beer from the keg. Edy laughed and opened her mouth, as if she'd drink right from the tap. Silas stared at her a moment, cursed, and then scooped her up caveman style.

Edy punched him in the back. "What the hell are you doing?" she cried.

Silas weaved through a crowd that largely parted for him. "Saving you from yourself," he called back. "You obviously don't know when you've had enough. You're wasted."

Edy flared and twisted, even as the jaunting steps he took threatened to make her hurl. "What do you know?" she shouted at his backside. "You don't know me! Put me down, you goddamned idiot." She pounded his back again for good measure.

It was then that she spotted Wyatt, moving fast and coming toward her.

"Put her down," Wyatt said.

Silas paused, no doubt looking at Wyatt like a bug

he meant to step on. Edy took the moment of confusion to wiggle free and straighten out her clothes. She could only imagine how much of a cleavage show she'd given riding on Silas' shoulder.

"Come on," Wyatt said. "Follow me."

For one wild moment, Edy forgot Silas, her dripping beer hair, and everything except the money Wyatt had given her. She wished she had it; she'd hand it back that second. Then she tried to remember all the questions she'd had after seeing him that day in the cafeteria. Edy swayed a bit on her feet, on those goddamned heels three of her teammates had talked her into. Two pairs of hands shot out to grab her. Over her head, Wyatt glared at Silas. She had no doubt that Silas glared right back.

"Can I talk to you for a minute, Edy?" Wyatt said, firm this time.

She blinked at him, slow. The music blared in her brain and she shivered from being soaked to the core.

"Yeah. Sure." This guy was her best friend, right? Why wouldn't they talk?

Wait. There was something wrong with that thought, Edy realized belatedly. But she couldn't for the life of her remember why. And why the hell was she so wet? Silas was too, though, so at least there was that.

A blonde girl appeared at Wyatt's side.

"Edy?" she chirped, with too much familiarity. "I'm Lottie, Wyatt's cousin!" She extended her hand for a shake.

Edy stared. His *cousin?* The same cousin he... Edy looked at Wyatt, then the girl, then Wyatt again. There was no way in hell her fumbling brain could make sense of this. "But I thought—"

Wyatt grabbed her by the wrist and pulled her away from the crowd. "Let's talk in private," he said.

"But I don't—"

"We really have to talk in private." He stopped, but he didn't let go of her wrist. "Just a second," he said, as if he thought she'd deny him. "One minute in private and you can go back. *Please.*"

She looked around in confusion, but returned to see only desperation in his eyes.

"Alright," Edy said. "One minute."

He led her back to the room, passing a wall lined with drinking guys. Unease bubbled in her stomach and briefly she thought to snatch away and run. He paused long enough to open a linen closet and retrieve two towels. Then they were in the room and Wyatt was locking the door.

She must've been drunk. She must have been absolutely smashed, because her judgment was all off... She didn't know what to make of herself. She didn't even know what was happening to her.

Maybe Silas was right. Maybe she was out of control.

"Edy," Wyatt said softly, then said nothing at all, his gaze sweeping over her again and again in open adoration. Only Hassan had ever said her name so gently.

She looked away, embarrassed. "Wyatt, if there's something you want to say…" Already, she was ready to leave.

"I think there was something you wanted to say," he countered. "I thought we should have some privacy for that, at least." Then he wrapped a towel around her shoulders. "Plus, I figured you wanted to get away from that asshole and dry off a bit."

Edy blushed. Drying off sounded good. Faintly, she dabbed at her face and hair, wondering for the first time just what the hell she looked like. She wandered over to the massive mirror he had and cringed at her damp, curling, gargantuan hair. Even her blouse, cut low and clinging to her cleavage, accentuated the swell of her breasts and hinted at — *Oh God.*

Edy threw the towel around her neck so that it dangled and covered her chest entirely. Then she turned to Wyatt. "I have to go," she said.

"Edy don't." He grabbed her wrist just a little too hard.

"Let go!" she snapped and snatched free.

Wyatt held up his hands in surrender. "I'm not — I just — please, listen. One minute, like you promised."

Edy took a step back and inhaled in an attempt at calm. "Fine then," she said. "But only if you tell me what you're doing."

"'Doing?'" he echoed. He looked down at her,

blankly. He'd gained another half inch, whereas she'd stopped growing.

"Why you're here," she said.

He lifted a shoulder. "It's my house."

Edy looked around, taking in the plush, massive bed, the impossibly lush bedding, and the bedroom set she recognized as expensive. It was the same way with the living room furniture. When she'd come in, she couldn't believe the way people were spilling liquor on it and scuffing up the floor.

"This is your place?" she balked, momentarily distracted from her original question of why he was in Baton Rouge. "This is your party?"

He nodded, his cheeks coloring a tad.

She shook her head, pivoting from the volley of questions that followed that one. Wyatt had never cared about parties and popularity before. Why the sudden change? What the hell was going on? Something felt... off.

"Your cousin," she said. "That's the same one..."

He opened his mouth, then shut. Wyatt nodded instead.

Edy's face crumpled. Nausea swept up and threatened to claim her. This was the closest he'd come to confessing to her. Now that he had, she couldn't even look him in the eye. She was going to be sick.

"I have to go," she mumbled, tripping over her tongue with the effort.

"Edy, please. Wait. I'm not supposed to tell you this,

but—"

She fought with the lock on the door now. Why the hell had he locked it anyway? The thought sent her into sheer panic. When Wyatt placed his hand over hers and the door knob, Edy jerked back, burned to her soul.

"Don't do this," he said. "Don't... be afraid. I swear, I worship the ground you walk on. I would never hurt you. You must know how I feel by now. Just... look at me. *Please!*" He shrieked the last bit as she resumed her fumbling. But his yelling had the opposite effect. Edy whirled on him, incensed.

"Do you honestly think I could want you after what you did to your cousin? You're sick, Wyatt! You're sick and you disgust me!"

He moved for her, as if to wrap her in an embrace. Edy shoved him so hard he fell, before she turned and unlocked the door.

"And what if I didn't do it?" he shouted from the floor. "What would you think of me then? Or are you like all the rest, with your mind made up at the start?"

She had the door open now and could have easily disappeared, but his words had bolted her to the floor.

"You're trying to trick me," Edy said quietly.

Wyatt's eyes began to fill. "I'm not. Ask her if you want."

Edy couldn't. She wouldn't ask a thing like that. But she gave Wyatt a single, cautious, confused glance before disappearing into the party.

She'd rode with London, who she asked to take her back to her dorm. She was soaking wet and trembling now from the blast of AC and her own rushing thoughts.

London wasn't ready to go, but maybe Tamela was, she suggested. A thorough search of the room revealed that Tamela had already left. Who else had drove? Kaylee-Courtney looked absolutely hammered. Considering she was a menace on the road during the best of times, Edy didn't think it wise to put her life in the girl's hands.

"Ready yet?" said a voice from behind.

Edy turned to see Silas. "Umm, for what?"

Silas raised a brow. "To go back to your room and get sober."

Edy hesitated, sure her leaving with him wouldn't look so good. But what were her other options? Stand there with her headlights on display because she'd entered a wet t-shirt contest without her consent? Or to ride with a drunk driver? She wasn't willing to take the chance on a total stranger, of course. So that left Silas.

"Yeah," she said. "Let's go."

Outside, she hesitated only once more with the realization that she'd be climbing on to the back of his motorcycle.

✼ ✼ ✼

Wyatt spent the rest of his party in bed, contemplating what he had done. When Kennedy slipped into the room with him and began rubbing his back, he slid over, putting distance between them. When she asked if she could stay the night, he ignored her. When she got up and left, he didn't care.

In the dead of the night, when the music quieted down, Lottie came to visit him. She wanted to know what had happened when he and Edy were alone together. He told her. After all, the blame laid with her just as much as anyone for his inability to get anywhere with the girl he loved. Lottie cringed at the story.

"She left with another guy," Lottie said. "The one she was dancing with."

At that, Wyatt sat up, certain he may swat her if she kept on talking. "What?" he said.

"She did. But all's not lost yet. We can turn these sour grapes into wine."

Wyatt wasn't in the mood for her scheming just now. He looked at her reluctantly, willing to marry himself to the faintest hope, to commit to it again and again. "Well?" he said when she didn't speak right away. "How's that?"

Lottie grinned. "You spent time alone with her. That guy took up so much of her time too. There were lots of witnesses to it."

"So?"

"So we'll talk about that whenever we can. Give

people ideas. It's bound to get back to Hassan eventually."

Yeah. It was bound to get back to Hassan, if his propensity to know every bit of gossip in high school was any indication. Wyatt thought of that ill temper of Hassan's and his love of jumping to conclusions. Slowly, surely, he began to smile.

Maybe the night hadn't been so bad, after all.

It was bound to get back to Hassan.

Twenty-One

Hassan stretched out on the floor and folded his hands behind his head. The room really was cooler where he was. What's more, his back still ached from the strain of breaking tackle after tackle against Iowa. He'd been out to prove something and had put up insane yards in the process. His teammates had chanted his name in the locker room, which he'd basked in until catching the other running back, Paul's, brutal glare. Then Freight had doused Hassan in ice cold water and it was over, with them looking forward to the next game. But the pain held on and now his back preferred the unforgiving hardness of the floor to his bed.

He had an appointment that day and man, was he looking forward to it. After ignoring phone call after phone call from his mother, Hassan had finally gotten the disposition up to talk to her. It turned out she wanted to discuss Mala, which wasn't a surprise. She wanted to tell him that Mala wasn't far from him at all, in college at Tulane, thanks to a family who wanted to keep her within his sights. Would he be interested in having dinner with her and her dad?

Hassan saw it as an opportunity. After all, Mala's

dad was the one pushing for this marriage, wasn't he? If he could only talk to him, maybe even show him how unwilling he was to marry the girl, then it was possible that he'd suggest calling things off. Who'd want their daughter married to a guy who wasn't interested?

Then there'd be the look on Edy's face when he told her he'd negotiated a way out of this problem—*his* problem. Because it was his problem that he had dragged her into. It was only right that he solved it.

"So, this girl was completely into me," Cash said. "She didn't even trip when I asked her if she had a friend to join in. She was cool with that too. 'Anything for you,' she said."

Laughter rang out around the room.

"You are so full of shit," Tennessee Jones said. He, along with Xavier and Lawrence, rounded out the team's elite wide receivers. "There was no girl, let alone two."

"Fuck you," Cash said. "There were two girls and I had them both."

Hassan seriously doubted that. Cash could get carried away with his stories. He had a way of confusing what he wanted to happen with what actually happened. But it was all funny just the same.

"I went to that off campus party I told you guys about. The one where there's, like, fountains of alcohol and weed everywhere," Xavier said.

"Yeah?" Hassan said, voice drifting with fatigue.

"How was that?"

Xavier snorted. "Ask your girl. She was there. Sexier than I thought, too. Bravo to you, pageant queen."

Hassan's eyes flew open. "Edy?"

He shrugged. "How many do you have? The dark one that's a dancer."

Freight eyed Hassan curiously. "When's the last time you talked to her?"

There was no way in hell Hassan was answering that. But he did want to know more about this party. How could he ask about it without sounding completely pathetic? He sat up, looking from X to Freight.

"So, she went to a party. Must've been with her teammates," Hassan said, trying on nonchalance. After all, he'd been to parties with his teammates. What was the big deal?

X laughed. "Went to a party? Your girl was the party. Shaking her shit up on the table. Getting sprayed with alcohol. And that outfit she had on…" He looked at Hassan and trailed off. "Never mind."

Tennessee cleared his throat. "There's one thing you should know," he said and it took a moment to decipher the expression on his face. Worry, maybe? Fear? He inhaled. "She spent a lot of time with this one guy. I noticed and kept an eye on her for you. You never can be too trusting with these girls, you know. Anyway, I was right about her. She went in the back with a guy. Then she left the party with another. Sorry, man."

Hassan swallowed. Suddenly there were too many eyes on him and he leapt to his feet.

"Sawn!" Lawrence called and Hassan burst out the room, down the hall, and away at a speed he would've thought impossible.

He didn't know how long he ran. He didn't know where he was heading. Not towards Edy, that was for sure, because something was happening. Something was happening between them and to them, and it happened without his permission.

A great well of pain swelled within him and he shoved back the two words that battered and bruised him: *Liar. Cheat. Liar. Cheat.*

He collapsed to his knees on a grassy Indian burial mound. A sob shuddered through him, shocking Hassan with its complete and utter power. Ragged breaths escaped and he bit down on his fist to fight back. He wanted to run further, harder, longer—long enough so that he collapsed, mindless with exhaustion. But his thoughts wouldn't let him. Edy owned him, of course. She always had.

"Sawn." It was Lawrence, pulling him up to his feet. Lawrence who dusted him off. "Come on," he said. "There are... eyes."

But Lawrence hadn't come alone. Cash came along, followed by Freight, slow runner that he was.

"I'll talk to her if you want," Lawrence said. "This is

Edy. There's got to be… some explanation."

But one look at Lawrence told Hassan that he was as skeptical as he was, that he had every right to be broken.

Freight suggested they go over to a stretch of lake, making Hassan realize how far he'd run and how fast. How worried had Freight been to even try to catch him? On a better day, that thought might have made him laugh. Freight was known for a lot of things, such as brute force, a formidable seize, devouring enormous bags of greasy food… but not speed. He was never known for speed.

Hassan shook his head. "I have to get back to the room. Mala and her dad will be here soon."

Lawrence raised a brow, but said nothing.

"Who's Mala?" Cash said.

Hassan hesitated. Hearing about Edy had made him vulnerable. He wasn't willing to share anything else just now. "No one. Someone from home. I've got to go."

He started off, without looking to see if they would follow.

Hassan barely had enough time for a shower and change of clothes before his cell phone rang and Mala's dad said they had arrived. Feeling nervous, Hassan inhaled deep and looked himself over in the mirror, wondering if the button up and slacks he wore were good enough for dinner. Surely he didn't need a tie, right?

Mala's father was tall and broad shouldered, a tanned man who shook by clasping Hassan's hand in both of his and jerking vigorously. He introduced his daughter.

"Lovely tonight, isn't she?" he said in aggressively accented English.

"Yes, of course," Hassan said. He wasn't there to insult the girl. He just didn't want to be with her.

Mala beamed.

Back in Boston, she'd worn a lot of traditional clothes, saris and the like. That night, she wore a slender, long sleeved dress that accented her slip of a figure and long, lean legs. Her hair, which looked long enough to tuck into a belt, shone under the dorm lights. She swept it into a tumbling, graceful up do.

Her father drove a Jaguar. When Hassan climbed into the back seat, folding uncomfortably, Mala's dad insisted she join him in the back. Awkward.

He looked out the window and thought of Edy. What was she doing now? Talking to the guy she left the party with? Laughing with him? Laughing at Hassan? How long had she been playing him for a fool exactly? What if she and Wyatt...?

He put that thought from his mind. This was Edy. He'd known her his whole life. He'd know if she was lying. And she'd never purposely hurt him. So what if it seemed to be no big deal that they hardly saw each other anymore? Unless that meant that she didn't feel the same as she used to.

What if she didn't love Hassan? What if she cared about him because they'd grown up together and stayed with him for that reason alone? A wave of nausea hit him at the thought and he wrestled with a prickling of tears. He was overreacting, wasn't he? There had to be an explanation why she would slip into a bedroom with a guy, then ride off into the night with another.

God. Hassan must've been an idiot.

"I enjoyed watching your Iowa game. You were very good," Mala said carefully.

"Yeah?" Hassan looked at her. "Thanks."

She appeared to pick at nothing on her dress. "You've been shown great favor in life with talent and… good looks." She blushed at her own words.

Hassan looked at her. Was she actually attracted to him? He hadn't even thought it possible. For him, the whole idea of her being forced on him made her the most unattractive option in existence. But if he looked at her, really looked at her, it was easy to see she was a pretty girl. Shy. Quiet.

She certainly wouldn't dance on fucking tables and ride off with some dick.

"Thanks," Hassan said and noticed Mala for the first time.

Twenty-Two

Edy was busy vomiting again. While Naomi tut tutted and rubbed comforting circles on her back, London laughed like a rabid hyena.

"And so he said to me, 'Well, have you got a friend to join in?' So, I grabbed Rhea by the waist and said, 'If we've got each other, we don't need you'."

Tamela and a few of the other girls laughed enthusiastically.

Edy heaved again. "So, do they really sleep together or what?" she said into the toilet.

"I'm not sure if they do, or if they just like people to think they do," Naomi said quietly.

Edy thought about this. The team had a wild reputation and it was one the upperclassmen made sure to perpetuate.

"How are you feeling?" Naomi said.

"Like shit," Edy said and dry heaved until her stomach spasmed.

Her roommate sighed in response. "I told you to drink more water. It's why you spent half the night smashed. Who was that cutie you rode out with, anyway?"

"You mean Silas?"

"If that's his name." She hesitated. "Does Hassan know Silas? Are they good friends or something?"

Edy lifted her head from the toilet. She knew where her roommate was going with this and she wasn't interested. "Leave it alone, Naomi."

"I'm just asking because he might take it the wrong way."

Did she really think Edy didn't know that? In her sober mind, she'd reeled over how many ways the previous night could have been interpreted. But what could she do, besides trust that Hassan knew better than to jump to false conclusions?

"He knows me better than anyone," Edy said weakly. She shuffled out to the bedroom with Naomi on her heels and sat down hard. "We've been through a lot. He trusts me."

"And if he doesn't," Tamela jumped in, "then fuck him. There are plenty of fish in the sea."

Edy looked up in time to catch London wink at her. She snapped her eyes to the floor, quickly.

The girls all chimed in, a chorus of agreement on how many men were out there for the taking. They didn't understand that there was one Hassan and he was her heart. She didn't even want to be having this conversation.

Before Edy realized what she was doing, she was up and pulling on shoes, grabbing keys, then heading for the door. Hassan's dorm was a hike away, but she had to see him. She had to talk to him before he heard any nastiness and interpreted it for himself. Every step brought her a new explosion of panic, before she took off running, then stopped to throw up. When the heaving subsided, she took a seat, willing herself to gather her thoughts, master her panic, and continue only once she had done so. The sun disappeared from the sky in the interim and, finally, Edy headed for Hassan's room.

❊ ❊ ❊

Hassan entered his room, feeling more confused than ever. He'd just had a nice dinner and an even nicer conversation with Mala and Mala's dad. They really were decent people. And when he brought up breaking off the engagement he'd never wanted, Mala's dad fixed him with a broad smile.

"You're young. You have a girlfriend, no?" he said.

For some reason, Hassan looked at Mala apologetically. "Yeah," he said, though he didn't know what the hell he and Edy were just now.

"I, too, had a girlfriend before I married. It's common everywhere. My daughter, she was upset at first, until I told her that this is what men must do. 'Do not interfere,' I told her. Hassan, you are a good boy and will make the right choice for your family, for my family, for us all. You are like all Indian boys: devoted to their parents."

Hassan had said nothing. 'The right choice,' Mala's father had said. Hassan had never been able to see it that way, no matter how desperately he'd wanted to. He'd wanted to make his parents happy. He'd wanted to give them what they asked for. But his soul had always gone its own way. It had gravitated to Edy, loved her, wanted her endlessly, for all the good that had done him. But if there was no Edy, would he be able to bend enough to accept Mala then?

He'd looked her over, taking in her sweet smile and her sweeping hair, and thought that if there was no Edy, what did it matter who he was with?

Now, he stood in his dorm room, witnessing a four-way argument with Lawrence and Freight, Cash and Xavier. Hassan had no idea what had happened while he was at dinner, and he seriously doubted he wanted to know either.

Silence echoed as they all stared at Hassan.

"Just tell him!" Freight blurted, and shoved Lawrence toward him.

Lawrence scowled. "You can't be sure..."

"We're leaving," Cash said. "You tell him." Cash grabbed Freight by the forearm and headed for the door. Hassan stepped aside to let them out. Xavier passed with an apologetic smile.

"Do I even want to know what that was about?" Hassan asked as he shut the door behind them.

Lawrence sighed. "I need to talk to you, I guess. About that party."

Hassan didn't think he had the stomach to hear anymore. He shot Lawrence a leery glance. "What about the party?"

Lawrence put his palms out as if staving off some attack. "Listen, it doesn't have to *mean* anything. It could all be coincidence."

"*What* could?"

"I think the party was Wyatt's. At least, a guy named Wyatt from Boston threw the party. He's off campus and…"

Hassan heard nothing else. This was the guy she'd danced with, disappeared into the bedroom with, and rode off on a motorcycle with. Wyatt. The two of them had made a fool of Hassan for the last time.

"You okay?" Lawrence said.

A knock sounded at the door. Hassan swore to Lord Shiva. If it was one of his teammates here to tell him more about Edy, the next one that mentioned her name caught a fist to the mouth automatically. He meant it.

He threw open the door to find Edy on the other side.

❊ ❊ ❊

He was all dressed up, Edy realized. It was a sharp contrast to the clinging t-shirt and track pants she wore. In dismay, she looked down and saw a splash of puke on her hem. God, what was happening to her?

"Yeah?" Hassan said harshly.

Edy nearly looked behind her to see who he was talking to. But his eyes bore into her with such unbridled anger that there could be no mistaking his target.

"Hi Edy, excuse me." Lawrence disappeared for a moment, returned with a backpack, and exited the room. "I'll be at Freight's if you need me," he said to Hassan.

Why would Hassan need him?

Edy looked past Hassan's shoulder into the room, realizing he'd yet to invite her in. So he'd heard. He'd heard and he was pissed.

"Can I come in so we can talk?"

His eyes went flat and hard and, for a moment, she thought he might say no. Then he stepped aside and she swept in, quick before he changed his mind.

He folded his arms and leaned against the door. He looked at the floor; he looked at the wall; he stared at everything but her.

"Hassan, I —"

"Wyatt?" he said. "It's been Wyatt this whole time, hasn't it?"

Her brows crinkled in confusion. "What?"

"I'm not stupid, Edy!" he exploded and swept past her in a huff. "All that time you two used to spend together? Him *here* all of a sudden?"

Edy froze. Swallowed. So he did know Wyatt was here. But his presence wasn't her fault. She hadn't invited him. Hell, this was America. People went where they wanted. "What do you want from me, Hassan? If you insist on being insecure —"

"You make me insecure! You dance on tables and take tips in the G-string by the sound of it!"

"What?" She hissed the word in a threatening whisper, moving in on him as she did.

"You heard me!" Hassan said. "You dance on tables and take ti —"

His head snapped to the side with the crack of Edy's slap. He stared at her, green eyes wide in disbelief.

Edy's chest rose and fell in convulsing heaps. "If you *ever* talk to me like that again, we are through."

He watched her for one long, endless minute. "I've got news for you. We are through now."

"What the hell is that supposed to mean?" Edy cried. She barely noticed when the tears flooded her eyes.

"You know what it means. Everything we were, are, and were ever meant to be is done, Edy. I've had about all I'm gonna take of this. Edy, Hassan and Wyatt, everywhere you look. He trails and you welcome it. I used to think you just didn't get it. But maybe you like the attention. Like the drama of two guys fighting over you. How about I find some girl to always hang around, trying to replace you?"

Edy clamped a hand over her mouth, desperate to stop the whimpering, the uncontrollable sobbing desperate to break free. She waited until she found some measure of control before she spoke again. "Maybe you already did," she said.

"What?" Hassan said.

"You heard me," she stood up straighter, and looked his clothes over. "Where were you tonight, Hassan?"

He looked at her in surprise. But his hesitation told her plenty.

"Tell me!" she cried.

He looked away. "I met with Mala and her dad. We went to dinner."

Mala was there? In Louisiana? How long had he known this?

And he'd gone out to dinner with them? It didn't take a dinner to tell them he wasn't interested in what they were offering. Edy could only think of one reason why he'd endure that much of their company.

And she didn't like it.

"Edy…"

"You talk about me," she said quietly, "when I've put up with you being engaged the whole fucking time. Now I'm supposed to sit aside while you have dinner with your fiancée?"

"She's not—"

"She is as long as you acknowledge the engagement! Not once, *not once*, have you ever said that you weren't engaged to her." Edy trembled under the weight of this truth. "So, tell me, Hassan. If Mala Bathlar's your fiancée, what does that make me?"

He opened his mouth and let it hang there for a

while.

"Oh, go to hell," Edy spat. And he'd had the gall to break up with her? "Go and have a nice life with your new family. Make your mother proud."

With that, she stormed out of his room and down the stairs, making it as far as the street before her insides heaved, tears and vomit making a violently awful mess of the sidewalk.

Twenty-Three

For the next few weeks, Hassan thought of nothing but football and classes, desperate to put Edy out of his mind. He worked out like a maniac in the gym, scrutinized play after play in their book, and studied without seeing half the time.

He played brutal football. Mississippi State. Missouri. Auburn. Week after week, he barely saw his opponents or the danger as he powered through blocks, savaged expectations, and ran rough, rude, and ruthless at each and every turn.

His teammates loved it. The fans loved it. He had bruises on his bruises and parts that never stopped aching, but no one cared about that, least of all him. Hassan ached when he walked and grunted just to sit, but he found it easy, so easy, to not care about himself.

He only had love for football just now.

She'd called him a handful of times. When she did, he stared at the phone, but never answered. He nearly called her back every day.

He couldn't bring himself to do it.

He saw Edy at the games and sometimes watched her without meaning to. She moved like a goddess and weakened him impossibly. But she wasn't for him, not anymore. Anytime she turned as if she might look in his direction when he was on the bench or otherwise had a spare moment, he made sure to look as far and fast in the other direction as he could manage.

He wasn't over Edy Phelps, but he was working on it.

At the same time, the competition between Hassan and Paul, the second string running back, seemed to be getting worse. He wasn't taking riding the bench for a freshman well at all. To aggravate matters more, Hassan's always-pissed-off attitude had a tendency to eek into every interaction they had. He provoked him, as sure as he did players on whatever team they happened to be facing. Paul couldn't handle the pressure. It was part of the reason he rode the bench. The other half, Hassan told him, was because he was supposed to. Coach used him as a battering ram to pick up inches and yards when Hassan needed a breather, but the guy played like he had no hips, running headlong into every goddamned block. Now, with Clemson in Death Valley, he was pulling the same shit.

When LSU's players started down the sideline, pulling off their helmets as they headed for the locker room, Hassan rushed to catch up with Paul.

"You gonna get any yards tonight?" he demanded.

Paul shot him a look. "I've got this, newbie," he said.

"You won't beat them with strength," Hassan said

firmly. "The line's stacked. You've gotta move quick. Three, four seconds tops. Hitting the hole before it closes is the only way."

Paul gave him a look of disgust. "One good game and you think you're on staff, freshman," he said. "Why don't you go pour me some water already?"

Hassan laughed harshly. "I was good enough to take your job. Coach sticks with me now. Have you noticed? Oh, I bet you have. But don't worry. He'll keep you around to get my water, I suppose."

He didn't hear what Paul said next as the marching band milled onto the field, Lady Tigers leading the way. A tall, dark-haired girl led the pack, followed by pairs of girls, the first of which were a blonde and Edy.

Around Hassan, players continued to stream by, pulling their helmets off, wiping their brows, and shouting appreciation at the girls. Lawrence, Cash and a few of the staff brought up the rear of the football pack.

The band streamed into formation, girls up front. Lawrence gave Hassan a shove and a nudge towards the locker room. He moved, but not because he should. He realized he'd have a better view of the performance from the entrance to the tunnel.

Once there, he stopped again, Lawrence on one side, Cash on the other, a few guys behind them.

The first note hit hard and the girls jumped to position. They moved again, shifting to a new pose with each note, diving in leaps of beauty.

He'd never seen Edy strut like that. And her hair. What the hell? It was jet-black and sleek, bone straight as it flung like a whip, slave to its master. God, he liked it.

She didn't so much move as throb, merciless to the music. Each step sharp and biting, no matter how quick the music flowed, no matter how demanding. Edy didn't just keep up, she overpowered. He understood why she was out in the front. When her hips thrust, his gaze dropped, when she kicked, his head snapped to follow. He might as well have been her puppy on a chain. He couldn't look away. He didn't dare look away. They dropped to their knees, sliding on turf. When they leaned back he caught a flash of abdomen and felt himself throb. Without knowing when, he'd begun chewing on his lip, breath held.

"God damn," came Freight's voice from behind.

Hassan had been thinking exactly the same.

"Boys! Lockers!" shouted the assistant coach. Reluctantly, they hustled indoors.

Once inside, Hassan pulled the offensive coordinator aside and said to him what he'd told Paul.

"And you think you can make the pocket in four seconds, five tops?"

Hassan nodded. "Why not?"

The coordinator grinned and promised to give him a go.

That he did. And Hassan had plenty of ammunition

for the game, thinking back to Wyatt following him and Edy south, back to breaking up with her, back to her saying he had always said he was engaged to Mala.

They lined up in a Wildcat Formation with blood pumping in his ears. Cash sat the play out, with Paul taking his place in the quarterback's position. That left Hassan with a spot on the far left, one end of an unbalanced line. At the hike, Hassan shot right with all the fury he could muster, punishing his own body from the second Paul slipped the ball into his hand. He hurdled right, then left, cavorting at a merciless pace, slamming into then through two blockers, before hauling ass at a slant faster than even he expected.

He was angry. Desperate. Plowing at top speed. This wasn't supposed to be his life. This wasn't supposed to be how it went. Him and Edy together and fighting, then not even together… he couldn't stand that thought. An upperclassman running back who'd sooner kill him than help him. And his mother: his mother was too convoluted to think about, too painful to try and understand.

Top speed. Faster. Faintly, Hassan registered the roar of Death Valley in his ears, a swarm of white jerseys on his ass. Closing in on the side was a free safety, fast, faster than expected. Curious, Hassan looked and regretted the motion, giving him enough hesitation to catch up. He had to rely on one ruthless stiff arm, but even with that, the other guy grabbed and held. So, Hassan dragged him and together they tumbled into the end zone.

The crowd exploded, but for him they barely registered. Teammates crowded around, yanking him onto his feet. He was slapped on the head, on his back, on his ass even, as the blare of stadium lights blinded him.

They were screaming his name in Death Valley.

But Hassan couldn't help but glance at the scoreboard.

He'd have to pull that off a few more times, thanks to Paul, unless the other guys stepped real quick.

Hassan glanced over at the stands, eyes trained to look for the dance girls, then winced. Had he just made eye contact with Edy? He was being stupid, he knew. But he was no one's chump and he wouldn't be dogged or cheated on. She'd had the ability to hurt him deeper than anyone on the planet and she'd done just that.

He refused to let her think she could pull it off again.

Hassan made up his mind to put his head back in the game. After all, they were in need of all the help they could get.

At the close of the third, Tennessee caught a pass from Cash that took them in deep and home for a touchdown. In the fourth, Hassan found the end zone again and looked up, like an idiot, to see if Edy was cheering from her place in the stands. She was screaming like crazy and refused to think of why that might be. He turned his attention to Clemson. They were so resilient that the entire stadium must've been on their feet by the time Hassan found himself behind the line of scrimmage again, down by one with less than a minute on the clock. He could do this. This was his moment. Clemson would expect them to go for the run, whittling away the minutes and hoping to close it out.

And that was exactly what they'd do.

The center hiked and Cash slipped it to Hassan. He started strong side, faked it, and ran weak, buying himself but a moment. His line was breaking. He saw Freight, his back and lineman atop him. It was his only choice. He took off in a fury, using Freight and the lineman as stairs, bought an opening and took it. A cornerback spied him and charged in, head low enough for Hassan to put a foot in his back and leap over.

Thirty.

Twenty.

Ten.

Home.

His teammates screamed as Death Valley rocked on its heels. They were so hysterical, team and fans alike, that Hassan would've thought a trophy ceremony came next. Somewhere in the crowd, a Pradhan chant started, and spread in an instant.

Hassan yanked off his helmet, and a reporter pulled him aside.

"Hassan!" A pale and rosy-lipped blonde shouted above the roar of the crowd. "What an *amazing* game! Three touchdowns and one hundred thirty-five rushing yards in a *single* half. What motivated your performance tonight?" She thrust the microphone nearly into his mouth.

"Losing," he said simply. "That's what we were doing."

One corner of the woman's mouth turned up as if wanting to laugh.

"Coming in, Clemson was favored because of a high-powered defense aimed at stifling the run. How were you able to overcome that?"

Hassan shrugged. "Words don't intimidate me. It's your job to say they can stop me, else no one would tune in. It's my job to prove you wrong."

She grinned now. "And what do you make of Coach's decision to bench you till the second half?"

He was rolling his eyes now. "How about you tell *me* what you think of that decision. Run my stats by me again?"

She hesitated, clearly bemused. "Three touchdowns tonight. One hundred thirty-five rushing yards."

"Right. And what do you have for Paul? Or did you even bother paying attention to him?"

Just then, Hassan was jostled by a handful of teammates, and instinctively grabbed Lawrence as he tumbled in the excitement of fellow players. "Why are we even talking about that train wreck? This is the man you want! First touchdown of the night! Lawrence Dyson, son of NFL All-Pro Receiver Steve Dyson!" Hassan hoisted a grinning Lawrence to his feet and shoved him before the camera.

"Lawrence, coming in tonight, most thought you'd have your work cut out for you with the Clemson defense, however you came out tonight looking a bit like your father. What can we expect from you and the LSU offense as you square off against Ole Miss?"

Lawrence beamed with the reference to his dad.

"Listen," Hassan interjected, "I've been playing with this guy for years. Put him up against any team. Put us —LSU—up against any team and we come out on top. Virginia Tech. Florida. Alabama. Auburn. You pick. You keep talking about Clemson's defense, but who are you standing here talking to?" He was warming to the old, high school version of himself that talked smack and hyped the team up in the process. "Our coach was a mad scientist when he put this team together, you understand? Now deal with the monster."

Lawrence let out a hoot of approval, quickly followed by the hollers of Freight, Cash, Tennessee and more as they tumbled straight into the interview.

"But Hassan, you didn't answer the question. Have you any final predictions for the game against Ole Miss?"

He thought he'd answered her just fine before, but he had no problem being blatantly clear. Hassan untangled from the pack enough to grab the mic and laughed. He was past on a roll now; he was showing his ass. "Ole Miss would better serve as our prom dates than opponents. Look for us in a championship game against Oklahoma." How'd she like that for a prediction?

His teammates liked it, judging by the hollers and catcalls he got in response.

Five minutes later—or maybe ten—Coach paced the width of the locker room three times over, his strides wide before he halted in front of Hassan.

"Of all the ignorant, stupid—" He picked up his walk once again. "Didn't you tell me your daddy was a professor up at Harvard?" Eyes on Hassan.

Hassan cringed. "Soooooo, you didn't like the interview?"

Coach tossed him one helluva evil eye, before he picked up the pace, eyes slitted, jaw tense.

"And Steve," he said, coming to a stop before Lawrence. "Hell, I know enough about Steve to know he'd never—"

He turned on Freight, Cash, and Tennessee. "And you three. Upperclassmen! How the hell don't you know any better?"

Cash dropped his head, thoroughly reprimanded. Freight shot Hassan a grin over their coach's head.

"Coach, it was my fault," Hassan said. His adrenaline had been going. He got carried away. "I just run my mouth sometimes."

"You're running it now! Shut the hell up! Did I even ask you to talk?"

"No."

"Then what are you talking for? Why're you even answering me?"

Hassan smothered a smile.

"See, I know what your problem is, son." He took a step closer to Hassan. "You've been up there in Massachusetts, where they went and built a golden calf to your likeness. But you're in Louisiana now. And down here, the golden calf's for me, boy. You got that?"

Hassan opened his mouth, remembered the warning, and shut it to nod instead.

"Now let's get a couple of things straight, Pradhan. If I wanna start a goddamned sock puppet at running back, then I'll do it. And you, you'll just shut the hell up and like it if that's what I want, too."

Hassan blinked.

Coach turned his attention to Lawrence, who sat ramrod-straight, and waited as if daring him to move. Satisfied, he turned back to Hassan.

"Good hustle out there, kid," he muttered and marched out the locker room.

They burst out laughing, but only once they were sure he was gone.

In the time it took to shower and dress, Hassan's teammates managed to pressure him into a frat party. He wasn't interested. He'd rather head back to the room and watch TV, hang out at the campus lounge designated for the football team, or maybe catch up on some sleep.

Alternatively, the guys were tired of him being pathetic. He'd had long enough to mourn the loss of Edy. He'd flinched at her name and told them he was getting along fine without her. He didn't look at Lawrence when he said this, because he knew that Lawrence knew better.

He was practically kidnapped for the Tri Beta house. There was no amount of convincing that would get the guys to leave him alone. Even Lawrence was in on the job, insisting that getting out might help him clear his head. So, he agreed. Next to Edy, no one knew him better than Lawrence. If his best friend figured the party was what he needed, then he'd give it a run and see.

Hassan had his Mustang now, so the guys divvied up between his car and Cash's beat up pickup. By the time they made it to the Tri Beta house, folks had already spilled out onto a littered front lawn. Lingering in clusters with clear cups of beer in their hands, the partygoers moved absentmindedly to the sharp beats and lazy lyrics of Deep South hip-hop.

Hassan and the guys were clapped on the back as they moved through the crowd, mingling, maneuvering, greeting strangers and familiars who shouted out their names. Once inside the sardined frat house, a shout rang out and a few Tri Betas grabbed them beers.

The music blasted indoors and threatened to rattle the fillings in Hassan's teeth. He could smell sweat and the tang of sour beer mingling with acrid cigarettes and marijuana.

"Okay! This right here is my song," Freight hollered and broke into a shuffle of disjointed steps, jolting his teammates and strangers alike.

"You need to stop that shit," Lawrence said.

"Freight! Come dance with me!" called a girl from the center of the crowd. She moved closer and repeated the request.

"Who's that?" Hassan asked and sipped his beer for something to do.

Freight shrugged. "Hell if I know," he said and moved to the dance floor.

"Boy, I tell ya, Pradhan. You showed your ass tonight. Sho' appreciate it," Cash called.

Hassan shrugged. Football was over and he couldn't think of it right then. Instead, the jerking, gyrating of everyone in sight made him think of Edy.

How the hell was this supposed to be a distraction?

He turned a sullen glare on Freight who was engaged in a shuffle of feet that managed to intermittently be gliding and stomping. Hassan grinned.

"Is that called something?" he asked.

Cash laughed. "Probably 'The Freight', knowing him."

Hassan moved in for a better view, glad for the laugh, and froze when he saw Edy clustered in a bevy of girls.

He noticed the straight hair again, dark, thick, and luscious, and imagined what it would feel like to touch it, to have his fingers tangle in it, to have it brush his face and sweep over his chest in the heat of a moment.

She wore makeup in gentle sweeps, hair hiding so much of her beauty that he ached to swipe it away. Her white V-neck dove to expose an expanse of dark, creamy skin, and skinny jeans hugged curving hips before tapering down to long, lean legs accentuated by pumps. Hassan's gaze traveled the length of her body in a greedy, slow and torturous stretch. When he looked up, it was to find her watching him with an unmistakable wrench of pain in her eyes.

He couldn't look away. He couldn't even breathe. No, his body had halted all that on meeting her gaze, rendering him wide-eyed and desperate as a want so severe knocked at the door of pain.

But this was a hopeless endeavor. They were better apart. Their families would be relieved. And the two of them… well, the two of them could get on with their lives.

Being apart was best. Sometimes, he had to remind himself that.

A tallish guy with dark hair and wide shoulders approached Edy. She wore a scowl at the sight of him before they exchanged a few harsh words. Hassan moved, prepared to rescue her, before Edy shook her head and burst out laughing. He glanced at his phone and Edy rolled her eyes, before snatching it from him. He didn't seem to mind. In fact, a few words from her while she rummaged through his phone had the other guy grinning. He eyed her openly while she had her head down.

Hassan swallowed, torn between grabbing the guy by his throat and dragging him bodily from the party and watching the two for as long as he could stand. He needed to watch, though. He needed to see how fast she had gotten over him. But just when he'd had that thought, Edy looked up, and choked him, tortured him even, with the gentle want he saw there.

God, she was beautiful.

She was devastating.

Twenty-Four

Edy hadn't expected to see Silas or Hassan at the Tri Beta party. Silas, for his part, had the habit of party-hopping over the weekends so it was easy to see how he wound up at the hottest post-game get-together. Edy was only there after an obnoxious amount of begging on the part of her teammates and their insistence that she had been aloof and standoffish for weeks. In fact, they argued, she hadn't been herself since the Iowa game. They thought the remedy to that was the Tri Betas, who were known for gorgeous frat brothers, unseemly pranks, and letting the alcohol flow at just about any event they pulled off. As Edy stood there discussing their school project with Silas, she tried her best not to acknowledge Hassan, and failed.

She didn't want to *want* him. He'd treated her horribly. He all but called her a stripper. He didn't trust her. He made insane accusations. He'd gone out with Mala behind her back. Try as she did to resist, Edy couldn't help but ask herself how many nights out he'd had with Mala without her knowing. Maybe his rejection of Mala had less to do with an arranged marriage *per se,* and more with him having tried the goods and turned his nose up at them.

What was she doing? What was she thinking? It didn't matter what he had or hadn't done, what he'd said or neglected to say. They'd broken up. They weren't even friends. They couldn't bear the sight of each other... And yet, every time Edy looked up at him, their eyes met. In them, she saw the unfathomable depths of her own pain, of this awful bed they'd made.

"You called me yesterday about the project?" Silas said. "Because my phone says you didn't. No missed calls from you. Nothing."

Edy snatched the phone from him, earning a laugh, before she glided through menu options in search of his call log. "I called," she said. "I called more than once."

"Yeah, but who you called is the question," Silas said.

Edy shot him a look. He could be such a butthole sometimes. Then she found what she'd been searching for, eyeing her phone number, not once but three times in the span of forty-eight hours. With weeks having passed, she'd experienced a rising panic corresponding with Silas' degree of calm and inability to simply get started on their work.

"There!" Edy called in triumph and thrust the phone in his face. "My number."

Silas shrugged, took the phone, and jammed it in his

pocket. "So, you called. I don't like the phone anyway."

That was his version of an apology, she figured.

Edy glanced over at Hassan and found herself unable to look away. Those green eyes met hers and there was no one else in the room, no one else on the planet. For one crazy moment, she thought to go over to him, to wrap her arms around him, to make him love her like he used to. Just what the hell had happened to them and why had they let it take place? She had so many unspoken regrets, but so much anger underneath all that. He'd called her a stripper, a cheater, a liar. He didn't trust her. They'd had an entire life together, and still her word wasn't enough for him.

Meanwhile, the reality of Mala had boiled over in epic proportion. What she'd said about him never denying their engagement, about him treating it as valid, had been a hidden hurt, one that she'd never meant to linger on, let alone share. She'd always told herself that he was in a difficult situation, that her support was what he needed. She'd concentrated on him to neglect her own wants and hurt, only to have it all erupt in a fit of fury. Now, when she wasn't basking in that same ill temper, she was close to tears, crying outright, or shoving him from her mind with weak desperation. What else was there? When would she get over him, exactly?

"Just go over there and talk to him if you like him so much," Silas said.

Edy glanced at him, only to find him openly glaring at Hassan.

Shit.

"I *don't* like him so much," she snapped.

Silas smirked. "Whatever you say, little rabbit."

"Why do you call me that?" she snapped irritably.

"Because you remind me of a little rabbit," Silas shot back. "Obviously."

A pale brunette in a form-fitting dress touched Hassan on the arm. The two exchanged words. He looked over at Edy, then moved to the dance floor with her.

Bastard.

Briefly, she glanced over at Silas, wondering if he'd be interested in dancing, then thought better of it. She wouldn't be petty like Hassan. Or at least, she thought he was being petty. What if it was all in her mind? What if he hadn't had a stray thought about her and instead was just enjoying the company of another girl? Maybe it was something he'd long wanted to do.

"So," Silas said on return, handing Edy a beer she hadn't asked for. "Are we dancing or what?"

Yeah. Yeah, they were. Silas was a great dancer and eye candy to boot. Why wouldn't she dance with him? Hassan had the slender brunette with the swaying hair. She'd have Silas.

"Who's the running back to you?" Silas asked, feet gliding absently in a complicated step that had to be his own impressive creation.

Edy watched for a second, measuring his count with bobs of her head, before mimicking his moves. When he nodded in approval, she grinned.

"How do you know he's anything to me?" she said defiantly. Then she betrayed herself by glancing over at Hassan.

Silas laughed. "One," he said and took a sip of his beer, "you two won't stop looking at each other. Two, he's the guy that felt you up on the field. Pradhan's kind of known. Especially with the good season we're having."

Edy scowled. "He did not feel me up."

"He did," Silas said. "And you liked it. Now, answer the question. Why is he out of rotation?"

Edy huffed. Maybe dancing with a busybody had been a bad idea. He'd been nosy at Wyatt's party too, a know-it-all who had decided for himself when she'd drunk too much, and took it upon himself to carry her off like a Fred Flintstone caveman. He hadn't stopped there, either. No, he'd parked his bike and walked her right up to the dorm. He would have walked her to her bedroom if she hadn't insisted that he leave her alone. Silas followed that up with a phone call to ensure she'd made it safely indoors. He'd surprised her by being as fussy as an old aunt.

"It's nothing," Edy mumbled unconvincingly.

"Meaning you don't want to talk about him," Silas said. "Must still be a pretty fresh wound, little rabbit."

He grabbed her hand as if it were an automatic

motion, getting her attention as he disrupted their makeshift dance routine to introduce another.

Again, she watched him, grabbing the gist of it faster than the last round. But then she shook her head, nudged off the group of guys who bumped her, and complicated Silas' moves a tad further, smoothing it out and improving it.

He rolled his eyes. "You're not a better dancer than me, little rabbit."

"But I am," Edy said and batted lashes at him.

Silas sighed. "One day, we'll have to settle that disagreement once and for all."

Edy nodded. "And when we do, you'll apologize to me."

This time, Silas was bumped, bringing him closer to her. Neither commented on it. Instead, he said, "What was with you and the guy who threw the party?"

"You mean Wyatt," she said.

"Yeah, whatever. He didn't want you to leave. I gave you five minutes in the room with him before I was about to come for you."

Edy looked up in surprise. "But why?"

Silas exhaled. "That is what I'm still trying to figure out."

Out the corner of her eye, Edy watched Hassan storm out the party.

Twenty-Five

Hassan laid flat on his back, bench beneath him with his eyes on the weight bar. He wrapped first the right hand then the left around cold steel and took a deep, bracing breath. Above him, the Strengths and Conditioning Coach, Brady Moss, stared down at him. He had a lean, red kidney bean face and thin lips. During Hassan's first week at LSU, he'd been pulled into Moss' office, where they devised a diet and workout routine meant to maintain his strength, speed, agility and endurance. His first week at LSU felt like a lifetime ago.

"Ready?" Moss said.

"Yeah."

Together, they lifted the bar. A look of agreement passed between them and Moss opened his hands.

"Let's go, Pradhan. Give it hell like you do."

He'd have to dig deep and find the requisite anger for that to work. Fury was his fuel for football. Given what had happened between him and Edy, Hassan found himself with no shortage of that.

Two twenty-five. It was the standard weight given at the NFL Combine to measure a player's strength.

While any mention of the league and his name in the same sentence was still years, the weight in his hands was still significant in terms of measuring himself and working towards that goal.

The first reps went splendidly. Steady, even, they flowed from chest to maximum height as his arms bent again and again. Gradually, he began to feel the eyes of his teammates on him. He was a shit talker, naturally, and used it to motivate others. Still, he couldn't max at this weight, otherwise he'd get plenty of what he'd been given. He'd deserve it and they'd enjoy it.

Hassan made ten and breathed a sigh of relief. The weight wasn't a new accomplishment for him, but a distraction, improper form, cramp, or hair in the eye could cause him to tap out. When he did, Freight, Cash, Tennessee and the rest wouldn't be soon to forget.

At twelve, Hassan started to feel the burn. It began in his upper arms and spread to his chest, tightening and thrumming with each lift. He thought of Edy. *Thirteen.* Edy and Wyatt. *Fourteen, fifteen.* Edy with the new guy. *Sixteen, seventeen, eighteen.* He slowed. Adjusted a tad. Breathed. Pushed up slow.

The weights tilted a shade and his arms trembled. He'd shoved Edy away. Broken up with her. She was with someone else now, someone who didn't see himself as engaged. Someone who wasn't an idiot like him.

"Come on, Pradhan. Push it," Moss hissed.

She was probably happy.

At that, Hassan shoved up once more, hard, before his belly clenched and the weights began to shift.

They disappeared, snatched away by Moss, and the room erupted in cheers.

Hassan closed his eyes. He felt so empty. So absolutely, utterly empty.

Next to him, Freight lifted a beastly amount of weight with smooth, crisp motions.

"You... going... with us... tonight?" he asked between puffs of breath.

"Going where?" Hassan asked. Wherever it was, he doubted he'd be tagging along.

"X and Tennessee say..." Freight's chest began to shudder, "that some Eta Chi girls —"

"No thanks," Hassan cut in. He wasn't ready to see Edy at another party.

Freight heaved his weights on their proper resting place and sat up. "Not a party," he said. "Just a get-together." Freight shot him a sly glance. "They asked for you by name..."

Hassan sighed. He swallowed the urge to scream.

"I don't *care*." He got up from the bench in a huff and strode over to the water cooler. "I *really* don't care."

"But man, you ain't seen these girls! Eta Chi sisters make ya wanna stick something in 'em!" X called from a nearby treadmill. He caught a glimpse of the slight blonde Sports Management intern near the bulletin board and cringed.

"My bad!" he called. "I didn't see you."

"Animal," Cash said, keeping his legs loose on a stationary bike. He took a swig of water from a bottle.

When Hassan passed Freight again, this time heading for a treadmill, the upperclassman tried again.

"They were twins, the girls that asked for you. Blonde. Best chests you ever saw. And handy, so I've heard."

"Sounds made up," Hassan said and stepped on the treadmill. He jabbed a few buttons and looked up to see Freight, Cash and Lawrence in a silent, gesturing, three-way argument from their respective places in the room. Freight was so caught up in the moment that he failed to notice Lawrence's repeated nods in Hassan's direction, an indication that he was watching.

"Yeah?" Hassan said when Freight finally looked at him.

"I'm going to come out and say this. You... need to start seeing other people. Ones who aren't your teammates," Freight said.

Lawrence promptly started his treadmill and stuck earbuds in his ears.

"Shut up, Freight," Hassan said. Though only warming up with a walk on the machine, he could already feel his heart rate gaining momentum.

"Best way to get over that heart break is to get back on the horse," Freight said.

Hassan said nothing.

"Get a friend or two. Nothing serious, you know? And just enjoy *her*."

Hassan glanced at him, but still said nothing.

"Hell, pageant queen, you were at the same party as us. She's doing the same thing right now. She's already back on the horse and riding it by the look of things," Freight said.

Hassan punched the stop button on his treadmill, climbed down, and crossed over to his teammate.

"Shut. The fuck. Up," he said, then went for the machine furthest from Freight. This time, he could hear Cash as he fussed at Freight, demanding to know why he always had to say the worst shit.

Hassan wondered the same thing.

He didn't care if Freight had a point. When Hassan wasn't in class, he was studying, on a football field, in the weight room, at the Player's Lounge, or locked in his room.

He found quiet times the hardest. On the rare occasion that his roommates were nowhere to be found, Hassan cranked up something loud and angry on the stereo and studied his playbook and whatever changes the coach had erected that week. When he grew tired of that, he studied the school's catalog and wondered for the umpteenth time whether he should pick up a Communications degree in addition to the Business degree he pursued, a Sports Administration one, or leave well enough alone. When the loneliness bore down on him, he'd look in the halls and catch a stray teammate. He'd dragged them into his room so they could go over the playbook together or strategize on how to strengthen the team for that week's opponent. Sometimes they'd review the highlight reels specially dubbed for him on request by the team's Audio/Visual Department. Occasionally, they'd watch ESPN, shoot the shit, and get to know each other better. It surprised even him how much he talked about Nathan. And Edy. Still.

Freight had been raised by an ailing Creole grandmother and was good-natured about all things — even his then-teenaged father abandoning his mother out of an apparent fear of responsibility. Freight still saw his mother here and there; he always got a card at Christmas and a tie in the mail at Easter, though drugs still claimed most of her money and time. "Don't worry," he'd told Hassan as he took in his teammate's troubled expression. "She'll clean up when the time is right. Some people struggle with discipline, you know." He kept a picture of his mother as a bright-eyed sixteen-year-old by his bed.

Then there was Cash. He came from a two-parent home filled with love. Both his parents worked hard, his mother as a maid, his father as a factory worker. He was the oldest of seven children, four of whom were boys. All of them were the best at everything, to hear Cash tell the tale.

Both X and Tennessee were chip-on-the-shoulder

inner city kids who'd never seen a football camp, elite training session, or gym membership in their lives. Tennessee lived five miles from the Titans' stadium and had never seen a game. Nonetheless, they were two of the toughest, most bad ass players Hassan had ever seen. They made him think and question. Though he had glimpsed poverty in Boston and India, he had never shook its hand and called it friend.

There were other stories, enough to fill a roster, and increasingly, Hassan came to believe he would know them all. They passed the time.

Despite being the one to dump Edy, Hassan still found himself staring off into space, taking out a picture of her or them, and a time or two having to brush away loathsome tears.

He'd been sitting on the edge of his bed the last time it happened. He'd bent over to pull off his favorite pair of Adidas and the engraved, silver dog tags, a sixteenth birthday gift from Edy, hit him in the face. He taken them off, read the lie, touched it, and stared at it endlessly. *He* was her favorite guy, in this life and the next. Not Wyatt. Not some other guy.

His vision blurred. Hassan snatched the dog tags from his throat and hurled them at the trashcan. Then he went after them to stomp them into oblivion, trampling again and again. It was Lawrence who pulled him away from the jewelry, making him stumble on the quick backtrack to his bed. And like that, it was over.

"It's okay," Lawrence said. "You're okay. I promise, you are."

Thursday night the football team stayed quarantined in their respective rooms and on Friday, they boarded a charter flight to Oxford, Mississippi. The flight was subdued, mostly on account of changes to the changes in the playbook. Those had the players up half the night studying. Never mind whatever school work they had to get done.

Had Hassan really thought he could handle a double major? With Edy, he'd felt some kind of superhero: anything had been within the realm of possibilities. But now, all alone, he mostly felt downtrodden, beaten, exhausted. His mind never stopped working. The anger never stopped coming. It mingled with a potent sort of nausea, as he contemplated yet another game without Edy's cool, steady voice, and warm, steadying touch.

When they arrived in Oxford, a bus shuttled them from the airport to a Marriott less than a mile from Vaught-Hemingway Stadium. They'd settle into their rooms, take lunch, and have a free evening before tomorrow's game.

On check-in, Hassan and Lawrence were assigned to room 419, where, to their surprise, they found a pretty pink corsage waiting on each of the two double beds. Four roses clustered together with a spray of ivy and a dusty rose ribbon. Curious, Hassan ventured over to the next room where Jacob Miller, a second string cornerback, and Gavin Cook, the free safety, were rooming. Jacob held up the same beautiful corsage with a frown on his face. Up and down the halls, players stepped out, each with an identical pink corsage and a look of confusion on their face.

Coach didn't parse words on the day of the game. He reminded them of the talent on their team and what it took to win. Then he told them to go and take what was theirs.

From the place in the tunnel, Hassan heard the fans, already at each other's throats with chants of "Go to Hell, LSU!" and "Go to Hell, Ole Miss!"

"Let's go!" shouted a voice from the front as the team trotted out. Boos rained down like hail from an enormous sea of red. In the stands were signs, mocking LSU tradition with "Geaux to Hell." He saw the "Geaux to Hell, Pradhan" signs and grinned. And then he noticed the flowers, dotting the breast of every man, woman, and child in Rebel Red. Pink corsages. Corsages like the ones that had been waiting for them at the hotel. In the crowds, on the home team sideline, on the overlay of every Pride of the South band member, and on the chest of every burly Ole Miss player. Each had the same pink corsage.

Their prom dates had arrived.

Twenty-Six

Silas and Edy crowded together, with the crown of their heads touching, as they looked down at his oversized phone.

"I'm not doing that one. Suggest another," he said.

"You suggest another!" Edy cried. "You've got too many stipulations. You think everything makes you look silly or dumb or not cool enough. You're so full of yourself that nothing'll do."

"Hush, rabbit. I've made some good suggestions that you shot down," he said.

"We can't *improvise* something historical," Edy said. "The whole point is that it's from the past and not contemporary."

"And you think she knows every dance that's ever been done before?" Silas was laughing at her now, his eyes told her that. "She doesn't, you know. We could tell her anything."

Edy's gaze narrowed. "You're doing this because you know I spazz over grades."

"I am," Silas agreed. He hit the power button on his phone, killing the dance suggestions they'd been Googling. "This really isn't a hard assignment, you know. You're the one who's making it hard by trying to go prehistorical."

"Yeah, and you want to pop and lock, as if that would give us a decent grade!"

They were in their usual standoff which Edy suspected would gain the usual outcome. Then Silas surprised her.

"Look, you move okay. If you think you could handle a lindy hop or a cha cha with me..."

"Handle?" Edy balked. The boy made a business of insulting her, she swore.

"Yes, handle. If you think you can handle it, then we'll do one of those. Assuming a fifty to sixty-year-old dance is old enough for Professor Martin."

It was the closest they'd come to a solution since getting the assignment. There was no way Edy would turn that down.

"We'll cha cha," Edy said. "That's the harder of the two."

Silas shrugged. "Can't say I've noticed a challenge with either."

What an ass.

After scrambling to find an open, adequate place to practice that met both their scheduling needs, they gave up and agreed to work at his place. He had an evening job bartending on Tuesdays, Thursdays and Fridays. Saturdays were game day for her and she still had dance practice in the afternoons and just after dinner. So, they agreed on Mondays and Wednesdays, with an occasional Sunday if needed. Silas would pick her up on his bike and they'd venture off campus to work on choreography in his living room.

He hadn't told her that he had a little brother, an adorable boy with expressive gray eyes and a smile that warmed her. He looked over at Silas and whispered in a too loud voice, "Silas, she's *beautiful*," only to have Silas elbow him so hard he stumbled.

Edy had a sudden urge to hug the little one. Not just because he'd called her beautiful and she couldn't remember the last time someone had. Not just because she knew he was a boy with no mother and father either. It was the eyes, she supposed, identical to Silas' yet warm instead of hard and forbidding. She had one wild moment where she imagined Silas looking at her in that way and she wanted it, she wanted that.

Edy shoved away the thought.

"I've got to make dinner first," Silas said. "I hope you don't mind." He looked her over. "You could probably use it, actually."

Edy scowled. Dinner hadn't been anything thrilling, just a weird pork sausage patty that she'd picked at, coupled with lima beans and roasted kale. But she wasn't going to validate Silas' sidelong insult about her being too thin or whatever he was implying.

"I'm fine," she said and marched over to the couch with her backpack.

She'd known that he would have a few things to do when he got home; he'd said as much. So, she'd come with the textbooks for her other classes and meant to catch up.

After a few minutes of fumbling with books and deciding to handle the history reading she'd yet to tackle, she heard Silas banging around with the pots and pans.

"Heard from Hassan?" he said.

Edy refused to look up. "Of course not. Why do you care?"

"I don't," Silas said. "But you seem to."

Now, she couldn't help but look up.

"Who's Hassan?" his little brother said.

"Mind your business. Go do some homework," Silas snapped, harder than Edy would've expected.

"I did it already!"

Silas snorted. "I doubt it." He gave the kid one withering look and he scampered away, slamming the door with a bang. Silas pulled out a chopping board and an assortment of produce from the refrigerator.

Edy returned to her reading.

"So, what happened with you two?" he said.

Edy sighed. "We broke up, that's what."

"I figured as much. Who did the breaking off?"

Edy shot him a cautious glance. There was no way she was venturing into such sensitive terrain with the crass, bullish, and arrogant Silas Swain.

He stopped chopping to stare at her. "He broke up with you," he said finally.

She looked away. Even when she didn't speak, the

truth rose plain on her face.

"It wasn't meant to be, that's all. He didn't trust me." For some reason, she couldn't stop gnawing on her lip. "And he had someone else," she said quietly.

"Sounds like an idiot," Silas said. He went to the fridge and peered inside. "You allergic to anything?"

Edy frowned. Hadn't she told him she wouldn't eat? "No," was what she said instead.

"We're having spaghetti. I go heavy on garlic so you'll have to forgive me."

"Just don't try to kiss me," Edy said. It was meant to be a joke, but somehow the laugh got lost. He only looked at her. She looked back.

"I'll try to remember that," he said.

A little more than an hour later, Edy sat sprawled on Silas' dumpling-like couch, where it was lumpy in all the right places according to him. She was on her second Pina colada and feeling spoiled. He'd made it with extra pineapple once she told him how much she liked them. In the time it took him to cook, they'd discussed her family, which seemed to fascinate him, and his brother, which was all the family he had. Levi was twelve and into robotics. He played football but understood that it wasn't his future. Silas planned for him to study engineering or some sort of science. Maybe even go to medical school.

Levi had questions at dinner, one after another, until Silas forbid him from speaking again. Where was she from? Why was her accent so funny? How did she meet his brother? Did she like his brother? "

That was where Silas ended the interview.

"Keep that up," he warned, "and you're heading for the room."

But that didn't have the effect he was hoping for as Levi looked from one to the other, let his eyebrows dance, and smirked at Silas knowingly.

Suddenly, Edy was aware of the time. And aware of how long she'd been in Louisiana—not long enough to be in some guy's apartment, she supposed. Last year, she hadn't known him at all. Didn't that mean that they hadn't known each other long enough for this?

Wait. What the hell was she saying? She was there to do school work. It just so happened that he had to feed his kid brother, that he insisted on her eating, and the conversations between them went on and on, approaching a comfort she would have never expected.

When dinner was done, Edy insisted on helping him and Levi with the dishes. Silas washed, she dried, and Levi put them away. They worked shoulder to shoulder trading little barbs about the thoroughness of one's work or the lack of work ethic. She claimed to see nonexistent stains, Silas swore she needed to buff the dishes to a high gloss, and he also swore that his kid brother put everything in the wrong place. When both Edy and Levi grew tired of Silas' mocking, she splashed him with dirty dish water. He, in turn, did the same to her. Levi disappeared, though when, Edy couldn't say. By the time they were ready to work on choreography, both were soaked and dingy to boot. Edy's white LSU shirt had an obscene wet spot dead center, complete with tomato splotches.

"I'd say I was sorry about that, but it would be insincere," Silas said. He ventured around the kitchen's island counter and down a short hall. Edy heard a squeaking door open. When he returned a moment later, he was shirtless and hard bodied before he pulled on a simple black tee.

"Want something to wear?" he said.

She nodded, eyes averted from him. Then he disappeared down the same hall.

"You're tiny," he said. "You can probably fit one of Levi's shirts. Mine would swamp you."

"Are you sure he wouldn't mind?"

Silas shrugged. "I grabbed an old one. It shouldn't be a big deal. Although…" he glanced down at her chest, "I'm not absolutely sure it will fit."

Edy felt her cheeks grow hot. She snatched the shirt from Silas and started down the hall.

"Second door on the right!" he called.

She slipped into the bathroom and changed. It turned out he was right. Levi's shirt practically strangled her chest. No way was she going out there like that.

"Well?" Silas called, his voice so close that Edy jumped. "What's the verdict?"

"It's tight," she called.

He snorted. "Judging by your jeans, I'd say you were into that."

Embarrassment flooded Edy. Was he flirting with her or making fun of her? With him, she could never tell.

"Just come out. You girls make a big deal out of everything. I'm sure…" He trailed off to nothing when Edy opened the door.

"Oh," Silas said. He didn't even make a point of lifting his gaze.

"See! You're being a pig!" she cried and swatted him on the arm.

"I'm not, I just…" For a moment, he wore a bizarre look on his face, as if even he wasn't sure what he was doing.

"Just what?" Edy said.

He shook off whatever he was about to say. "Let's get some work done. It's getting late and I know you have a curfew."

Edy nodded.

Right. Work. That's what she was there for.

Later that night, back in her room, Edy puzzled over that weird moment with Silas. He'd been looking at her, outright looking at her chest, and she'd accused him of being a pig. It wasn't that she'd felt objectified though she implied as much. No, she had felt something else, something frightening, something she'd only experienced with Hassan.

She put the thought out her mind. There had never

been anyone for her but the boy next door.

Edy and Silas didn't get to practice again until the week after they faced Florida. Since there was no game and therefore no performance for Edy and her teammates, she thought it the perfect time for them to apply themselves to the assignment.

And it was. They managed to put together the beginnings of a decent performance, although it was shorter than Edy would have liked. And she got some great cooking out of the deal, too. Chicken alfredo. Jambalaya. Salisbury steak. On one night, there were barbecue ribs she moaned over. Edy was halfway through those and sure she had sauce on her face when Silas sat down, took a deep breath, and said, "Go out with me."

She looked up, bone in her hands, sauce all over, and stared at him horrified. "Why?"

He shrugged. Studied the table, the floor. "Cause I think it would be good for you. You still think about him, don't you?"

Edy sat the bone down and wiped her face with a napkin. Then she wiped her hands, trying and failing during all that to come up with an adequate response.

"So, yes. You do," Silas said dryly.

He had a way of reading her that she didn't understand. Rarely did she give him a straight answer. Rarely did he need one.

"Where would we go?" she said softly, trying to imagine herself out with someone other than Hassan.

She sighed at that absolutely pathetic thought, then looked Silas in the eye.

He was trying to help her get over this hurdle. He was being a good friend. Maybe going out was what she needed. He seemed to understand her so well; maybe he understood that.

Silas shrugged. "We'll figure something out."

And suddenly, she was looking forward to it.

On Edy's first free Saturday since arriving in Louisiana, she spent a good part of it frowning at her closet, at a loss for what to wear. How could she possibly dress appropriately when she had no idea where Silas was taking her?

"Well, it will have to be jeans or pants or whatever because he rides a bike, right?" Naomi said helpfully.

"Yeah." That helped a little.

"And a cute shirt. Make sure it's tight," Cassie said from her place on Edy's bed. "That's always sexy."

"Who says I'm going for sexy?" Edy said.

"What else could you possibly be going for?" Cassie asked and looked at Naomi as if she could help.

"I think it's nice that you're going out again. Getting back up on the horse, so to speak," said Willow.

Edy closed her closet door with a sigh. "It's not a date, for the umpteenth time. We're just two friends hanging out."

"When you hang out with us you don't obsess over your clothes," Cassie pointed out.

"I do when we go to parties," Edy tried, afraid to

admit that she saw the logic in the argument.

"Maybe because Silas is at all of them," Cassie said.

"And Hassan," Willow said.

"Wow, Edy, do you think they'll fight over you eventually?" Cassie asked. She seemed thrilled by the notion.

"Shut up, Cassie. Please. This isn't a date and Hassan hasn't spoken to me since he dumped me. Does that sound like two guys willing to fight over me?"

"Maybe," Willow said softly.

Edy murdered her with a look.

"But he did ask you to go out with him," Naomi said finally. "Those were his exact words, weren't they?"

Edy sighed. Naomi was always the last bastion of sanity. If she had hopped up to join the chorus, then the whole conversation had gone off the cliff already.

"Yes," Edy said. "But it wasn't like that. Trust me, I was there."

Several hours later, Edy donned a blouse that revealed more skin than she would have preferred and black leather tights. She'd ditched the high pumps for a lower pair.

Silas had the wild and stylish hair, a white V-neck tee underneath an open blazer and a pair of rich, blue jeans that hung awfully well. When Edy met him in the parking lot, his gaze swept over her discreetly before he touched her cheek with a stray finger. Then she climbed onto the back of his bike.

"Ready, rabbit?" he said.

Her hands slipped around him low on the waist. She leaned forward so her chest pressed against the heat and hardness of his back. Instinctively, her thighs squeezed his. In the days since she'd begun riding with him—more and more often it seemed—she'd learned how to lean into turns with him and how to tamp down on her fright when he was accelerating at break neck speeds.

That night, he wouldn't tell her where they were going. It turned out to be dinner, where he promised her the best Cajun of her life. Second to him, of course.

"I didn't know you were Cajun," was what she chose to say.

"Hell yeah, I'm Cajun," he said and slipped an arm around her as the hostess led them to a table.

Since Edy didn't know what to try, they settled on a greedy array of dishes: smoked boudin, spicy jambalaya, three kinds of thick gumbo, and crawfish, which she had never had. At this obscene declaration, he'd dragged his chair closer to her, went to work cracking shells, and explained to her how to suck the head. When she demonstrated, he watched her with gray eyes that darkened and absolutely smoldered.

"Do another," he said and made his eyebrows dance.

Edy swatted him. But the crawfish were good, so she ate another.

Their conversation flowed easy as they continued to

eat, with talk turning to her parents, and eventually… his. Both his mom and dad had been dancers, with his father being a tap dancer and his mother a ballerina, both of regional renown. There had been no question of whether he'd study dance, only of how good he'd become. He only hoped that he managed to live up to his parents' expectations, whatever they were.

She told him about how her parents had the absolute opposite dream for her, how lowly they looked at dance, and how art was a noble expression for other people.

"And yet you're doing it anyway," Silas said with a quiet note of admiration.

When she looked up at him in surprise, he fed her a lopsided smile.

After dinner, they hit the bike again for a dash across town to what looked like an alley-side courtyard attached to a coffeehouse. Except the courtyard had a full-fledged band complete with fiddle, playing a wildly vibrant, up-tempo tune.

Edy looked at Silas in wonder.

"It's zydeco, Boston. Now let's see how fast you learn."

Twenty-Seven

Once again, Wyatt realized, Lottie's plan had gone to shit. He wasn't spending more time with Edy. He wasn't spending any time with Edy. He'd thrown the parties and eventually she came, only to be scared off by the sight of him. He continued throwing the parties in the hopes that she'd return, and she hadn't. They'd made sure that anyone who would listen knew about Edy being at his house, knew about Edy being in his room, and knew about Edy dancing on his coffee table. She and Hassan had broken up, rumor had it, but afterwards she'd taken to spending time with another guy.

Wyatt was tired of the noise and tired of the crowds; he was tired of never having a stray moment to himself. The parties were worthless and Lottie was spending too much of his cash. Not only did Wyatt absolutely support her, but he had Matteo and Lincoln and sometimes Kennedy too. Everyone lived on Wyatt Green's dollar but, for his trouble, Edy was no closer. For his trouble, she had taken up with some tall, dark biker who could two-step.

"He was very pretty though," Lottie said. She and

Lincoln and Matteo had seen Edy and the new guy while out to dinner one night. "You really can't blame her for that."

Wyatt rolled his eyes. "So, what now?"

Matteo and Lincoln exchanged a familiar look. They had long ago told him to give up on the Edy conquest. There were plenty of hot girls, they'd told him. As if that was all Edy was.

Lottie had her head in Matteo's lap and her feet in Lincoln's. Lincoln massaged between her toes as Matteo rubbed her scalp. She could only purr and flutter her lashes.

"You can't give up on love, Wyatt," she finally said. "And at the very least you should get to screw her once for all the trouble you've gone to."

It was an attractive principle, but one he couldn't put any stock in. After all, he wanted—needed—Edy to see him as worth the trouble, too. While having Hassan out of the way was a definite step in the right direction, Wyatt figured that he would have conquered Edy by the time he reached old age. Oh well, maybe all the competition would have died out by then.

Lottie closed her eyes. "Kennedy wants to come over. I told her you weren't having a party or anything, but still, she wants to see you."

Wyatt sighed.

"Really, Wyatt, why don't you just bang her?" Lottie said. "She's into you. She might even make you forget Edy."

They had had this conversation a million times, and a million times after that too.

"We came here for Edy," Wyatt said. "If we're giving up on that then I'm going back to Boston."

Like always, that killed all Lottie's talk of giving up the goal.

"What do you want to do then?" Lottie said. "Send her expensive gifts?"

Wyatt shook his head. "She'd never accept them from me. We've had that fight before."

"Then send them anonymously," Matteo suggested.

"For what?" Lottie said. "So the other guy can get all the credit? Or Hassan?"

It would likely be Hassan. Everything worked to the benefit of Hassan. Always.

"Why don't you go see her and be completely honest," Matteo said. "Tell her you beat your meat to her every night."

Lincoln burst out laughing. "True love," he sang sweetly.

Heat shot through Wyatt as he realized they were making fun of him again. He was about to ask what Matteo beat his meat to—Lottie or Lincoln—since the three of them kept the same bed most nights. Then he realized that he didn't give a shit.

Sandra had taken up calling Wyatt and texting and leaving voicemail messages for him to call her back. He never did. All she did was worry and fuss over him and tell him that she didn't like him all the way off in

Louisiana in pursuit of a girl. She also didn't like him down there with Lottie. She didn't trust Lottie.

She never had.

"At this point, all you can do is throw your hat in the ring," Lincoln said. "Go up to her and ask her on a date."

"Tell her you love her," Lottie said.

"Hell no," Matteo said. "Play things cool. The most you can say is that you want to be with her. A girl can take that a whole lot of ways."

Lottie slapped his arm. "Ass. That's what you said to me."

Matteo nodded. "I rest my case."

Okay. So, it was *Matteo* who was with Lottie.

"I wouldn't even tell her that much," Lincoln said. "You're loaded, man. You've got girls at your house all the time. In your face, grinning. Tell her to give you one night for you to try and make her happy. She'll say, hey, what's one night? I bet you'll get to fuck."

Lottie kicked him.

"Let me guess," Matteo said blandly. "He said something like that to you."

Wyatt got up and went to the fridge. He found it empty.

"I'm ordering pizza. What do you guys want?"

Lottie jumped up. "We'll pick up food and get Kennedy. You wait here. Take a shower or something."

Yeah. Sure. Whatever.

Wyatt flipped through Lady Tiger photos online while he waited for them to return. He'd been to every home game, sometimes ponying over a grand for him, Lottie, Matteo, Lincoln, Tristan, Kennedy and whoever else they hoisted on him. He never cared, so long as he saw Edy sashaying in those tight, skimpy outfits, working hard to inspire plenty of his chubs. He always had good seats, as close to the front section where the Lady Tigers stood as possible. He'd pay any amount for that view.

Once, Kennedy had grown sullen watching Wyatt gawk at Edy. He'd only known because Lottie had nudged him, warning him that he was being a little too obvious and had to at least pretend to watch the football game. But why? They were in his seats paid for with his money and he wasn't even the one who had invited Kennedy. Who had invited her anyway?

Wyatt hadn't heard from her for a week after that. During that time, Lottie made it her business to guilt him into something resembling an apology. It hadn't taken much to get back in Kennedy's good graces: a text message saying that he hadn't meant to be rude. Even when he'd been thumbing in half ass messages to Kennedy, he'd been thinking of Edy and wondering if he'd ever get up the nerve to text her.

He could do it now, he realized. What were the odds that Edy had changed her number? He could think of no reason why she would.

Wyatt went through his phone until he found her

name, complete with the updated photo of her in Tiger uniform, cropped from a website picture. Man, those legs inspired wet dreams. To have them wrapped around his waist just once? To hear her say his name, to whisper it as if Wyatt was the only thing she wanted? He'd give anything for that.

Anything at all.

Wyatt went into his bedroom, locked the door, and put some thought into the message he would send Edy. After all, he was the only one who truly knew her. He knew how she thought. He knew her worth. Of course, Lottie would encourage him to sleep with somebody else, anybody else. She wasn't the most discriminating girl herself.

But this was about Edy. He needed a message that would make her want to respond, a message that wouldn't be easy to ignore.

Then he remembered what Matteo said about telling her the truth.

EDY, IT FEELS LIKE EVERYONE IN MY LIFE HAS ABANDONED ME. MY MOTHER, FATHER, FAMILY, AND NOW YOU TOO. IT HURTS WHAT YOU DO TO ME.

He never expected her response to come so fast.

I'M ON MY WAY.

Twenty-Eight

"So," Lawrence said from his place on the bed. "You've been leading Mala on all this time because you're mad with Edy and *now* you want my opinion?"

Hassan tamped down on the fury and failed. It seeped into his pores and through his bloodstream, strengthening with every pump of his heart.

"I'm not leading Mala on," he said quietly.

Lawrence sniffed.

Hassan whirled on him, the folding of his clean laundry forgotten. "I'm *not*. But you've obviously got a lot to say. Speak up." He balled and flexed his hands until they cracked.

Lawrence looked him over, then slid an abandoned biology textbook into his lap. "Forget it. Just... don't ask my opinion and get pissed when it isn't what you like."

And he had asked his opinion. Only Edy had been the topic, not Mala.

"Were you even listening?" Hassan demanded. Edy was with another guy already. She'd forgotten him... already. How could she do that?

"My hearing's fine," Lawrence said absently and

flipped a few pages.

Hassan could fucking pound this guy some days. No matter what was happening, no matter how dire, he kept the same offhand tone.

Lawrence glanced up at him as if he'd read his thoughts. "You're being an ass," he said.

Maybe he was. But Edy was with another guy. Hassan had even seen her whip past the practice field on his bike. Everyone had.

"She's forgotten about me." Hassan slumped to his bed, suddenly weak. "All these years and..." He shrugged, unable to say the words again.

Seeing her with that other guy had dislodged something in him, rendering him weak, shaky, ineffective at practice. Maybe he had never really given credence to the notion of them broken up. Maybe he had been too sure of them even within his doubts and thought himself in the midst of the world's worst tantrum. Edy had always been a fixture in his life, and Hassan one in hers. There was no way to undo that sort of bond, no way to break it with mere words. But break it he had. It took a pretty boy on a bike to show Hassan that. He'd nearly thrown up as he dropped to his knees. His stomach had cramped viciously and the cry of rage building within him had been so potent, so savage and horrified and exposed, aimed so much at himself as at them. He had done this to them. *She* had done this to them. And how could she? *How could she?*

Mala put Edy out of his mind. He knew that. It wouldn't have been fair to Mala if she didn't know about Edy, but she did. Everyone did. Mala and her father had only been relieved when Hassan told them that things were over in his old relationship. Mala and her dad had visited him a second time since that first dinner. The three of them saw a movie and Hassan spent most of the time convincing himself that he wasn't on a chaperoned date. After that, her father had returned to India, but Mala and a few of her friends had visited a couple more times: attending Hassan's games and even hanging out once, awkwardly, with Lawrence and some of the guys. She called him to talk and mostly he held the phone in silence. Either way, Hassan's mother was thrilled with his abrupt pivot away from Edy. She called him regularly now.

"Edy hasn't forgotten about you," Lawrence said, "anymore than you've forgotten about her."

The anger returned, magnified tenfold. Had the bastard been paying attention to the last few months? Edy was dating someone else. When Hassan said so, Lawrence laughed.

"And so are you," he said.

He wasn't.

Hassan thought back to the last time Mala visited. She was with two girls from Tulane's India Association club, Prisha and Divit. Both had blushed on meeting him. Divit was at least a football fan and had hurriedly gone on about Hassan's Heisman prospects and how unusual it was for a freshman to be considered. He'd told her that he had absolutely zero chance, because he was a freshman, because several other really good guys were being considered, and because one of those guys was his own teammate, Cash.

They'd blushed more when his idiotic teammates had shown up: Cash with his bullshit charm meant to lure the panties off any girl, Freight with his gleeful jesting and over-the-top flattery, and both Xavier and Tennessee, who were promptly escorted away by Lawrence when they began to come on too strong. Mala, for her part, had barely glanced at the other guys, so complete was her attention on Hassan. At the time, he had credited her with being able to see through the bullshit, but now, he wondered if her eyes had only been for him. She did still refer to them as engaged.

And then it occurred to him. God, he was a dick. They were engaged, just like Edy'd said. Never once had he flat out told Mala that they weren't, that he refused to acknowledge it. He'd only tried to wriggle away from the agreement, but even in doing so there was a tacit acknowledgement, a legitimacy to their relationship. Now he'd begun seeing her—every week. They were getting to know each other. Maybe because he'd told her father that he could never marry a girl without knowing and liking her. So, he was spending time with her.

They were dating.

"Fuck," Hassan cursed. "Fuck!"

When his phone rang, he plucked it from their desk and heaved it straight at the wall, watching it shatter with a note of satisfaction.

Lawrence glanced at him and went back to his book.

Twenty-Nine

"Silas, I need help with this question. Tell me what you think," Levi said.

Silas laughed. "I think you should ask Edy." He propped his feet on the coffee table and picked up the remote.

"Fine. She's better at this stuff than you anyway." Levi scooped up his binder and textbook before dropping on the couch next to Edy.

Silas shrugged, but the upturn of his lips was unmistakable. "Look. I've told you before. I'm an artistic sort of fellow. Academia isn't where my talents lie." He nodded at Edy. "Help him, would you, rabbit?"

Edy looked up from her laptop and her butchered history essay. "Sure. What's the question?" It really was getting late. If she could help Levi wrap up his homework, she would. They usually waited until he went to bed before practicing.

"I can't remember who the first civil engineer was." He looked put out by the idea of not remembering anything.

"Oh, it's Imhotep," Edy supplied. "He designed the

Saqqara Step Pyramid outside of Memphis." She'd visited it with Hassan and their dads. Their fathers had been working in Egypt, back when it wasn't so subject to random outbursts of violence, and had taken them on a grand tour in a beastly summer heat. They'd seen Giza and the Sphinx, ventured inside Khufu, and they even saw the burial chamber in Dashur.

It seemed like another life and another girl.

"Sweet," Levi said. "Thanks."

He'd swept Edy from her mournful reverie.

"Get to bed," Silas said. "Stop dawdling."

Levi packed up his belongings and gave his brother a fist bump. He fixed Edy with a shimmering smile, which she returned absentmindedly, before bounding off for the night.

"You're thinking about him," Silas said.

Edy started guiltily. "No, I'm not." Well, she didn't want to, anyway. What was the point?

Silas closed her laptop and set it aside. He studied her with cool gray eyes. Scrutinizing. Calculating.

Edy wondered what it would be like for Silas to lose control. For him to weaken at the caress of another, to fumble, reaching, desperate to feel teeth, tongue, touch. Those cool gray eyes would heat like molten steel. She cleared her throat nosily at the thought and looked away.

"According to you," Silas said, "you're never thinking of him. You must be over him. So, prove it. Kiss me."

Her breath caught at the thought and her gaze dropped, automatically, to his lips. His tongue dipped out, wetting them, and her breath came a little slower.

She was a liar, of course. She thought of Hassan so much. But Silas was right, in a way. If she was over Hassan, she would probably be able to kiss him. She needed to get over Hassan, too. He had absolutely proven her right regarding Mala, wasting no time in openly seeing her after parting ways with Edy. She tried not to think of what that meant. Though at night, when the room was still, it hit like a brick to the skull. She'd break down and sob with wounds so fresh she knew she hadn't done any healing. Maybe Silas could help her with that.

"Well?" he said.

Edy decided to try on some of his nonchalance. "Sure. I'll kiss you, if you want."

He cocked a brow, laughing at her with his eyes. Then his gaze dropped to her mouth.

She could do this. It was nothing, right? Just skin and wetness and emotions, maybe.

Edy scooted a little closer. Silas did the same. She held her breath, counting backwards from three before swooping.

His little chuckle cut off with a sharp inhale and, for a moment, Edy swore that he wouldn't respond at all.

Boy, was she wrong.

Their lips met and a groan escaped Silas. Both his hands found her hair and pulled her in hard, shoving heat through every part of her body. But that was okay. They were young and sexual tension was normal. It didn't have to mean anything. It didn't have to mean...

She was pulling away unsteadily, light headed and breathless all at once, searching his face for some sign that what had just happened meant nothing. That she was nothing to him and he had been joking.

He reached for her again, mouth coming down hard. Their lips parted, tongues meeting in a crash of heat. He was gathering her up now, pulling and pressing her closer with hands that ran down her back, tightening at her waist and bringing her in. Edy came willingly, confused by the heat that stirred within her. She whimpered involuntarily and her phone rang. When she tore away from him, he sighed.

Wyatt. A message from Wyatt. She read it over, then read it again to be sure.

"What is it?" Silas said. "What's wrong?"

"I... have to go." She keyed in her response.

"Edy," Silas said, "we're kind of in the middle of something."

She looked up guiltily. "I—" She didn't know how to explain Wyatt to him. She didn't know how to explain Wyatt to anyone. "I still have to go," she said.

He looked her over and it was then she saw it: the molten steel she'd imagined, the barely contained passion she'd pictured.

"If that's Hassan..." he warned.

"It's not," she said. She didn't even know how he could think that. "I wouldn't…"

She had no idea how to phrase it. But whatever she'd been trying to say, Silas seemed to understand. He gave a curt not.

"Fine," he said. "Let me get the helmets. I don't want you having a heart attack over what might happen."

She'd been lecturing him into oblivion about his inability to wear a helmet. At the very least, he now wore one because of her. He'd even bought a second one, 'just in case' he'd said. Half the time, Edy kept it in her room.

"Where are we going?" he said, when he'd returned with the gear.

This part would be sticky. "To Wyatt's house. The place where we partied together and got sprayed with beer."

He went still. "I remember it." His eyes hinted at all kinds of assumptions about her and Wyatt Green.

So, it wasn't just Hassan.

"He was a friend," Edy said. "Only ever a friend." For some reason, it felt important that Silas knew that.

"Was?" he echoed.

Damn, the boy didn't miss a thing.

"Was," Edy said firmly and met his gaze so that he knew the conversation was over.

Silas shrugged. "Let's go. I don't want Levi to miss me."

The two of them hopped on Silas' bike and made the way from Port Allen to Jim Taylor Drive, making record time. When they arrived, Edy leaped from the motorcycle, earning a shout of alarm from Silas, before his arm shot out and captured her by the wrist.

"Remember how I told you that your weight and balance affect the bike?" He looked absolutely pissed.

Edy nodded and dragged her gaze to the townhouse.

"Good," Silas said. "Don't forget it again. Now do you mind telling me what the hell we're doing here?"

She bit her lip, momentarily torn with indecision. Then, deciding it would be faster to tell him what was happening, and probably best considering the likelihood that he was walking into a volatile situation, she said, "I think he's going to hurt himself. He sent me a really weird message. It was scary."

Silas cursed. "Let's go then." And it was he who dragged her along, as he hadn't let her go yet.

They tore up the stairs and banged on the front door, first Edy, then Silas.

He looked at her. "Do you think we'll have to break it down?"

She had no idea how people did that outside of movies. "Maybe using a window would be a better idea."

"We're on the second floor." He banged again and the door flew open in his face.

Wyatt scowled. He looked from Silas to Edy, face

purpling right before them. Then his gaze dropped down to where they were holding hands. In fact, hers was squeezing the color right out of Silas'. When had that happened?

"Let us in, Wyatt," Edy said and slipped her hand free of Silas'. He said nothing, but he glanced down as if he hadn't known they were holding hands either.

Wyatt stormed off, leaving the front door opened. Edy went after him. They tore through the living room, past the foyer and dining room, before rushing down a hallway she remembered from before. He turned on her, halfway down, and choked, red-faced.

"Why'd you have to bring him with you? Why do you always..." He trailed off, eyes glistening with tears.

Edy frowned. "Why do I always what?" she said gently.

He shook his head. "It doesn't matter, does it? Nothing I do. It will never make a difference. I'm no one. I'm nothing."

She was frightened now, so afraid of what he might be thinking. "Wyatt, please," Edy said and realized she was trembling. Her own vision blurred. "Don't talk like that."

"Like what? Like the truth? You'll never want me! There'll always be some other guy. Hassan, or... or this one."

Edy's tears evaporated. "What does this have to do with me? I don't understand."

"It has everything to do with you!" he exploded. "I'm here because of you! I love you, Edy, and you're goddamned killing me. You don't even care. It doesn't matter what I say, what I do, I can't get you to see me. Please... tell me how to change. Tell me what you want. Muscles? They've both got muscles. I'll go to the gym three times a week. I'll go every day. I've got money now. You can have that, too. Just... love me back."

God, this was a mess. She could feel her stomach churning. He meant these words. He loved her. He loved her so much he forgot to love himself. He loved her to the point of possession and beyond. He'd do anything to own her.

"I can't," Edy whispered.

"I didn't do it!" he screamed. "I didn't rape her. I know you think I did, but I didn't rape my cousin. I've never even had sex before. I've been holding out for you. Hoping for you."

"Wyatt..." She should leave. She never should have come.

"I'd never even kissed anyone until I came down here." He hardened with these words, eyes going flat and angry. "She wants to have sex with me. Girls want to have sex with me now. Do you know that?"

Edy hesitated. "They're not the right kind of girls, Wyatt."

"What do you know about it? You don't want me! You've been rejecting me for years, making me out to be a laughingstock. Now you want to tell me who's right for me? It's you! Haven't you been listening?"

"It's not, Wyatt. I swear, it's not. When you meet the right girl, you both will feel something. Not just you. Not just her. And she won't care whether you have money or not."

He broke out with a sob, then stamped it out by pressing his fist to his mouth.

"You don't feel anything for me?" he asked eventually.

She never had. "No," she said. "I'm sorry." She only hoped that this was the right thing to do—that honesty was the right thing to do and that she wasn't pushing him over some edge. He'd had a hard life, and if it was true that he hadn't hurt his cousin, then he deserved much better—better than Edy even, who couldn't love him the way he deserved.

Wyatt disappeared into his room, slammed the door, and bolted it.

Eventually, Silas retrieved her from where she stood in the hall.

Thirty

The campus reeked with hysteria in the days leading up to the game. Every night there was a party causing fewer and fewer students to attend class the next day, until by Friday classes were getting cancelled altogether.

There was good cause for the hype. LSU and Alabama were top ranked teams in the nation. Their performance on the field would do more than bestow bragging rights for the rivalry. A win would all but guarantee a slot in the College Football Playoff and a chance to compete for the Bowl Championship. A loss would drop said team from serious contention. Also, there was Hassan. He'd talked a boatload of shit about the Alabama match-up, swearing in one interview that the team was packed full of fat boys. He hadn't been able to help it. They'd booed him insanely back at Ole Miss. It got his juices going. It got his mouth going. He'd been forced to run laps around the practice field endlessly for the wagging tongue.

But for all the talk of football, Alabama, and Heismans (he still couldn't believe that one), Hassan mostly had a single thought on his mind: Mala. The thought of dating her had sent shockwaves of panic through his system. It told him everything he needed to know. While he had agreed to meet her in a sullen bout of anger, he realized, in hindsight, how utterly stupid that was. How that single decision affected others and erected hope for them. He would have to tear it all down. He would have to straighten out this mess once and for all.

He couldn't meet her in the days leading up to the Alabama game, given that New Orleans and Tulane were a good hour away. She'd called him a few times that week though, and, in a panic, he sent her to voicemail a few times, unsure of what to say but certain it needed to be said in person. Finally, with her persistence he answered, only to mostly hold the phone and field her awkward talk of football, her fumbling compliments regarding the game, and one pulse stumbling moment when she outright called him *∂a zrra armaana me*, or, her heart's desire. He'd held the phone as if he thought Mala and the moment would disappear if he'd only stop breathing. Neither did, and the anxiety snaked through him so fiercely, so completely, that he had to excuse himself from the phone. What the hell was he doing? Marrying Mala Bathlar because Edy didn't want him anymore?

Wait. He'd been the one to break up with Edy. Some days, he had to remind himself.

He decided to concentrate on football. And school. He'd decided to major in Business and in

Communications. Or maybe Sports Administration. It was still early.

There'd be no more phone calls with Mala until he was ready to have the talk with her. After their discussion, there would be no more acknowledgment on his part of the engagement. He finally understood what Edy meant. *He'd* been the problem all along. He had given the arrangement legitimacy by recognizing it, but claiming to want out of the relationship. He had never said that he was not engaged. It meant that he'd tacitly agreed that he was. God, he'd been an idiot. Poor Edy. Poor Mala, even.

Hassan spent the week prepping for the game. In English class, he cast surreptitious glances at Edy as he tried to determine whether she was happy. Did the other guy make her happy? No doubt he wasn't engaged. He didn't have a mother either who labored diligently to keep them apart. At least she could be happy now. He really did want that for her.

His heart ached still. He loved the girl; there was no point in denying that. Any talk of her with another bled jealousy off him in waves. He didn't bother to hide it. Even Freight and Cash had asked him why he didn't just take her back if he was so crazy with her. But how could he? He'd said some awful things. She'd moved on so effectively. Only Hassan drowned in the past. Only Hassan swam in memories so deep.

Alabama came. The madness was like nothing Hassan had ever seen. The reaching and screaming during the walk to the stadium was tremendous. Fans screamed their lungs dry, waving flags and banners, begging for pictures, shouting compliments. A little one asked Hassan for an autograph. An old guy cursed himself cross-eyed as he cheered them on. Hassan stopped and hugged and signed because he couldn't *not*. These people loved him. He couldn't help but love them back.

Once at the stadium, Hassan knew this game would be different. Both teams played faithfully in the most difficult division of the most difficult conference in college football. Each year the Crimson Tide and the LSU Tigers gathered for one of the most hostile games in football. More than players competed. Cheerleader against cheerleader, dancer against dancer, mascot against mascot, crowd against crowd—all determined to stake a claim to superiority for their team. Up in the stands, Edy's girls had new uniforms that looked specially made for the game. Glittering black tops with 'LSU' emblazoned across the front and teensy shorts of the same black material. Hassan held his breath, then forced himself to look away, certain he wouldn't play right should he ruminate too long on Edy's outfit and how it clung to those curves.

Hassan entered the stadium and got hit with a cup of Coca-Cola in the face.

Had he not been looking at Edy, he would've sworn it was her. Had it been last week, he would have guessed it was Mala. Or his mom. Who knew with the number of people he pissed off daily.

But this was only a red-faced Alabama fan. Security moved quickly in his direction as an LSU staff member supplied Hassan with a towel.

"I can see you have adoring fans everywhere," Lawrence said, before pulling him along. They made their way to the field for stretching and the soda to the face was soon forgotten.

❁ ❁ ❁

Edy watched the field with trepidation. More than once, Tamela had to tell her to uncross her arms and sit like the other girls. They were not to ball their fists and curse, especially.

She had seen the big wad of a man who threw a soda at Hassan. She had nearly gone there herself, until Naomi grabbed her wrist the second she moved. Frustration mounted nonetheless and Edy sent a silent prayer that the guy would be forced to pass her on his escorted exit out, so she could at least trip him as payback. He didn't, leaving her to cross her arms and give one epic sigh. Tamela was on her in an instant, about her facial expression, her posture, her ability to get distracted at these games, and 'Oh, by the way, I thought you two had broken up,' she threw in for good measure, which straightened Edy out like nothing else could.

She had Silas to think about, too. Things were

weird between them. Since that first kiss, they'd made out twice... the first time after a grinding, frustrating evening of cha-chaing in his living room. She'd been swung and flung and dropped and pressed up against him and in between they'd argued about whether right was left or left should have been right. All night they'd been at each other's throats, him with his asshole snarky comments and her insisting he was the worst dancer she'd ever seen. They should have killed each other. Even Levi had been forced to step out of the room and tell them that they were making too much noise and that he couldn't sleep. The second his door closed, Silas called her a brat and a moron. Edy told him she wasn't above slapping him. Then they were up for another round of the routine, except one of them went the wrong way, and when Edy turned to argue, Silas grabbed her face and kissed her. He kissed her hard enough to steal her breath, to muffle whatever argument she'd been about to make. When he broke, it was with a grin. "Sorry," he'd said. "I've been meaning to do that."

Their third kiss had been more of an equal opportunity participation endeavor. They'd been at the same zydeco dig as before, with Edy picking up on more of the quick swings and quicker footwork. For Silas' part, he was an excellent teacher, explaining to her the various open and closed positions, when she should counter him with opposite moves, and what counts were used when. She never thought that dancing to an accordion and washboard could be so fun.

He watched her with those gray eyes when she danced, all alight. She'd noticed how those gorgeous eyes of his went from steel guards to dreamy stars. Like her, he lived when he danced.

She drank a lot that night. Silas drank a lot that night. Through it all, Edy wondered when she'd learned to toss back shots like that. They still gave her one hell of a hangover, mind you, but she was at least able to hold a few down. That had been her thought when she and Silas had climbed back on his bike for the trek back to campus. Then he stopped for what looked like no apparent reason, pulled her to the wall of a shuttered bakery, and kissed the breath out of her. She'd kissed him back and her hands had roamed, because he was Silas and absolutely gorgeous, and her body *did* respond to him and he made her forget Hassan. Except, nothing made her forget Hassan, and so, in her mind, he became her ex and also not her ex, making her kiss him and shove him away at the same time. She'd choked out an emotional 'Sorry' with one hand over her mouth and another on her stomach. Silas had glared like he knew every thought she'd ever had about Hassan. Then he huffed that she'd better get back on his bike, before they sped away without another word.

Maybe a friendship with Hassan would settle things for her. Maybe having him in her life the way he used to be might make things easier for her. Maybe she could even see Silas as more once she settled whatever lasting tension remained between her and Hassan.

Rani had called her, but Edy didn't answer. She didn't want to be the one to tell her that the reason she'd tossed Edy away no longer existed, that they were free to go back to the old days. She wouldn't tell her that, because she couldn't. There was no way she and Rani could ever be what they were.

"Goddamn it, Edy, pay attention!" Tamela hissed and Edy leapt to her feet, the last girl in a stand routine that had already begun.

She resolved to put boys out of her mind and concentrate on what mattered.

Dance, of course.

The LSU offense hit the field for the start of the game. Things went at breakneck speed. First down and nothing. Second down and a short pass, leaving plenty to be gained on the third. On the third, it was Lawrence who kept the drive alive.

LSU crawled downfield, fighting for inches, practically bleeding on every play. Edy refused to bite her nails, then sat on her hands, to be sure. Alabama, she saw, was determined to shut down the run, the pass, and LSU altogether. They were doing a good job of it too.

With the start of the second quarter, the LSU crowd got antsy. They were used to sloshing drinks, especially at night games like this, leaping and shouting obscenities. They tended to have points on the board by the second quarter and hardly ever cause for much worry. But this here was different. Seven on the board for the opposition, nothing for them, and that with their primetime boys on the field.

Something had to give.

And then it did.

With seconds on the clock till half time and a swift, brutal Hail Mary pass caught haphazardly by Lawrence, they were finally in the Red Zone.

They'd go for the run, and everyone knew it. That meant Hassan.

The crowd stood, collectively holding one breath, as he and his teammates moved to their spots behind the line of scrimmage. Edy's hands found her mouth, heart thrumming a wild tune, as she waited, waited, waited.

"Come on," she whispered. "You can do this. I swear you can."

The quarterback lobbed the ball to Hassan, but the defense expected this, and barreled towards him, a firing squad turned in on one man. LSU's line struggled against oversized Alabama boys as Hassan hesitated, veered left, then pitched the other way.

He was scrambling, desperate for an opening that didn't exist. With the clock threatening zero, possession would belong to Alabama after half time, after this play. He had to score now.

He barreled right, in that hard, desperate pound that was three parts talent and one part so much of that angry determination he'd been demonstrating lately. Edy shrieked when he collided with a defender headlong and disappeared into a sea of red shirts.

She jumped up, knowing she'd be in so much trouble later. Lady Tigers were poised, pretty, and collected. They did not scream and dance around maniacally, which Edy had done a few times. They did not shout obscenities after bad calls. And they didn't lean forward in an attempt to see a scramble better and practically spill their junk in the process. But it wasn't Edy's fault their uniforms looked like underwear.

Muscles strained, bodies struggled as the crowd leaned in collectively. They could see nothing, except the dog pile that was Crimson Tide fighting for a piece of Hassan. Edy could hear herself breathing. Her fears were real in that moment. Would they hurt him? They couldn't. She couldn't stand if they did.

The clock was dead. The play was over. And suddenly, "Touchdown!" shouted the referee.

LSU exploded. No one saw how he did it. No one cared. Jumping, shouting, screaming, Edy wildest among them. Tamela gave her a look. The strangest look, really. One she didn't understand until they made their way to the field for the halftime show.

"You must not know," Tamela said quietly. "If you did, you wouldn't be embarrassing yourself so much."

Edy stared at her. She had no idea what she was going on about.

"You're the guy's number one fan. But you're not the only one," she said.

The stadium echoed in Edy's ears.

"What are you talking about?" she heard herself say. She didn't bother to tell herself that she wouldn't care.

"He's seeing someone else. A cousin of mine told me. He's pretty reliable." Tamela shrugged. "I'll point her out after the game if you want."

"No. Yes. I don't…" Edy wondered. Was it possible to get this nauseous this fast?

"We don't have time for this," London said. "Let's get ready for one helluva show." Still, she cast Edy a worried glance after she said it.

"He's just a guy," Tamela said. "And I warned you about those football players."

"You did," Edy heard herself say. She sounded hollow. Empty inside.

Later, her teammates told her that she didn't make a single mistake during the halftime show. Edy barely remembered performing it. But she did remember after the game, when Tamela pointed Mala out in the crowd.

Thirty-One

They beat Alabama, and in the post-game interview Hassan talked like he always knew they would do just that. He was getting damned good at being a bullshitter. Who knew college would help him with that?

After the game, Hassan returned to his room in order to shower for at least one of the zillion parties his teammates insisted he had to attend. No sooner had he showered and dressed than did Lawrence tap on the bathroom door.

"You've got company," he said.

For one wild moment, Hassan imagined it was Edy, there to get back together. His heart beat wild at the thought. But she wouldn't do that. Not after the way he talked to her. Not after he'd accused her of so much.

He no longer thought all that was true, though. He wasn't sure if he'd believed to start with. Oh, he knew she partied hard now, but he didn't think this new partying spirit included being unfaithful to him. What on earth had made him accuse her of that?

For whatever reason she'd come, he'd apologize for

what he said. He'd gauge her. See if she wanted to try again. The thought ate into every rational thought he had—he saw her everywhere, after all, even in his sleep. But the jealousy stayed there, too. He hated what it did to him. How it made him feel.

Maybe, he could make her understand.

"E—" Hassan stepped out the bathroom and froze at the sight of Mala.

"Hello, Hassan. You did very well tonight. You must be pleased."

He stared at her. What was she doing here when he'd asked her not to come?

"I... uh, yeah. Sure," he said.

Lawrence snorted. Hassan shot him a look of desperation over Mala's shoulder.

"Where are your friends, Mala?" Lawrence said. "You came in alone."

Was that a warning of some sort? Hassan couldn't think straight. He hadn't planned on talking to the girl again, much less seeing her, until the words he'd planned for breaking things off with her had come together.

How did he get in these messes, anyway?

"Oh, they got caught up in the hall. Cash, I think his name was? He saw them. And Xavier."

Oh Lord.

"I'll go and check on them," Lawrence suggested.

"Good idea," Hassan said. With that his friend disappeared.

Hassan took a deep breath. He'd have to do this now.

"Let's sit down," he said. "We, er, need to talk."

"Alright," Mala said in that gentle, dulcet voice. Just the sound of it made Hassan feel awfully guilty.

The two stared at each other for a minute from their awkward perches on the end of his bed.

Mala dropped her gaze. "I am thinking of when we were in high school and you came to see me. You said that we could not get married if I was unwilling to have even a conversation with you. I said that you were dishonoring me by even speaking to me without a chaperone."

That wasn't quite how it went, but close. Also, he'd been trying to break things off with her, not get to know her better.

"I remember," was what Hassan said. He'd wanted to convince her to rebel against the marriage, thinking their united front would seal its fate. But he hadn't known back then that she'd never rebel against her parents. She would marry Hassan or whoever else her parents insisted on.

"I am…" she shifted so her hand came to cover Hassan's, "glad you are wise enough to be practical. I would like to make you happy in this."

Hassan stared at her hand. What the hell did she think she was doing?

"I don't think—" he said, before her mouth pressed into his completely.

He had a moment of complete brain trauma, of blankness, of denial, before understanding dropped down on him like so many bricks. She was *kissing* him. Mala Bathlar had her mouth on his.

Hassan shot back hard enough to tumble from the bed. Then he scrambled, crab-like, backwards, to put distance between them. Only the edge of Lawrence's bed stopped him.

"What are you *doing?*" he cried.

Mala frowned. "I am not... practiced in this. If you could teach me — "

"No! What? No?" Realizing he looked like a fool, Hassan clamored to his feet. "You're misunderstanding me. Maybe purposely." He took up a pace, back and forth, in that tiny center of room between his bed and Lawrence's. Intermittently, he glanced at Mala, realizing that he'd made several gross miscalculations. He'd underestimated her devotion to her parents and the lengths she'd go to obey. He'd purposely ignored her little compliments toward him, whether about his appearance, or his talent, or whatever. He'd thought those part of whatever game the Bathlars were playing. But he hadn't anticipated this. Could she really be attracted to him? Could he really have led her on?

"I'm sorry," Hassan said quietly. "I didn't..." He shook his head. His reasons for screwing up didn't matter. He simply had a mess to fix. Except, what he blurted surprised even him.

"I love Edy," he said. Not that it mattered. He'd fucked that up, too.

"I understand," she said, in that same sweet voice. "You need time."

The girl was not hearing him. He was about to tear his hair out. "No. I'm in love with Edy. I want her."

"But you broke up with her. You told me so," Mala said simply. As if anything in life were simple.

Hassan looked away. Took a deep breath. Dove in.

"I'm an ass," he said. "Yeah, I broke up with her, but there isn't a day I don't think about it. Mala, you're nice. You're really nice. You'll be a wonderful wife for some guy someday. But it won't be me."

"Because of Edith."

"Because I'll chose my own wife," Hassan said. "And... it won't be you."

Mala stood, stalked the two steps towards him, and jutted out her chin like a taunting boxer. "You are an embarrassment to your parents. You disobey them. You gloat and misbehave on the field. And you are in love with an ignorant, faithless, unclean, non-believer."

"Who the fuck—" Hassan bit down on the rest of that when Mala gasped. He'd really let things go too far. "You need to go," he said. "And you need to forget you ever heard my name."

"Your parents will owe a lot of money," she warned.

"Money that you're willing to be traded for? Get lost. I'm done with you." He stormed for the door and opened it wide.

Mala sniffed and gathered her purse. "I'd expect you to be rather passionate about her. I'm told the two of you have been passionate in a most inappropriate way."

"Congratulations. I'll get to work on that medal for you. Now disappear. And if you ever open your mouth about Edy again, you won't find me so polite."

Thirty-Two

Another party. Some sorority. Another random crowd. People were using the Alabama win to get smashed. Edy found it to be a good enough excuse. Maybe with enough beers she could forget seeing Mala at the game.

With an almost-smile, she brought the cheap beer to her lips, thinking of what her father would say if he could see her.

The girls had been hovering ever since Tamela had pointed out Mala to her. They'd also been arguing in hushed whispers that Edy pretended not to notice.

She didn't feel like dancing that night. She didn't feel like thinking. Yet, round and round her mind went, contemplating Mala's appearance.

Surely he wasn't giving her a chance because things didn't work out between them. That was crazy. Maybe, though, with the distance from his parents and the emotional baggage there, plus the grand way they'd come apart, he'd simply felt the need to be close to someone. Maybe he had been close to her all along.

Maybe they'd slept together.

Okay. Clearly, she wanted to torture herself that

night. She'd been having thoughts like that since she'd seen Mala. It reminded her of how Mala had shown up in Boston. Now she was in Baton Rouge. To think Hassan had gone all ballistic over Wyatt's appearance. He needed to explain Mala's.

Wait. No he didn't. They weren't together. They weren't even friends. He could sleep with her, for all Edy cared.

She nearly burst into tears at the thought.

"Edy? You okay?" Naomi said.

Edy glanced at her, annoyed suddenly. They'd been treating her as if she might break. As if she was made of spun glass meant to hang from a Christmas tree.

Oh God. Christmas. Holidays. What would they do about those?

"Yeah," Edy said, and realized it came out as a whisper that could never be heard at a party. She nodded instead.

"Are you sure? Because he just showed up," Naomi said.

What? Edy whipped around and sure enough, there was Hassan dressed all in black and nestled between a half dozen other players. He looked tense.

"It doesn't matter," Edy said, though she was sure Naomi couldn't hear her. But it was okay, she was mostly speaking to herself. After all, she'd occupied places with Hassan before: football stadiums, English class, the bed.

He went for the keg and disappeared in a swarm of

what looked like admirers. Edy didn't care. She couldn't care less. She didn't admire him, that was for sure.

"I'm going to dance," Naomi said, "unless you need me."

Edy shook her head. She was bad company and she knew it. "I'll be fine," she said. "Have fun."

Naomi nodded and squeezed her shoulder before taking off. There was a guy on the football team she'd been admiring from afar. Tamela's anti-football player attitude had her keeping mum about which one it was. A late night of whispers when it was just Edy and her roommate alone would probably get the truth out of her.

Whoever it was, Edy hoped she fared better than her in love.

An image came to her unbidden. Maybe it was brought on by her birthday, which she had been forcing out of her mind anytime she had the misfortune of remembering it. She saw the two of them dancing, Edy in her little tiara, Hassan a prince to her princess. God, when he smiled everything seemed possible.

Edy stood there and drank, buoyed by her own despondency, accepting one cup after another as she sank deep into her own intoxicated abyss. Tamela brought her a beer with a mutter of encouragement. It was too late now for her to be feeling guilt over the delivery of the day's earlier news. So what if she'd screamed or whispered about Mala, anyway? It all packed the same gut-wrenching punch.

There was another cup of beer, then another—passed by one or more faceless teammates as Edy spent her time tripping over her own thoughts. Across the room, Hassan drained beer after beer likewise, then something that couldn't possibly have been beer at all. Their gazes met and it was her who snapped away, unwilling to glimpse even a moment of those conquering green eyes. She couldn't stand him was what she told herself. Everything was over; that's what she had to believe. Then Edy wondered at all why she hadn't believed that already. Suddenly, she was making for the keg herself.

***

Hassan leaned against the wall, something dark and strong in his cup, lids heavy, eyes on the dance floor. In the thick of it he saw his girl, rocking and pitching with the music. And then he remembered: she wasn't his anymore. Those had been his dumbass words. Maybe they could forget them?

He tossed back the last of his drink, moved towards her, then behind her, and slid a hand around her waist.

Fuck. That last drink was… something. Hassan carded a hand through his hair and crushed his cup, surprised when a splash of the dark drink hit his shirt.

Whatever.

Pop music tonight. Muted in and out… Edy wasn't dancing though. Maybe he'd make her dance.

He took a few steps for her and collided with every damned body in the way. Why were there so many people? One guy he hit so hard he had to grab him on his bounce to the floor. Alcohol had only slowed Hassan's reflexes some. He was still able to make the rescue. Sort of.

She wouldn't look in his direction. Why?

Oh, this was a good song. Out of one corner of his eye, Hassan spotted his teammates all clustered and hopping as if getting hyped for a game. When an arm shot out to pull him into the fray, he slapped it away, lids lowered and on his goal. Edy.

Edy.

She really should have been dancing. She could curl a man's soul in on himself with the way she moved. Maybe she needed encouragement.

Hassan went right by her and snorted when she averted her eyes. Like they hadn't been looking at each other for a lifetime.

Wait. Did that make sense?

He was able to squeeze in behind her and start swaying to the music. When she turned on him, fast, he slid an arm around her waist, determined to keep it there until the day he died.

Edy's faced wrenched into a horrible expression before it cracked into a peal of giggles.

"What are you *doing*?" she cried. But she was

laughing and he swore he could get drunk on it. Drunk*er.*

"Dancing." He pressed into her. "C'mon. Keep up."

He threaded his fingers through hers and forced her arms around his. That felt good. So good that he forgot about moving for a second and pressed into her.

"You're sooooo…" Edy paused, speech lazy, lids heavy. For a second, they closed as if she'd drifted off to sleep. "Drunk," she said.

Hassan grinned. "Guilty."

He ran his hands over her hips, down, up, over her back, swaying like he could seduce her with the grinding of his hips. But everyone else was moving too fast. Or too slow. He couldn't remember which.

Just then a tray of Jägerbombs sailed by. Hassan grabbed two, threw one back and offered the other to Edy. When she shyly admitted she'd never had one, he snorted in disbelief, having forgotten that his first taste had been only an hour and a half ago.

He guided her over to the wall, where she willingly tilted her head back and offered an open mouth to him.

Fuck. Just… fuck.

He brought the cup to her mouth, tilting its contents down her throat. His fingers brushed wet lips and lingered, and when he pulled away, she licked at him teasingly and smiled. Then he drank his own, set their emptied cups on a littered end table and missed.

Somehow, his fingers found those pouty wet lips of

hers. When she licked his fingertips, Hassan grunted.

"Don't," he whispered and moved in a little closer. "Not unless…" His hand dropped to drag over that oh-so-tight abdomen. She trembled. Shit.

He couldn't look away from her lips, moist from dark liquor.

"Cake," Hassan said and gripped her by the button of her jeans. He used the leverage to pull her flush against him so his lips could travel the length of her throat. She quivered and he quivered and when he nipped, then tugged, at the lobe of her ear, she whimpered like a wounded kitten and squirmed.

"Don't tease me," she gasped. "I—*oh*."

He moved to her mouth and it fell open for him, leaving him plummeting, drowning. "I love you, Cake. I want you."

She mewled against his mouth. Closed her eyes. Slipped an arm around his shoulders.

That was good enough for him.

Hassan grabbed her wrist, weaved them through the crowd, and stumbled towards a room upstairs. Halfway there, he glanced back idiotically, as if to make sure Edy was still with him and the swerve of the movement had him pawing for the bannister.

Edy bleated in laughter. He tugged her along.

They ducked into a room partway down the hall and Hassan had the presence of mind to lock the door. The second after, he went for her, capturing her face in both hands and crushing her mouth under his. He was

Shewanda Pugh

suddenly all out of time and backing her to the bed. They were hands and tongue and pressing bodies, with him clamoring on top of her and her pulling him in tight. Dressed, they moved as one, compact, desperate, trembling in need. He shoved up her shirt and grinned when he saw the front snap bra, before her hand buried in his hair and pulled his face down hard to hers. Hassan gripped and kneaded, then pulled at her jeans, pausing long enough to fumble out of his.

He couldn't move fast enough to get back to her. With his help, she got rid of her jeans and panties in one go. Then he clamored up, grabbing her leg as he went, and thrust in harder than he ever had. They both cried out in a tortured sort of pleasure. He drove in again, fiercer still, and she gripped him to her with a shuddering cry. There was no way he could last like this, but he was so greedy for her, so desperate, that he couldn't hope to stand it.

He pounded her into the mattress with relentlessly thrusting, savage strokes, half-crazy from her stuttering his name, moaning and shouting, mixing it all with mindless 'pleases' that he kissed, open-mouthed, away.

There was no one else but this girl for him. There was nothing else but this moment. Sweat pricked his brow and he picked up even more speed, brutal, slapping, grunting with need. And her, her thrusting up and into him, taking him, accepting him.

He was losing it. He was losing his fucking mind,

his soul to this girl. Distantly, he heard the drudging breaths he took and the wild pound of his heart between his ears. He drew back, flipped her over, pulled her up by the waist.

He drove into her, punishing, grinding, slamming until she jabbered, until she shook and took up the begging. He gripped her hips possessively, pressed kisses to her back, and drove into her with harsh, punctuating thrusts. She was his. She was his, she swore. And he, he said something that made no damned sense.

Edy bucked beneath him, signaling her finish, and jerked hard enough to trigger one in him.

He shot on a cry of pleasure and gripped her tight, certain he wasn't ready to let go.

Not now. Not ever.

Thirty-Three

The curtains came into view first: lilac monstrosities slightly parted to let in a gruesome beam of sunlight. Edy squinted at it, briefly wondering when Naomi had picked up such ugly window dressing. Then the sunlight assaulted her skull and she threw up a hand and groaned.

Behind her, a body shifted in bed. For one brief, horrible moment, Edy froze, unsure of who she'd find. Silas? No, she wouldn't. Not even drunk at a party. She wasn't ready for that. Not now. Maybe not ever. But did her drunk mind know that?

She turned, hesitant, unwilling to see, and exhaled audibly at the sight of Hassan. She could deal with this. She could deal with having slept with him, though it complicated things considerably. He stared back at her, studying critically, thoughts creasing his face. When his features twisted belatedly into a grimace, Edy recoiled.

"What?" she whispered, not sure she wanted to know.

"You," he spat. "You've slept with him, didn't you? You fucking slept with him!" He practically tumbled from the bed in his rush to get up.

He could not be serious right now. Not when he was spending weekends with Mala. Not when it was him that dumped her.

"You think you get a right to question what I have or haven't done?" Edy said. "You broke up with me, Hassan. We're done, remember?"

For some reason, it was this declaration that flared his nostrils and had him baring his teeth like some brazen bull.

"Done, huh?" Hassan said. "Yeah, well, we looked pretty done last night, didn't we? Can we be done again in a few minutes?"

"Fuck you, Hassan!" Edy's cheeks heated with the memory of how desperately their bodies had met only hours ago. "I'm not yours and you're not mine, and it was you that made sure of that."

"Yeah, because I can't trust you and clearly your new friend can't trust you either!" Hassan roared.

She could kill him. She would kill him. For him to throw everything back in her face like that?

Edy didn't know how or when she made it across the room, only that she was thrashing him with an open hand that he swept away. It freed her other hand though, and distracted him, which she used to ball into a fist and pop him in the cheek.

Hassan cursed. "Ow! Will you fucking stop?"

He fumbled with her arms before grabbing her firmly by the wrists and forcing them down by her side. Edy huffed and struggled in vain. He pushed her back and the two fell atop the bed.

She was distinctly aware of their nakedness now and reminded of the night before.

"Get off me," Edy hissed. "You don't get to screw me then say I'm a slut afterwards."

"And you don't get to beat the shit out of me!" he said.

They stared at each other for one defiant moment, neither willing to bend to the other's will. Then Edy shifted and his manhood slipped from its resting place against her thigh to the spot between them. He responded by hardening immediately.

"Edy…" Hassan said.

"Get the hell off me," Edy said.

He pulled back, coloring visibly, and clamored away.

"There is nothing you can say to me," Edy said, "when you had a fiancée the entire time we dated. When you started seeing her yourself the second you got away from me. Maybe you've been seeing her the whole time. Maybe I was just too stupid to know."

A knock sounded at the door, rescuing him from whatever nonsense response he could come up with. Simultaneously, they glanced at it. Edy rushed for her clothes. He went to block the door.

"What is it?" Hassan said into the crack.

"Party's over," sang a girl sweetly. "Time to go."

He nodded as if she could see him. "Yeah, sure.

Already getting dressed."

He looked down at the lock and jiggled the knob to be sure it was secure. Edy, now in her bra and panties, went for the rest of her party ensemble.

Hassan turned back to her. "Edy, listen to me. Me and Mala are through. I'm not—"

"You're *through*, you bastard? I just saw her at the game! And you have the nerve to talk about me. Everyone talks at this school, you know. They've told me about how she comes to see you every weekend. About you and your friends hanging out with her and her friends. Sounds very cozy. Sounds like something special is happening."

His silence poured on. Eventually, another knock sounded at the door. Still, he didn't move. In his eyes was the conversation Edy didn't want to have: one full of hurts and accusations and way too much emotion. There was too much between them and never enough time. They could never get the words right and they were addicted to hurting each other now.

"Edy, you can't think—"

"Don't tell me what I can't think when you just accused me of sleeping with Silas!"

At the mere mention of the other boy's name, raw fury stiffened his features, deadening then dulling his eyes to the coldest shade of moss. The bedroom door rattled as if it might lose every last hinge, but Hassan didn't so much as glance in its direction.

"Well?" he said. "Have you?"

Edy clamped down on her next thought. She made up her mind not to give a damn about him and Mala. Like she'd told him, they were done. He wasn't hers and she wasn't his. They were free to do or be with who they liked.

She ignored the awful tug at her heart.

"Tell you what," she said, and pulled her fitted tee down over her bra. When the tears came, she ignored them. "Why don't we agree to never do or go through all this again? Why don't we agree that you and I are a nightmare and can't even be in the same room together?"

Hassan got dressed slowly and made a point of not looking at her now. "Fine. Whatever you want."

She was done here. Done with him. Done with hope. "Have a nice life, Hassan. Since I won't get a chance to tell you later, congratulations on the Heisman."

Thirty-Four

By the time Hassan returned to his room, his face had begun to throb. The tightness there told him it was swelling, the tenderness that it was bruised. Edy had given him a damned contusion.

At least the floor of his dorm was quiet when he returned. With any luck, he could slip into bed without encountering anyone and bury his woes in a few hours of sleep.

Things had gone bad. Achingly, devastatingly bad. For the whole of his life, he'd had Edy by his side and, because of that, some part of him knew she'd always be there. They'd belonged to each other, right from the start. Two tots stumbling along the beach. Him and her hand-in-hand as kids, gliding along the ice at Frog Pond. Never had he imagined that this part of him would cease to exist, that the *them* part of his world wouldn't be populated with new sights, sounds, whims, with the fullness of Edy. Now he had nothing. Bitter emptiness—no, less than emptiness, he had a hollow caving in his soul that beckoned to be filled. It didn't get better with time like he'd stupidly hoped. No, it whispered day after day in a pain-filled pulse:

they were through, they were through, they were through. Some days it was his only thought. And now, now she'd punched him in the face, damnit.

The door to his room squeaked when it opened and Lawrence's head snapped up. The flinch was immediate. Hassan chose to ignore it as he made his way to his side of the room and his bed, where he would bury his face from the world.

"Things went that well, huh?" Lawrence said.

Hassan didn't bother to kick off his sneakers before he flopped, face down on the bed. "I don't know what you're talking about," he said.

"I saw you go up," Lawrence said so quietly Hassan had to strain to hear it. "With Edy."

Oh.

"And since you're just getting back…"

"I don't want to talk about this," Hassan said into the pillow.

The worst part of ruining it all with Edy was the knowledge that he had pushed her into the arms of the dancer guy, or Wyatt, or someone. Someone who would comfort her and verify that Hassan was an asshole unworthy of her tears. He'd be willing to be there for her. He'd hold her for as long as it took. Then he'd kiss her.

Hassan looked down to find his hand balled so tight his fingernails drew blood. Great. At the rate he was going, he'd have more injuries than after game day.

He sighed.

"Well," Lawrence said. "Whatever happened, I'm sure your mouth got you that mark on your face."

He did not need this right now.

"Thanks," Hassan murmured into the pillow. "Glad to know whose side you're on."

Lawrence snorted. "Don't be dramatic. I don't have a side."

A knock sounded at the door. Hassan swore. If it was one of his goddamned teammates stopping by this early in the morning, they'd better have a good reason.

"There's something I should tell you," Lawrence said quickly. "Before they get in."

Hassan looked at him, saw Lawrence flinch, then remembered that his own face looked like shit. "What is it?" Hassan said into the bed.

"It's about the Heisman," Lawrence said.

"I don't give a shit about the Heisman," Hassan said. "You guys can get all worked up if you want to, but I know the history of the award and my chances are next to nil of getting the prize."

"Fine," Lawrence said. "Then I'll get the door."

Less than a minute later, the sound of Freight had Hassan wishing he'd gone elsewhere.

"Hassan back?" Freight said.

"No," Hassan answered.

"We saw you go up with her," Freight said. "Are you back together?"

There was shuffling, letting Hassan know that Freight wasn't alone.

"I'm telling you, pageant queen just went to get some ass. I don't think the other girl puts out," Cash said.

Hassan couldn't take it. He was up and shouting at them in an instant. "Would you two shut the fuck —"

"Shit!" the two cried together. Then, "Who beat your ass?" That was Freight.

"It wasn't that pretty boy on the motorcycle, was it? If you let that ballerina kick your ass…" Cash said.

"Nobody kicked my ass," Hassan said. "I just… had an accident with some weights."

Now they were rolling. Freight and Cash fell all over each other, wild with their laughter.

"Okay, let's all relax," Lawrence said. "The man said he had an accident."

Hassan shot him a grateful look.

Freight straightened up first and gave him a knowing look. "Listen, I understand. I had an accident like that last year when I was dating Tamela Carpenter and Ashley Martin at the same time. This weight hit me in the eye, nose, mouth, stomach, and back. If you look at last year's team photo, I've got a busted lip in it."

Hassan got up. He'd had all he was going to take of this. He marched over to the door and opened it. "Get out. Now."

Cash and Freight looked unimpressed.

"Tell us this," Cash said. "Are you just getting back from last night's party? Or did you stop somewhere else?"

Maybe he could get rid of them if he shared this tidbit. It was nothing in the scheme of things overall.

"I'm just getting back," Hassan said and opened the door wider.

Cash and Freight glanced at each other.

"And Edy gave you that, right?" Freight pointed at Hassan's face, finger so close it got slapped away.

That he wouldn't share. It told far too much and it revealed him for the pain-filled idiot he was.

"Leave him alone." Lawrence was up and at Hassan's side. "Can't you guys ever take a hint? Everything doesn't need to be said. When shit goes foul you need to let it be."

Somehow, for some reason, this worked. Lawrence was able to push the two out the door with Freight even casting a sympathetic glance Hassan's way. But before the door closed, Cash said, "Did you see the Heisman list? We're both on it!"

Now, for that, Hassan could conjure some enthusiasm. Cash had a much better chance of being honored as a damn talented quarterback and upperclassmen. But his addition was late.

They gripped hands enthusiastically before it turned into a one-armed embrace. Once Cash had the benefit of Hassan's ear alone, he said quickly, quietly, "She'll come back to you in time."

They broke the hug with Hassan looking slightly starry-eyed. He needed something to do, so he jammed his hands in his pockets before giving the guys a nod of goodbye. After all, Cash wasn't exactly the romantic or reassuring type. Hell, had he ever seen the guy hug someone? What was happening here?

Lawrence stared at Hassan awhile. "You okay?" he finally said.

Hassan shook his head. No. Never. Was 'okay' part of his existence anymore? It felt like he simply managed to get by.

The days passed at a crawl. Hassan spent them telling himself that what had happened with Edy was for the best. He spent those same days telling himself that he'd spend the rest of his life thinking of her, wanting her, and wondering what she was doing at that moment. Would she eventually get married? The thought twisted his stomach and caused him physical pain. If Hassan and Edy ever calmed enough to be civil towards each other, then he'd be forced to look this other guy in the eye, shake his hand, and even smile at him. Would he sense the jealously coming off him like a viper? Would he know just how badly Hassan wanted to take his place or how he had been in his place and fucked it all up like the world's most practiced idiot?

Yeah, the days passed like that. Football was his only solace. Arkansas. Florida. Texas A&M. He played savagely, without a care for his body or what happened to it. He ran on autopilot. He cursed the opposition. They thought they had him all figured out, that he did this for something as cheap as screen time or attention. As if the attention he wanted could be had this way. Idiots.

As if anything he wanted now could be had this way.

Thirty-Five

"How long do we have to watch this fucking channel?" Lincoln said from somewhere distant, possibly Mars.

"As long as he wants to, love, it's his place," Lottie said.

"I think he should eat something," Matteo said. "Wouldn't you like to eat something, Wyatt?"

Wyatt sniffed and wiped at his nose with the sleeve of his shirt. On TV, LSU scored their zillionth touchdown.

"That's settled," Matteo said happily. "I'll make salsa and chips."

"That's all you ever make," Lincoln snapped.

"And just what the hell do you make?" Matteo said.

It was so much trouble following them, so much trouble being *aware*. All Wyatt had was hurt and pain and misery, a wellspring of it so deep he feared its bottom.

She did not want him. She would not ever want him.

Wyatt sniffed and wiped his nose again.

"You're crying, Wyatt," Lincoln said bluntly. "In

case you wanted to know."

That surprised him. He had hardly drunk water, so he didn't think he had the physical capacity for tears. And anyway, how could a person sit there, crying, and not know it?

"You're an asshole," Matteo said. "I don't know why I deal with you."

"Fuck off," Lincoln said.

"Don't fight. I do *not* want the two of you fighting," Lottie said. "I have enough on my hands."

Matteo sighed. "Noted."

How long had life been happening around Wyatt? He couldn't say. The first days after Edy's outburst were filled with outbursts of his own, screaming, lung-emptying rages where, for the first time, he'd called her every filthy word he'd known—and he knew a lot thanks to his dad—before folding like the crepes at Edy's birthday party and sobbing face down into the floor.

He had never believed he had anything in common with his father before that day. That day he learned he was his father and his father was Wyatt. Once the man had been a boy neglected by his own father, Wyatt's grandfather, before he became the crude, revolting figure of today. Wyatt had been on his trajectory without even knowing it, and it took a string of profanity to prove it.

There were more days of screaming curses to the rafters—curses for Edy, for Hassan, for himself. Some of what he bellowed was nonsense no one could make out, delivered amidst a cacophony of tears. Sometimes he panted with a very real pain in his chest or gut; other times he locked himself in the room and wept into his pillows with brief rests for something like sleep.

This was what he had fallen to now, he supposed, these silent tears, as he locked his every word, his every thought in a vessel so deep even Wyatt had trouble finding it.

He'd turned on football days ago and sat there, on the couch, as the people and the noise and the activity around him changed. He had brief bathroom breaks. Sometimes Matteo forced water or salsa and chips — the only "dish" he knew how to make — down his throat.

"Cabrona! Fuck!" Matteo cried as he undoubtedly chopped at his hand again.

"Jeez, Matteo. Could you *not* put your life's blood in our food, for once?" Lincoln said.

"And could you not pick on him so much? He takes it to heart, you know," Lottie said.

They were all so far away.

"You're worried about him when your cousin is fucking comatose?" Lincoln laughed. "You're weird, girl."

"He'll come around!" Lottie cried. "Isn't that right, Wyatt?" He felt a cool, smooth touch of skin atop his hand and flinched away, knowing it to be hers. He didn't know why, but he didn't like her much anymore.

"Maybe soup would be better," Matteo said. "I could pick up a can."

Lincoln sighed dramatically. "He just needs to get laid. It's an animalistic need we all have," he said matter-of-factly.

"She's not worth this, *mi amigo*," Matteo said. "I've seen what you've been going through and no one is worth it."

"I am," Lincoln said.

"Not you," he said firmly.

"And yet you stick around," Lincoln said.

Lottie seemed to be cooing at Lincoln or some other such weird thing. Wyatt couldn't be troubled to turn his head.

"You *are* worth it," she murmured to him.

Matteo scoffed.

"It's not a matter of being right or wrong," Lincoln said. "Wyatt has gone to an awful lot of trouble for this girl. He was her best friend in high school, which got him bullied by her meathead boyfriend and his friends. Before he could finish the twelfth grade, loving her had got him *shot*. Now, with his life pieced together, what does he do? Seek her out like the true romantic he is. But she spits on that. She wants the common jock, everybody's pretty boy." He waved a hand impatiently. "Babe, give me one of Wyatt's cigarettes from the drawer there, would you?"

A bit of shuffling commenced before the familiar

spark of the lighter, and oh yes, Wyatt imagined the nicotine filling the other boy's soul. It wouldn't be bad to have one of those.

Wyatt turned his head to him.

In silent acknowledgment, Lincoln offered him the cigarette. He took it with every pair of eyes plastered to him.

"Was that about the lay of the land, Wyatt? What I was saying about Edy?" Lincoln said.

Wyatt nodded. No one had ever reached in him quite that way and pulled out those troubling thoughts he'd had.

"You deserve her. You should have her at least once. I think so. Your cousin thinks so, too. Want to?" Lincoln plucked the cigarette from between Wyatt's fingers. He felt bereft without it.

Still, he managed to nod.

"Once might get her out of your system," Lottie said quietly.

Why were they doing this to him? It wasn't possible. She didn't want him. She'd never want him. Wyatt's hands scrunched in fists and came undone over and over and over. His chest seemed to furl the same way. He needed them to stop. There was no way he could ever have her. And yet, his first words spoken after so much silence were said at a near-whisper.

"Tell me," he said.

"I've got this friend," Lincoln said and took another drag of Wyatt's cigarette, "and he's got a friend, too.

Well, this friend's friend can get you roofies, if you need them."

"Roofies," Wyatt repeated. He knew the word and yet it meant nothing to him in that moment.

Lottie giggled. "I told you he's an innocent."

For some reason, Matteo's chopping became really loud.

"Roofies," Lincoln said. "You know, benzodiazepine. GHB rendered to, uh, make a particular person unconscious. Then, when said person is unconscious, you have a good time, wake them up, and send them on their way."

Wyatt stared at him. "You mean…" He had to be able to say it. Yet, he couldn't. He didn't want to hear this. He wanted to stop considering it. But God, the thought of having Edy, actually having her naked, in his bed, underneath him, taking *him* instead of that asshole *Hassan*, shot through him like a punch through the wall. She'd be completely naked. He'd finally see those incredible breasts she'd grown, ones that he'd imagined in so many ways. He still hadn't forgotten her end of summer visit to his house when she'd given him a stiffy. He'd only thought he'd been hard then. He couldn't even stand to think of the possibilities. He'd never been so hard in his life.

"Uh," Wyatt said. Realizing that the others probably could see his erection, he quickly sought for a way to turn the attention from him.

Matteo looked him over. "Any chance I can help

you with that problem?" he said.

Wyatt's face burned. Now his friend was coming on to him. There had to be a way to end this.

"Help him?" Lincoln said. "Just how the hell would you do that?"

"Same ways I help you," Matteo said. "And you never seem to complain."

Okay, that was enough of that.

"Hey," Wyatt said, and was horrified to find his voice low and husky. "How would you expect me to get her back over here after all that's happened?"

"Wyatt!" Matteo said. "You cannot seriously be contemplating this shit. It's rape. She's just a girl."

"You don't even like girls. How would you know?" Wyatt snapped.

He hadn't meant it, even before Matteo gasped, threw down his knife, and spat a string of obscenities Wyatt couldn't understand.

"I'm sorry," Wyatt murmured. "Tell him I'm sorry," he said to no one in particular.

Lincoln waved a hand. "Forget that. Let's get back to the matter at hand."

Rape.

Thirty-Six

Edy glanced at Silas, found him looking at her, and then blushed. She couldn't help but look away. For the umpteenth time, she stared at the black and white checkered pattern of the restaurant's floor. It had been this way as they'd practiced for weeks, steps confident, flirty, splashing with swagger, even as she blushed and never said much. Now that they'd come to the end of it all, they sat at a blindingly white ice cream parlor to celebrate.

"How is it?" Silas said.

Absentmindedly, he reached over, tilted her chin so that she faced him, and brushed a thumb across her lower lip. When it dipped into her mouth, she gasped, cheeks flaming and jerked away.

She had agreed to meet him like this so she could break things off, but every step of the way he had been anticipating and toying with her.

"Silas, I —'

"Whipped cream," he interrupted.

Edy's eyelashes fluttered. "What?" she said. Belatedly, she looked down at her sundae, remembering it was topped with whipped cream.

"Your lips," he said, "had whipped cream on them. I'd ask if you minded me removing it, but I'm already pretty familiar with the exploratory side of your mouth, aren't I?"

God, she could drop through the floor. Silas returned to his own dessert as if he hadn't said a word, as if he hadn't conjured the memory of the near-half dozen times they'd made out—one of which included his *hands* getting exploratory. And that was it. Edy had figured it out. He knew why she'd asked to see him. He knew that this was where their story ended.

"You know why I want to see you, don't you?" she said.

He looked up, gray eyes cool as a morning before rain. Yet… at their edges lay the storm. A storm of colossal magnitude.

"How could I possibly know?" he said smoothly.

Silas sat completely still and waited, even as the cherry on his sundae slumped to one side.

She sighed. "Silas, listen to me, I really like you—"

"But ever since you fucked Hassan at the Iota Rho party, you just haven't got eyes for me."

Edy recoiled at the malice in his voice. Still, she recovered herself, shaking off the urge to scurry under the table in embarrassment. "Don't you *dare* talk to me like that. Whatever happened between me and Hassan is just that, between me and Hassan." She recovered herself a tad. "Look, just because you're hurting—"

He laughed in that nasty way bullies did. "Hurt?

Really? You're the wounded one who goes around using people and getting used."

Edy had no idea when she'd begun to tremble. She gripped the edge of the table as she worked on maintaining some semblance of control. He would not get a rise out of her. He was right to some degree. Despite his rough exterior, she had recognized his feelings. Maybe she shouldn't have taken him up on his offer to use him as a catalyst to purge herself of Hassan. No matter what, Silas hadn't been able to take possession of her heart. Edy had no idea if that was what he'd been hoping for. She had no idea if that was what she'd been hoping for. Either way, she was sorry for this pitiful end.

"I'm going now," Edy said quietly, pushing her ice cream towards him. She had only a few dollars in her pocket and there was no way she'd put them on the table. "But I am sorry. In the end, there was just too much between me and Hassan, even if I did have feelings for you."

Silas glared at her. "Well, did you or not?"

She looked at him blankly for a moment. "Yeah. Definitely. If there were never a Hassan Pradhan then you and I could've been something. Thank you for letting me test the waters and try to get over him."

He nodded thoughtfully, face creased in the deepest of frowns.

Once outside, Edy called one of the Lady Tigers to pick her up. Of course, London wasn't available but

Tamela would be there straight away. Cringing, she calculated the distance back to campus.

"Night," Silas said, and revved his engine in the parking lot. Without a backwards glance, he peeled off.

Tamela arrived soon after.

❈ ❈ ❈

Wyatt couldn't sleep. He stared at the ceiling, practicing the deep breathing techniques that his therapist had taught him, but more and more they blended with the lush, eager sounds of lust from next door. It absolutely boggled his mind how he—the virgin—had been accused of all manners of depravity with Lottie, a girl who had slept with Lincoln, Lincoln and Matteo together, the brewer's son, Solomon, and a drunken guy from the Florida Away party all since they'd been in Baton Rouge. He didn't care though; Lottie had made a fairly eloquent argument as to how promiscuity was a label wielded by men to control women. She said that guys called girls sluts even as they congratulated each other for as much sex with as many partners as possible. Despite all that, he'd nearly taken a pitchfork up the ass for supposedly violating an innocence she didn't have.

Eventually, Wyatt was only able to sleep after grabbing a bottle of hand lotion and jerking off feverishly to the image of taking Edy as she slept. He'd been rougher with her than he would have anticipated, angrier even, with all traces of the boy who thought her perfect gone.

But he still wanted her like mad.

Yeah, perhaps the circumstances were right for a one-and-done kind of deal. Once he did the deed, who would know, except him? It wasn't like she was a virgin. She was probably screwing the new guy now. What was one more? How would she even be able to tell?

She wouldn't, Wyatt figured. With that thought, he drifted off to sleep.

That night, Wyatt dreamed of Edy. Edy spread across his sheets and reaching for him as she wore a silk pink nightie that made him gasp.

There was no mistaking her intentions as she looked up at him with soft and luminous, half-lidded eyes. He climbed into bed with her, pausing only to tug off his t-shirt and ease out his boxers. His prick bounced back at him like a sling shot, taut and ready to go. She only smiled at him, then giggled a little, making him smile back and giggle a little more.

Wyatt lowered his mouth to hers, conscious even in his dreams that this would be their first kiss. But even as he had that thought, he had another. He absolutely could not wait for her. He would not wait. So he pried open her knees, clamored in between, and adjusted himself for action. God, his heart could barely stand the moment; it threatened to stamp right out his chest.

Edy reached up with both hands to cup his face, causing him to bite down hard on his lower lip. In and out. That was all there was to it, right? Wyatt hovered, then shifted. Inch by inch he went. At the moment he felt a brush of quivering, sweet, softness, Edy opened her mouth and screamed.

Wyatt jerked in confusion, until she began batting at him and shrieking, her mouth cracking open in blind terror. Viciously, she clawed at his face, drawing blood, slashing deep, before he could even throw up his arms in defense. He thought to stop her, with a kiss or a slap, and leaned in to the fray eventually with his lips. Edy froze, eyes wide in unmistakable terror.

Were those eyes for him? Did she fear him? He needed to tell her that he would never hurt her, never allow another to hurt her, but as he leaned forward to pin her arms—she shuddered, as if gripped in a seismic, mounting terror. She had to calm down. He handed her a cup of seltzer water from the nightstand and begged her to calm down. This was Wyatt, remember? Her best friend.

Almost immediately her eyes began to roll back to the whites and her body went rigid, muscles stiff as bone as she moaned. Briefly, she vomited. When she went still, Wyatt didn't need to be told she was dead.

Then he woke up.

Wyatt's dad, Roland, called a few days later. Though they weren't supposed to talk, Wyatt figured that his grandfather had no way of knowing who he spoke to or when, and therefore couldn't restrict his inheritance on those grounds.

Roland asked how he was faring down in New Orleans. Wyatt asked him how he'd gotten his cell phone number. Roland laughed, told him he'd given Sandra a sob story, and asked Wyatt for some money. Figuring it had to be for a forgotten light bill or some groceries, Wyatt told him to name his number.

"Oh, big man, are you? 'Name your number.' So big you can't call your old man. Never mind that I raised you all those years. Think on that, why don't you?"

"I didn't mean it that way, Dad," Wyatt said. Though his father had been drunk and forgetful and verbally abusive, he did keep Wyatt out of the cold. And he had helped with his conception. He'd buried a lot of sullen resentment towards his dad, years of sulking and bitterness brewing. They'd have time for that though. Right now, he could simply be his son.

Wyatt sighed. "What can I do for you, Dad?"

"Give me about three-fifty thousand dollars for a house in Providence, Rhode Island. I want to head back home."

"Three-fifty thousand dollars!" Wyatt sputtered. "I don't even have a house!"

"Yeah, but you're in school. You'll get one when you're done. What's that you're studying again?"

He hesitated. He made the mistake of hesitating. Then compounding on his error with, "Dad..." What he should have said was that he was undecided, not hint that he wanted his father to stop talking.

"Are you even in school, Wyatt?"

"What? Yeah, of course," Wyatt said.

"Because I know you followed the Indian boy and that black girl down there. I told you, I worked your cousin over, told her I was worried and all that. She told me everything I needed to know. Now I'm just wondering if you're a student," he said.

This was his father. Not only was the man skilled at bullshit himself, but he knew Wyatt well enough to know when he was attempting it.

"I'm in school," Wyatt said simply.

"All I can say is that I hope she's playing the Indian boy for a fool, because if you're not getting any ass after all this work—"

"Dad, I should go," Wyatt said.

"About that money—" his father said.

"I don't have that much!" he cried. "Lottie's been down here bleeding me dry. She's supposed to be helping me, but—"

"Lottie? I thought I told you to stay away from that girl!" his father said.

"Dad, listen—"

"No, you listen. I never wanted you near the girl, but you've always wanted what you can't have. So she became your favorite cousin. It's no wonder why. The damned girl's even crazier than you are."

"You believed I hurt her," Wyatt said.

"Between you two anything was possible, including

that. Yeah, I'll say it."

"You said I went off the rails! You said I better not go off the rails again!"

"You're the reason I don't own a gun anymore. You waving it at my boss' son, half the kids from Cobblestone, and then sticking it in your own mouth is why we had to make goddamned tracks. Thank God I didn't keep the thing loaded."

Wyatt held the phone for a while. "I tried to shoot myself?" He hated his life, yes, but why would he choose to end it over an act he agreed to feign guilt over? Granted, he hadn't known the consequences of going along with Lottie would be so high, but it was often that way with Lottie. She was so beautiful and innocent-looking. Her slight size and soft speech conjured an instant protective need and, Wyatt was discovering more and more, it was a need best left unfollowed.

"Look, I don't have the education of your precious black girl's family, but I'm no fool, either. I know a few things. I know that Lottie's a little older than you and a lot more experienced in the ways of life. I know her dad used to brag about raising her the British way or some shit, and giving her equal involvement in her upbringing. She used to watch HBO and Cinemax and all them types of shows too, and not just the daytime ones either. Her daddy talked about it over coffee with the others—not me, of course, I was too lowly for something like a straight conversation, even though our kids were first cousins. Anyway, he let her watch what she wanted when she wanted and called it learning about the world. He said folks who care about ratings are helicoptering, whatever the fuck that means. Anyway, the girl knew a lot more about the world than you, so I wasn't too keen on you being around her... figuring she'd take advantage of you easily. But you know how you are."

"Tell me about my shooting myself. Or trying to. I don't remember it. Why don't I remember it?"

"Hell if I know. You acted a right damned fool. I had to rush down from the plant to the house, through all those crazy ass teenagers. Some of 'em were throwing rocks. All of that to get to my son still holding a gun. But by the time I got there, you were just holding it loose by your side, like. I didn't understand the look in your eyes. Like you'd went to visit somewhere in your damned head or something. Off the goddamned rails."

Something tightened in Wyatt's chest. He strained to remember this day, though he did so with fear. What if he reached for death again once he recalled the anguish he felt? What if a kitchen knife became handy? Or he opened the oven and stuck his head in?

No. Whatever else he could have said, he was not that same hopeless boy. He had known some happiness now. He had danced at a party. Kissed a girl. Shared cocoa on the roof of another beautiful girl's home and stared at the stars. He was rich now, too.

Was he happy enough to remember? Secure enough in his mind?

Wyatt doubted it. So he shoved the want away.

"I should go now," he said quietly.

"Hey! Are you gonna give me the money for the house?" his dad said.

"No! Maybe when I've invested some of it, you know. Turned a bit of a profit."

"You bastard."

"Bye, Dad."

"You rotten little shit."

Wyatt disconnected the line.

So, his dad had been as worried about Lottie being around him as he was worried about Wyatt being around Lottie.

If the earth quaked beneath him, he couldn't have trembled more.

The next evening, he sent Edy a text message. He didn't trust his voice not to shake, so he couldn't, of course, call her. He'd spent some time considering his words and what she would respond to now, as well as his need to keep her around long enough to serve her a drink after she arrived.

Then he had the problem of the motorcycle guy. What if he wanted to come? How could Wyatt control all these variables? He put his mind to it, considered it, and considered what he knew about Edy. Then he came up with a solution.

IT'S ME. I NEED TO TALK TO YOU. IT'S ABOUT THE DAY I GOT SHOT.

Her answer took longer to come than before.

WHAT IS IT?

He had considered which way to go with this for a while, wrestling with several possibilities before settling on his answer.

JUST SOME FOLLOW UP QUESTIONS MY THERAPIST HAD. I KNOW YOU'LL PROBABLY SAY NO, BUT IS IT POSSIBLE YOU COULD STOP BY? JUST FOR A FEW MINUTES? IT'S EASIER, THAT'S ALL. IF IT MAKES YOU MORE COMFORTABLE, WE CAN STAY ON MY PORCH.

He waited, praying she'd simply say she didn't have a ride instead of leaving him to ask whether she'd bring the pretty baboon with her this time. Getting rid of him would be trickier. But she didn't have a ride and reluctantly wound up letting him pick her up in his rented Mustang.

They sat on his porch with Matteo's mint juleps, served up by Lottie, who wore a peculiar smile as she did so. Wyatt wished she wouldn't.

Edy left her drink for a long while, sitting in one of the cushioned porch chairs as Wyatt shuffled through his endless papers. That was also part of his ploy. He knew exactly what he wanted to ask and when—had it memorized, in fact—but the shuffling would leave her with nothing to do but drink. Her drink had been spiked.

Her drink had been spiked.

Wyatt sat back, inauthentic papers in hand, and eyed the condensation on the outside of her glass. She had been his friend. His best friend. His only friend. His friend after so much had gone wrong in his life. Would he really hurt that girl? The ballerina he used to watch from the back of the classroom? The girl he'd shared floats with and drunk cocoa with and loved with all his heart?

No. He—he wanted the warmth that surrounded her endlessly, the warmth that beat from her very heart, so that he could wrap himself in its protection forever. He'd wanted the goodness from her soul because he had known so little. And the kindness. There had been so much *want* and *she*, Edy, had been the first unfortunate soul to replenish him. But even what she gave had never been enough.

What he needed wouldn't be found with Edy.

She reached for her drink, and he watched her, as if from a daze.

Then he remembered.

Wyatt flailed, knocking the glass from her hand so that the drink spilled all over her blouse and shorts.

"God, I'm so sorry. Let me get you home so you can clean up," he said.

"But you can give me a shirt, can't you? We might as well finish—"

"We are finished, Edy," Wyatt said. "Let's get

going."

Thirty-Seven

Coach wanted to see him in his office. Hassan figured it could be for any number of reasons. Something off he'd said to the press, a fan he'd flipped off, anything. So, he took his time getting there. Over to the Football Operations Center he went, jammed his Mustang between a sporty coupe and a beaten hatchback, and strode on over to the coach's office. Hands deep in his pockets, head down, he considered his likely punishment. He'd been brazenly disrespectful, so much so that his father had called and said that Mr. Agre down the street had asked him whether the wild one at LSU was his son. Oh, that had warranted a long conversation, made longer when Hassan had taken the time to confirm that he was talking about the butcher. *That* earned him a scalding earful about looking down on people who were earning a decent living. Which he wasn't. Not that it mattered.

Hassan arrived at the coach's office too soon. He could've done with another walk around the block. Just as he considered it, the door flew open and out flew Cash with a look of absolute murder. He paused long enough to consider Hassan, but there was none of the encouragement from before, none of the love. This looked as if he'd tackle him in a dark alley and slip two hands around his throat. Politely, Hassan stepped to one side. He had no idea what that was about, nor any interest in finding out. Coach wanted to see him and that was the end of that story.

Cash shouldered past him and disappeared.

Still rubbing his wounded shoulder, Hassan stepped into the coach's opulent office when called and fell into the chair before his desk.

The smoothest, darkest mahogany Hassan had ever seen comprised the coach's desk and the cabinets behind it that held LSU's glittering trophies of the past. He dropped his gaze back to his hands, however, and waited.

"Pradhan," Coach said to him, "I have news. You should be among the first to hear it."

Hassan looked up at his tone. He couldn't understand it. It was... enthusiastic?

"Let me shake your hand. You're a Heisman nominee, kid." And to make it all worse, he came around his desk, this man with so much distinction, with so many accolades—that man came around his desk and thrust his hand at Hassan as if they were something like equals. Hassan stared at it, blinked twice, then gave it a firm grasp. Coach laughed at the moment Hassan worked on swallowing the lump in his throat. What the hell was happening here? This couldn't be. He had to tell them. He had to tell someone.

"But I'm a freshman," he managed to croak.

Coach laughed big as the waves back home on the Cape. "I know. You're also incredible. Thank God those idiots saw it."

"You think I'm incredible?"

Good thing Hassan was sitting, because standing wouldn't be advisable at the moment. Had he had vertigo before? He couldn't recall being bothered by it.

"Pradhan, I start you in every game. You give me exactly what I ask for," Coach said.

"Except when it comes to the press," Hassan said sheepishly.

Coach whipped a look his way that warned him: he better not go there.

The Heisman. God. Was he dreaming?

"Coach?" Hassan said, getting to his feet. "I'm not dreaming, am I?" Because his mind was already elsewhere if he wasn't. His thoughts were with a certain girl who'd congratulated him on winning the Heisman even when she'd been angry. And it clicked for him in that moment. She'd always been there, hadn't she? In anger. In joy. In one sleepless night after another.

Coach laughed at him. "No, kid. This isn't a dream."

"Good," Hassan said. "Thank you." He paused. Looked around. "What do I do next?"

Coach handed him a few pieces of paper. "You'll go

to New York for a ceremony and do the usual media rounds. Then there will be much pomp and circumstance before you're honored." He stepped closer to Hassan, much closer than he would have liked, and placed a hand on each of his shoulders. "Listen, kid. Enjoy what they do for you, because you do deserve it, eh? You're a damned fine athlete. Don't forget that."

Hassan inhaled all the air in the room and held it. Then he nodded and marched out, crumpling whatever coach had given him. He went straight to his Mustang on numb feet, pressed the necessary button to unlock his door and sped across campus. There was no thought to where he went, no concern for the stares he got as he powered through the lobby or bounded up the stairs. Hassan even banged on the door like a madman and stared in confusion, breathless and sweaty when Edy's roommate Naomi answered instead.

"Yes?" she said. "How can I help you?"

"Edy," Hassan managed. Then, "Please."

Naomi studied him for a moment as if considering. That exchange meant she knew all about him and them and what they were to each other. She knew he had no business being there.

"Yes?" Edy said. She still wore her pajamas, though they were some that he didn't know. This pair had a Winnie the Pooh Piglet stretching in a big yawn. The tank top had been coupled with a little snatch of shorts that had Hassan biting his lower lip.

"I'm a Heisman nominee, Edy," he said.

He saw it right away, that spark of something beautiful, before her mouth opened, then closed and she had to close her eyes.

"That's wonderful, Hassan," was what she said.

"Thank you," was what he said, while feeling like an ass.

He took an interest in his feet. Black Jordans. His favorite pair. He'd need a new pair soon.

"Hassan?" Edy said.

"Yes?" He practically broke his neck looking up.

"I'm really happy for you," she said.

"Oh. Yeah." He nodded to himself. He could do this. He just got shortlisted for a fucking Heisman. He could talk to a girl, right? Especially one he'd known all his life.

"Edy," Hassan said, and this time it was her head that snapped up. But that didn't make things any easier for him. Maybe it made things a bit harder. Maybe it would have been easier if she'd been looking the other way. He just didn't know at this point. "Edy, I want you to come to the Heisman ceremony with me."

She frowned. "Me? Why?"

"You know why, Edy." He dared to take a step closer, narrowing the space between them. "I want you there because this doesn't make sense without you. It's all been fueled by this anger at not having you. I don't know how to explain it. I just... I want you back. I need you in my life. Be my confidante again, be my friend. Be there for me. I need you beside me. We were everything to each other once, remember?" He flinched at her tears. Why had she begun to cry? "Cake, please don't, cry," he said.

She shook her head. "I can't help it. I'm sorry." As soon as she wiped a trail away a fresh spill replaced it on her cheek. Hassan looked around, helpless. He'd never been able to stand her tears. He found nothing to wipe them with and decided to use the hem of his shirt. With the fabric of his tee wrapped around one hand, he stepped in and reached up, poignantly aware of every inch of her body and every breath she took. He dabbed at her face gently, wanting to cup it, to caress it, but never daring. At last his hand lowered pretty pathetically. His gaze followed and her lips captured his.

She'd pulled him to her by the face entirely, then slipped in, mouth parting his, tongue questing and shattering what little calm he had with those succulent, feather-like swoops.

Then she was gone.

Gone from arms he hadn't known he'd been holding her in. Gone from lips that demanded her touch.

Edy's eyes went wide. She threw a hand over her mouth. "I'm sorry. I didn't mean—I mean, I don't know what I was thinking."

Hassan grinned. "Don't apologize for taking what's

definitely yours."

This time he swooped in with arms around her waist, pulling her in flush, and God, that tongue of hers, oh did he miss it, oh did he miss *her* and her laugh and the way she went on about dance or nothing or the little things that only she remembered. He missed everything about her, including this, including her body against his, and the instincts between them and how a graze here or an open-mouthed shiver were all the words he ever needed. And now, please, he'd never let her go if only she'd come back to him.

Because he knew Edy, well. And she hadn't agreed to go to the Heisman ceremony yet.

"Cake?" Hassan said.

She pulled him inside. "What about your parents?" she said.

"I don't give a shit about my parents. I need you."

Naomi let out a low whistle.

Edy shot her a warning look.

"As long as you're sure," Edy said.

"I'm rock solid on this one," Hassan said.

Edy threw herself at him, practically rocking him in place as they hugged. For Hassan, it felt like coming home.

Thirty-Eight

After finals and the SEC Championship that LSU wrested from Georgia—a game in which Lawrence had to face his brothers on defense, and both Lawrence and Hassan were subjected to a bit of pre-game tussling from the twins—Edy and Hassan headed home on the same flight. Weeks ago, they both would have probably found it horrifying to be on the same plane. Months ago, they had found it thrilling. Life really did turn full circle.

"You want the window?" Hassan said.

"Like you want anything but the aisle," Edy answered. Those shoulders seemed to have broadened in his time down south. He'd certainly thickened and picked up even more mass. She couldn't believe how imposing he looked these days.

They dropped into their seats and it wasn't long before a bit of pre-flight commotion began. A cluster of football faithfuls had gathered near his seat and eventually the word 'Heisman' drifted through the cabin. Hassan wound up signing autographs until the flight crew insisted that everyone take their seats. Then he was called into the cockpit to sign two more for the captains.

When he returned to buckle in, Edy smiled sympathetically. This was his life now. Record breaker. Heisman hopeful. Loved by the multitude. She could get with that.

He slipped his hand into hers.

They could make this work. The alternative was unthinkable.

They kept the stop in Boston brief. An awkward apology from her dad about not having her back when it came to Hassan or LSU and another for his out-of-character behavior while he was in Baton Rouge. She'd already forgiven him for that and could forgive him endlessly—he was her dad. That, for some reason, had him wiping at his eyes and hugging her like he never had before.

She did some quick shopping with her mom at a few exclusive shops on Newberry, since Rebecca had always been particular about appearances and wouldn't have her daughter at a high-profile event looking "mangy." Afterwards there was repacking as some of the Heisman coverage took place in and around the Pradhan house. They wanted to see Hassan's house, his childhood bedroom, even Edy's backyard, where he first learned to toss a ball with Nathan. Hassan made sure to mention that it was Edy's backyard, oddly enough, to point out just how close their homes were, and to remind them that they had come to LSU together. Horrifyingly enough that prompted the crew to descend on Edy after they'd finished taping that segment for a bit of Q&A that they warned her they might not use. In their follow-up, they wanted to know her earliest memories of Hassan and football. She talked about his wish to get everything just so, even when they were small. Holding the ball right. Throwing the ball sure. "He spent so much time with the Dysons," Edy had said, "and for a while, I think he lived in their shadow." She'd twisted her hands together, hesitant to admit this, but believing it was just what he needed. "You know, thinking himself a poser, some kind of pretender around the great Steve Dyson and three sons with massive talent." Edy had glanced at Hassan then, to find him frozen, staring at her with the world's widest eyes. "I think now he knows Steve Dyson had four sons with massive talent."

And his eyes began to water, grass plains flooding at her words. He dashed a hand at his face. "Shut up," Hassan said and they both laughed.

She was pretty sure they were using that segment.

They took a flight to New York that night and checked into the Marriott Marquis. It sat on the shoulder of the PlayStation Theater, both on Broadway. The Heisman ceremony and a ton more coverage would take place at the theater. Hassan swore it would be cheesy from then on out, stuff like him and the other Heisman hopefuls tossing a football around in their suits, on the sidewalk, as they answered random questions. Stuff like the four of them pretending to be friends at a diner as they filmed cheesy promo. Stuff like each of them entering the theater for the ceremony. Edy didn't need to ask him if he was nervous. Though he stood relaxed and reached for her hand casually when he could, each time she found it slick with sweat. Each time, she gripped it in her own as she was the one frightened.

A little nervous, yes, but confident, too.

In fact, Edy worried more about the words she'd exchange with Rani and when she'd exchange them. Her mom told her that Rani had been positively smug when Edy and Hassan broke up. Clearly, Hassan hadn't bothered to tell her there'd been a change in scheduling, judging by the death his mother tried to glare into her. But on arriving in New York, they hadn't said a word.

Oddly enough, while Hassan was out being a celeb, she spent her time playing the tourist with Ali and her dad. It was almost like the old days, walking between the two men, having Ali trying to guess what she wanted and then getting it, with her own father quietly hovering. After he'd cancelled her credit cards in a hissy fit, he'd been distant, absent. That day, however, he'd muttered something like an apology, so she supposed they were okay now. Something near normal, at least. But Ali wasn't letting him off that easy. As the three of them shopped, he took every opportunity to chastise her dad, to question his sanity, and his thought process. To Edy's surprise, he insisted that if her father ever lost so much common sense again, she should call him for money.

She could only imagine how that would go over with Rani.

Speaking of which, Hassan's mom had claimed another one of her headaches, but this time hadn't bothered with a pretense of pain. She said she'd meet her sister at the spa and then, maybe, do a bit of shopping.

Their days leading up to the ceremony were spent like that: Edy, in the company of both dads and her mom, with Rani as far away from them as she could get. Surprisingly, Edy couldn't say she minded.

Hassan busied himself early on the morning of the ceremony with a bit of his nervous vomiting. Edy held his hair up, rubbed his shoulders and back, and reminded him once again that he had nothing to worry about.

"But I don't even want it," he lied. "I'm a freshman. Some other guy should have it. Do you know my quarterback was on the list? He should be here, not me."

"You should be here and you are," Edy said.

He threw up again. Acid, no doubt because he hadn't had breakfast and hadn't had much of an appetite for dinner, either.

"I don't even want the Heisman," he told her again, face down in the bowl. "There are other guys, older ones, like Cash…"

Edy shushed him and laid her head on his back.

The Heisman festivities kicked off on Saturday. Hassan spent the latter part of the morning doing interviews and such. That afternoon, the family joined him at a pre-announcement cocktail reception. It was pretty star-studded, positively dripping with famous athletes, and Edy spent it in one corner gripping virgin daiquiri. Rani stood next to her in silence. For all of Hassan's nervousness, he worked the room like he was a celeb among peers, reacquainting himself with old friends. His presence was insane. For all Edy's talk, she had to dab her forehead with a napkin repeatedly.

The Dinner Gala followed. Edy positively squealed when she caught a glimpse of Steve Dyson making his way to their table, followed by the entire Dyson clan. Edy glanced at Hassan, who shook his head slightly, indicating that, no, he hadn't known they'd be there. He looked touched though. It must've been Steve who'd sprung for the table, and maybe for Edy and her dad to play tag along at the cocktail reception, too. What did that cost him? Tens of thousands, she was sure.

They spent hours honoring this person and that person's Heisman anniversary. They remembered a few deaths. They laughed at a few jokes, though more from the twins than any up on stage. Finally, finally it was time to move on to the auditorium for the proper announcement. One glimpse of Hassan said that he might pass away. Edy had to think of something. Any second now, cameras would descend on him, capturing his every flinch and smile, grinding fodder for ESPN, YouTube, and a million memes.

She gripped his hand, tucked her elbow under his so he knew to tilt a bit. This was their secret language. When she had his ear, she said, "You are absolutely it for me, Hassan Pradhan. And you're it for these people. Can't you feel it?"

His skin flushed rose as the corners of his mouth turned up. Hassan's fingers had her chin, tilting her eyes up to face him.

"You mean that?" he whispered. "That I'm it for you?" Even as others milled out around them, carrying on nosily as they went, there was no mistaking the heavy rise and fall of his chest, or the intensity of his stare.

"Yes." And she knew she did.

"Yes," he echoed.

Edy swallowed as those green eyes continued to watch her, searching endlessly for something. But then he nodded just as surely as if she'd whispered some magic word to him.

"Wish me luck," he said, turning towards their group. He exchanged a hug with his parents, Edy's dad, who said something extra, Steve and Tessa, the latter of whom was teary-eyed, and each of the Dyson boys—even Lawrence, who looked uncomfortable.

One final time, he turned to Edy, and pressed a kiss

on the corner of her mouth. Afterwards, he made towards the press, and towards the main event. He would go it alone from there.

Edy exhaled a breath she hadn't known she was holding.

Rani stepped into Edy's line of view and gave her a pointed look. "Remember what I told you about boys being guided with the wrong head. *You* led him away from his mother, Edith. I hope you're pleased."

"Really?" Edy hissed. "With your son on the cusp of the greatest trophy a college athlete could hold, you still want to talk about how I'm taking him away from you? *Life* is taking him away from you. Growing up is. He's still your son, but he's becoming a man. His own man, whether you like it or not."

Rani bared her teeth at Edy, indicating that the answer was 'not.'

The Heisman finalists sat at the front of the auditorium, four large bodies with their backs to the entirety of the darkened theater. Family members along the first row. For their purposes, only the Pradhans, her dad, and herself were able to get seats there. The Dysons made it just behind.

She endured opening remarks pretty well, even chuckled at one or two dry football jokes. But the day had been long, between Hassan's morning vomiting, the day's itinerary, and Rani's nonstop glaring. All she wanted now was to hear the Heisman winner and head back to Boston. Correction, all she wanted now was to hear that Hassan was the Heisman winner and head back to Boston.

A Heisman Trustee had spent a considerable amount of time describing what they did and the charities they benefitted. Meanwhile, the thin sheen of sweat had returned to Edy's forehead. A touch of Hassan's nausea was attacking her, too. What must it be doing to him?

She made a business of chewing on her bottom lip, lip gloss be damned. The pits of her dress were drenched. God, her mother would be so embarrassed by her. Nonetheless, she shoved that thought from her mind and replaced it with one mindless mantra: *Please say Hassan's name. Please say Hassan's name.*

Okay. He was about to announce the winner. He'd just promised to announce the winner. But first, he had to tell them about John Heisman, for whom the trophy was named.

Jesus Christ and Sunshine. Hassan had leaned forward, elbows to knees, and Edy had a momentary bout of panic. Should she switch to praying that he didn't throw up or continue asking for the Heisman?

Fuck that.

Give us a Heisman, Jesus. *Please.*

"Without further ado, the winner of this year's Heisman Trophy is… Hassan Pradhan."

Edy screeched, feet kicking out, before both hands clapped over her mouth. Hassan's parents hugged, then Ali and Nathan hugged, as Hassan trotted up to the stage. Edy hugged her dad, then Ali, before sliding her gaze to Rani. She'd already taken her seat.

The auditorium sounded reckless. There was so much cheering for Hassan, Edy's heart might've burst. "God, thank you, God," she whispered and her eyes fell shut.

Eventually, the room fell silent. Edy opened her eyes. Hassan still hadn't spoken. He swallowed and swallowed again, enormous gulps magnified on a big screen.

"Thank you. To those people who cheered for me, voted for me, prayed for me, loved me in their own way. Thank you especially to my *mām* and *pitā*." Hassan sniffed. "I had something prepared to say, but I need to go off script." He waved a crumpled sheet of paper. "So I'd like to begin with my thank yous." He rattled off a long list that Edy had helped him with. It included the Dysons and an assortment of coaches, including one who had not even coached him. "Now that that's done, can I tell you all a story?"

Some girl from the rafters shouted "Yes!" Heffa.

He smiled his infectious grin. "My next-door neighbor, Nathan, has always been like a dad to me. He and my father met in college and they've been best friends since. It was Nathan that taught me the game. He put a football in my hand when I was five, began teaching me the fundamentals not long after. But one of my earliest memories was of Nathan putting his daughter's hand in mine."

From a few chairs down, Edy heard Rani make the sound of a choking chipmunk.

"Edy Phelps and I grew up as close as two kids could. When I failed to make the junior varsity team in the sixth grade—yes, folks, JV—"

Edy threatened to rear up at all the mumbling. Only her father's hand on her arm steadied her, though that didn't keep her from glaring around mutinously.

"I went straight to her house when the team's list came out." He laughed a little, though pain rained down beneath it. "I must've been the only guy who didn't make it. *Lawrence* even made it."

A smatter of laughter rang out as Edy careened around for the look on Lawrence's face, only to see him throw up his hands as if to ask why he deserved *that*.

Hassan shook his head. "But I had it in my head to quit. I marched straight up to her room and started snatching down every piece of football-related *anything* I'd left there. We both tugged at a lot of stuff." He rubbed the back of his neck in trademark embarrassment. "I trashed what I could get away from her, slumped in a corner, and started crying." He sighed. "The two of us must have sat there forever… long enough for the room to get dark. She wiped my tears that day and told me that we'd stick out football until the ball got up and left."

He waited for the laughter to die down. Then he looked up at her as if they were alone, as if he weren't magnified for millions to watch.

"I want to be there for you that way, Edy Phelps. There's no question in my heart about you. So, um," He stepped away from the podium, abandoning his Heisman momentarily. Then he darted off stage and straight up to her with lightening quick speed.

Then he knelt before her.

"Marry me," Hassan said.

Edy's eyes flew huge. She couldn't move. She couldn't think. She could only… stare.

"If you meant what you said," Hassan said quietly, "if you meant that I'm it for you, then marry me. Not now, of course. After school. After whatever you want. Just…please."

Edy exhaled. Inhaled. Exhaled nosily and closed her eyes.

One word entered her mind.

"Yes," she said.

Sign up at http://ShewandaPugh.blogspot.com for email updates on new releases.

If you enjoyed this book, please consider leaving a review. This author appreciates even a few words.

Acknowledgements

As always, I owe a debt of gratitude to so many. This novel, long in coming, wouldn't have been possible without the advice, encouragement, and helping hands of others. Thank you to my husband, Pierre, and son, Caleb for their love, enthusiasm, and boundless encouragement. Thank you to my parents and family, who have shown unwavering support during tough times. Thank you to my writing ace, Lashanta Charles, whose patience and dedication helped make Wrecked a reality. Thank you also to my editor, Stephanie Dagg, cover designer, Regina Wamba, and formatter, Christopher Morgan. Their work contributed to the product before you. And where would I be without these girls? Carletta Hall, Allyn Key, and Catrina Sparkman combed through earlier, rougher versions of this novel and shared their unique insights. Thank you to my respective alma maters, Alabama A&M University and Nova Southeastern University, for the guidance, love, and friendships I found there. They continue to sustain me. A whopping thanks goes out to my uncle, John HL Newton II, for his unique way of kicking my head back into the game. Also, I'd like to thank the doctors and staff of Massachusetts General Hospital, particularly my neurologist, Dr. Michael Bowley, and my rheumatologist, Dr. Sebastian H. Unizony. These people are in the resurrection game; I swear.

Finally, there's you. If you've made it this far, I'd like to thank you. Whether this is the first adventure we've taken together or the sixth, I'm grateful for the time we've shared.

About the Author

Shewanda Pugh's a tomboy who's been writing romance since an inappropriate age. While she's been shortlisted for a few awards and snagged a bestsellers list or two, there's nothing she enjoys more than hearing from her readers.

In another life, she earned a BA from Alabama A&M University and an MA in Writing from Nova Southeastern University. Though a hardcore native of Boston, MA, she now lives in Miami, FL, where she sulks in the sunshine, guzzles coffee, and puzzles over her next novel.

http://www.facebook.com/groups/shewandapugh/

http://www.facebook.com/Author.ShewandaPugh/

http://twitter.com/shewandap/

http://www.instagram.com/shewandapugh/

http://shewandapugh.blogspot.com/